# FLAT-OUT CELESTE

From the *New York Times* Bestselling Author of
**Flat-Out Love**

# JESSICA PARK

*For Andrew, of course. Every day—without fail—I am staggered by our friendship and by you. Thank you for being my clarity.*

# CHAPTER 1
# WHAT WAS BEST

"AND SO IN short, that is what is meant by *reductio ad absurdum*." Celeste beamed at the class and closed her laptop. This past month had been worth it. And the joy of finally releasing her pent-up energy and excitement over this philosophy presentation had paid off. It had gone flawlessly. "So the next time that you find yourself in a situation in which you must prove that something is true by showing it to be false, you'll be sensationally equipped."

It really had been quite the fantastic and thorough presentation, although her classmates' blank expressions did not appear to reflect it. A boy in a blue skull cap looked as though a medically induced coma might cause more of a reaction, and the girl with the possibly illegal-length mini-skirt was shooting a death stare in her direction. Celeste looked to her teacher, Mr. Gil, to see if his response was different. He appeared stunned. Something was wrong. Something had happened. What, however, she didn't know. She shut her eyes for a moment and ran over the past forty-five minutes. Had she forgotten something? It didn't matter what they thought, though.

Mr. Gil pursed his lips and appeared to be holding back a smile as he left his seat near the window. She didn't see anything the least bit amusing about the situation. In fact, her spirits were plummeting dramatically. "That was... quite... It was quite brilliant. Are we sure you're a senior in high school and not already defending a dissertation?" He winked just as the bell sounded loudly, and Celeste could breathe again.

Students brushed past her, one bumping her laptop and another not-so-accidentally stepping on her foot. Celeste looked straight forward and let their faces fly past her in a haze. It would not be good to focus now. She could see the eye rolls, and even under the clamor of the bell, she could hear the mumblings.

*What a nut bag. Who understood anything she said?*

*I have, like, never been so bored in my entire life.*

*I don't care how totally hot she is; that was not normal.*

*Freak. Loser. Weirdo.*

She clutched her laptop into her body until the room emptied.

"Celeste?"

The bell had stopped, and now a new noise took over in her head, reminiscent of wind or static.

"Celeste? Are you all right?"

"Oh? Me? Yes, of course. I'm quite all right." She turned and smiled at Mr. Gil. She liked him. He was a kind man and always spoke in a gentle voice. He also smelled chronically of wet leaves, but she could forgive that because he should not be faulted for an unfortunate cologne choice.

"Are you sure? Your report was very detailed. I would imagine it might have been exhausting to present. You packed a lot of information in. As always, I'm impressed, and I admire how hard you clearly worked on it."

"I enjoy research. It is energizing and inspiring," she said. Smiling hurt her cheeks, but she did it anyway.

"You sure you're okay? I'm sorry if the class didn't respond with as much interest as you hoped. Some of the material may have been a bit beyond them."

"I *had* expected the turnip metaphor to go over better, but it seems not everyone appreciates a clever philosophically grounded root vegetable reference." Celeste stepped to her desk and put her computer and folder into her red messenger bag.

"I thought it was spot on and very clever indeed." He paused. "Just because this is an excellent private school and the student body is largely bright and thoughtful doesn't mean that they are capable of what you just did. Or that they can understand it. It's okay, you know? You're in a league well above that of your peers; you must know that. It's nothing to be ashamed of."

"I am not ashamed," she said too quickly. "Sorry. It is just that I do quite enjoy higher-level thinking. I had hoped to properly convey my enthusiasm for this subject to you, and I have done that."

"You did well. I'd like to write you a reference for college. I imagine that you're applying to all of the Ivy Leagues?"

"Yes, thank you. A reference would be most welcome."

"It's only October, I know, but I thought you might be going for early decision at some. Are you applying anywhere outside of the Ivies? I have ideas for alternatives, if you're interested."

"Alternatives? Why would I need alternatives?" Celeste lifted her bag over her shoulder and took a step forward. The room began to spin slightly, and she stopped, dropping her gaze down. "I apologize. It seems that I am a bit overtaken by the rush of adrenaline after my philosophy oration."

Mr. Gil frowned. "Would you like some water?"

"I have a free period now. I shall get some and regroup." Her bag weighed heavily on her shoulder, and she momentarily feared it might just bore her through the floor and into geological oblivion.

"Well, anyway, congratulations on a job well done. You should be proud." Mr. Gil buttoned his shawl cardigan and popped a piece of gum into his mouth before taking a seat behind his wooden desk. "I'll see you tomorrow, kiddo."

Celeste lifted her head and took a deep breath. The door to the hall felt unnecessarily heavy, and she sighed as she shuffled from the classroom. Usually the dark wood floors and brass fixtures of the school's architecture were comforting, but the sound in her head had not quieted. What *was* that sound?

She should be happy. Today had mostly gone as she hoped it would; she had given a successful presentation with no response from or interaction with her peers. It's how she liked things. Not to have an effect on them, not even to be noticed. She could have done without the snide remarks following her oral report, but they were expected and short lived. Yet she was not elated.

Most students were in class now, and Celeste would use her free period to curl up in the school's library and read. She didn't have homework to do, so it might be a good time to reread some Jane Austen. She reached her locker and slowly worked the combination. It wouldn't open. She tried again. By the third try, she understood that it was hard to see the numbers on the dial because her eyes were watering. Blinking furiously eventually cleared her vision, and she was able to undo the lock. What in the world was wrong with her today?

As she slipped her bag into the locker, she was jolted by a crash when a girl with long, hot-pink hair slammed into the few lockers next to her.

"That report totally rocked." The girl grinned and rested her head against the metal doors.

Celeste took her in. Yes, this girl was in her philosophy class. Considering her choice of hair color, she was hard to miss, but Celeste hadn't spoken to her before. Not that Celeste spoke to a lot of people anymore. Her social isolation was a choice that she was comfortable with. This girl was invading her territory, but Celeste would be polite anyway.

"Your name is Dallas. Is that correct?" Celeste asked. "You often sit near the window and look outside instead of listening to our instructor."

The girl laughed. "You're a straight shooter. Yes, I'm Dallas. But, no, I'm not lost in thought. I learn better when I'm not distracted by Mr. Gil's tragic comb-over."

"Oh. I suppose he does have imperfect hair."

"And one time during class, a bird flew smack into the window and died on impact. It was completely disgusting, but

I keep an eye on the window so that I don't miss any other suicides."

"That is understandable."

"So. Your presentation was killer. Loved it."

It was hard to tell whether or not Dallas was sincere. It seemed unlikely. So Celeste said nothing.

Dallas waited the few moments while Celeste fiddled with folders and papers in her locker. "I'm sorry. Did I say something wrong? You look really pissed off at me."

"Sorry. No, you have done nothing wrong." Celeste delicately shut her locker and then looked at Dallas, her outrageous hair somehow clashing in a most pleasing manner with her seventies-inspired brown leather jacket. "I quite like your jacket. You have an impeccable and original fashion sense."

"Yeah? Thanks. But look at you. You have blonde ringlets down to the middle of your back that most girls would kill for, and you're wearing a sick ensemble that makes you look like you stepped out of Vogue." She waved her hand around Celeste's top. "What is that? A cashmere hoodie? And riding boots? Hot. Love it."

Celeste glanced down at her boots. She and her mother had bought these together just last week, part of a neutral ensemble that she hoped would let her fade into a crowd. They were supposed to bring her luck today.

"You kinda set the bar high by going first. But that's how you do it, hot stuff!" Dallas held her hand up above her head, palm out.

Celeste looked up and raised her eyebrows questioningly.

"Go on. Slap my hand. You earned it."

Tentatively, Celeste touched her palm to Dallas's.

"Oh, jeez. C'mon. Harder! This is celebration time!"

Celeste bit her lip, but smacked her hand against the one belonging to her pink-haired classmate.

"Babe." A deep voice echoed in the hall.

Dallas turned and then bounced on her toes. "There you are!"

An undeniably handsome senior strode their way. Celeste recognized Troy immediately. Tall, certainly what one would call "strapping," and oozing confidence. Troy was well known on their campus. He slid an arm around Dallas's waist and pulled her in, kissing her noisily on her cheek.

"Stop that!" Dallas said, giggling. "Troy, do you know Celeste? Celeste, this is my boyfriend, Troy."

Troy stuck out a hand. "Pleasure."

Celeste tentatively put her hand in his. His jet black eyeliner matched his hair exactly, and she found it to be a nice contrast with his simple button-down shirt over a navy tee and jeans. "It is very nice to meet you."

"Celeste just rocked our socks off in philosophy class. No one is going to want to go next now. I'm sure my talk on Thursday will be a nightmare. She was just great. You should've been there, Troy. You would've loved it."

"Yeah? That's cool." He smiled warmly at Celeste.

"So Celeste, we're heading off campus to that diner down the street. Want to come?"

"Do you have special privileges that allow you to go off campus during school hours?"

Troy laughed. "We don't."

"Scandalous," Dallas squealed.

"You have no concerns about being discovered by a school official and penalized with a demerit that can never be removed from your record?"

"Nope, not a one. The risk makes it all the more thrilling, don't you think?"

"Oh… well, certainly. Yes, I can see that." Celeste nodded vigorously.

"But that's what makes it fun. Come with us!" Dallas leaned her body against Troy's and rested her head on his chest.

"I do appreciate the invitation, but I was planning to go to the library in order to read some Jane Austen."

"I totally love Austen. But," Dallas started as she groped in her bag, "try this." She held out a book. "This is romance, too. Just less formal."

Celeste took the book. The black and white cover showcased a semi-naked man's muscled torso, with barely an inch of skin that was not tattooed, clutching a woman in a clearly intimate embrace. "I see that they are on a motorcycle. I have concerns about where the handlebars might end up."

"Don't worry. Nothing creepy happens with the handlebars."

"I am unsure about this selection. I have not read these types of books before."

"Try it."

"My expectations are not high."

"Then the odds of your being disappointed just dropped astronomically."

"I will read it with gusto and a positive attitude." Celeste nodded.

"Cool beans. Well, we better hurry now. If I'm late for calculus, I'm dead, but I need me a bacon omelet something fierce. I had fun chatting with you, Celeste." Dallas took Troy's hand and led him to the exit doors.

What an entirely unexpected encounter. How disconcerting. And did anyone else in the world say "cool beans" besides Dallas?

Celeste looked down again at the romance book in her hand. While she didn't have much interest in reading this book, there was still a pang in her heart because she was unlikely to ever have any sort of romance, either on or off of a motorcycle.

Celeste took a deep breath. She would give this book a try, however. Maybe she would learn something about the real world from this love story.

This confusing, overwhelming, daunting world.

The one that she imagined might one day swallow her whole.

# CHAPTER 2
# THE SLAP HEARD 'ROUND THE WORLD

CELESTE PACED THE floor of her bedroom. She noticed that she was fidgeting with her hands. She dropped them to her sides and continued pacing. Sounds from the dining room echoed up to the second floor, and she tried to brush aside the guilt she had developed after ignoring the meal that was intended to celebrate her successful philosophy presentation. It had been hard enough to lie to her parents when they'd come home from work ("The class loved every insightful moment! I did not have the time to address all of their comments and questions!"), but regaling them with an overly enthusiastic retelling of her presentation over the course of an entire meal would have been impossible. Feigning exhaustion and a desire to unwind by browsing through college applications bought her an escape to her room.

Her reflection in the floor-length mirror glared back at her.

"Shut up. So what if I am a vile, flagrant liar and unworthy of ever being trusted again?"

She took a few steps closer. Celeste knew that, according to societal standards at least, she was attractive, but she didn't quite understand why those standards existed in the first place. Her appearance had nothing to do with the strange creature that she was. While she had inherited her mother's height, and her legs were long and lean, it seemed to her that her height just made her gangly and more awkward than she already felt. And these more recent curves on her hips and her chest? She was most uncomfortable. Men looked at her. She did her best to wear loose tops, but there was really no hiding her figure. Celeste liked modestly cut earth tones, clothing made from textured fabrics, body-engulfing wraps, and cozy sweaters. Things that flowed. Things that were, ironically enough, romantic in their aesthetic

She shrieked at the mirror. "Lecherous stares are unwarranted, given my aberrant character."

Social and romantic endeavors were not her strong suit. An Ivy League college was in her future, and that was the only area of her life in which she would excel. Celeste knew that there was no boy who would want her once he got past the physical. That was the simple truth.

It was devastating. And it was devastating that she even cared, because her value system was not one that contemplated a woman's happiness being dependent on the presence of a fairytale love life.

She sat down at her desk and took some deep breaths, rearranging the already-organized white storage containers. Her email sounded, and she clicked it open.

*Hi, Celeste!*

*My name is Justin Milano, and I'm a sophomore at Barton College in San Diego. While I've settled in to the warm weather here nicely, I'm originally from Needham, Massachusetts, so not too far from where you are in Cambridge. After hearing about you, Barton would really love the chance to connect with you. I'm a student liaison for the college. I "woo" applicants and answer any questions they might have. I'm going to be part of a Barton meet-up night for prospective students soon. We hope you can attend! I imagine that you must be busy with lots of college application stuff, but have you checked out the materials that the school sent yet?*

*I love it here and couldn't imagine a better liberal arts education.*

*I hope you can attend the meet-up!*

*-Thanks, Justin*


Barton College? Celeste didn't know anything about this Barton College. How did they know about her? And when was this meet-up thing? She usually did not participate in "meet-ups."

Her email sounded again.

*Celeste-*

*Oh God, sorry. The meet-up is next Saturday afternoon at 5 p.m.*

*-Justin*

Before she could even hit the delete button, he wrote again.

*Seriously, I'm really sorry. By "next Saturday" I mean the one after the one this weekend. Next week's Saturday, not the next Saturday that arrives. Hold on; I'll check the date.*

*Okay, it's Saturday the 15th.*

*-Justin*

Celeste stared at the emails. This Justin was not one for details. At least not condensed details. So where exactly was she to go if she, in fact, did want to attend this "meet-up" for this unheard of college?

*Celeste, I'm really sorry. I tend to just fire off emails and don't always pay attention. The meet-up is in Harvard Square at Border Cafe. I haven't been there in ages, but they used to make this awesome Camptown shrimp dish that was amazing? Do you like shrimp? Half the menu is Cajun; the other half Tex-Mex.*

*My apologies for all of these emails. And this started off so well!*

*-Justin*

It hadn't started off *that* well, she thought. She did like shrimp, but that was not enough to entice her to venture out to a social event for a college that was not on her list, nor for her to do so just to please this person who needlessly sent multiple messages. She did note that it was quite bold of Barton to hold this affair in the middle of Harvard territory, and that confidence piqued her interest slightly. Still, this was not for her. There would be conversations to be had, and awkward exchanges, all of which were unnecessary because she was applying to other schools. Applying via written applications and one-on-one interviews with academic and professional people from those schools. People who would be appreciative of her intellect and not judge her on her ability to make small talk while eating crustaceans.

There was a knock at the door, and Matt leaned in, swinging a brown paper bag in her direction. "I heard Mom made stuffed peppers tonight. Last time she made those, I nearly died from flatulence. I assume she stuffed them with her usual repulsive ground chicken, quinoa, Brussels sprouts, and pomegranate seed mix?"

Just the sound of Matt's voice made Celeste relax. She smiled at him. "Based on the smell, I believe you're right."

"So you didn't eat then? I was right!" Matt flopped onto her bed and lay down, his long body scrunching up the neat white comforter that she had spent ten minutes arranging before she'd gone to school this morning. "I thought I'd take a break from studying and bring you something edible."

"It smells like a burger from Mr. Bartley's," she said as she got up and took a seat next to Matt. "Hand it over, thoughtful brother."

He tightened a hand around the top of the bag. "You have to guess which kind I brought you first."

"How am I supposed to know?"

"Close your eyes."

She did as instructed and felt him move the bag under her

nose. Sweet, spicy… a bit garlicky. "Aha! Boursin cheese and bacon! The Mark Zuckerberg burger!"

"And sweet potato fries and a bottle of iced tea, but you win. A burger named after the so-called 'richest geek in America.'"

"You will be the richest geek in America after you finish your Ph.D. Program," Celeste said through a mouthful of fries.

"If M.I.T. doesn't land me in a psych unit first."

"You only have this year left to endure. And you will hardly find yourself in need of psychiatric care, Matthew. You are doing stupendously."

"I'm scraping by." Matt reached into the bag to grab a handful of fries and opened her iced tea.

"You are not 'scraping by.' You are teaching classes, excelling in your own, and in all ways performing to standards that exceed even the high ones our mother set for you." She frowned as he chewed on the fries. "Did you not eat?"

"I did. A Big Papi burger and a Fiscal Cliff. But you can never have enough sweet potato fries."

"I have a finite amount of my own from which you are stealing. But I shall not complain because this was very kind of you."

Matt chewed and studied her. "Are you okay?"

"Why do you ask?"

"No contractions. When you're stressed out, they disappear."

"I know. But most days, I do not care to use them. If it is an effort, then I do not push."

"Okay. I get it." He chewed for a minute. "I heard your presentation went well. Did your friends like it?"

"It went marvelously. My friend Dallas took me aside to offer quite the list of compliments."

"That's great, Celeste." He was downing half of her iced tea.

"And then I bitch-slapped her."

Matt choked on the drink and desperately tried to clear his airway. "I'm sorry. You did what?"

She cocked her head. "I bitch-slapped her."

"That... that can't be right," he sputtered. "I mean, I hope it's not."

"I slapped my hand against her hand. Up in the air." She looked at Matt blankly. "Is that not the right term?"

"Thank God, no, it's not. I think you mean a high-five."

"If you say so. Well, either way, it happened. You know I have trouble with colloquialisms, so I resent your shocked reaction."

"I do know that about you, and I apologize."

"Since we are on the subject, there is something else I would like for you to clarify."

"Shoot."

"What is meant by 'nut bag'? Is that a testicular reference or merely the identification of a satchel of cashews or pecans?"

Matt groaned. "This conversation has gotten really weird. Could we just talk about— Wait a minute. Why are you asking me this? Did someone say that to you?" He looked angry.

Celeste picked at her fry. "No. Certainly not. I heard the term and had a natural curiosity."

"Okay then…" Her brother crumpled up the paper bag and then smoothed it out in his hands. Then crumpled it again. "It's the same as 'nuts.' You know, crazy."

"Thank you for the definition." She took the last bite of her burger and wiped her hands on one of the paper napkins. It shouldn't matter what her classmates thought of her. Celeste would just be strong about this. She would move on. "I got an email from someone at a college in San Diego."

"Oh?" Matt continued to avoid looking at her.

"Yes. It's called Barton College. It's in San Diego," she said pointedly.

"I heard you the first time."

"Julie is in Los Angeles."

"I know where Julie is."

She waited, but Matt said nothing else. "Maybe I will go to school there, and then you will be forced to come visit me, and you two will be in the same state."

Matt sat up and threw the bag across the room and into the trash can. "Celeste… Knock it off, okay?"

The door to her room swinging open and a simultaneous knock interrupted them.

"Celeste? Oh, hey, Matt! What are you doing here?" Their father, Roger, stepped into the room, still in his corduroy pants and cable-knit sweater that he'd worn to work. "I didn't hear you sneak in, but— Oh, you brought food? What is that I smell? Burgers?" He gently shut the door and tiptoed across the room. "Gimme, gimme!"

Celeste had to laugh. "We have already eaten."

"Oh, that's nice, Celeste. You left me alone to eat all of

that couscous lasagna that your mother made? I'm all for experimenting, but that thing was a dud."

"I did not ask Matthew to bring me a burger, but I am sorry that you had an unpleasant meal. We were afraid it was stuffed peppers tonight, but that sounds even worse."

Matt made gagging noises. "And how exactly does one turn couscous into lasagna?"

"I don't know… Overcooking couscous and then flattening it into something resembling sheets… Well, never mind. Do you have fries at least?" He looked desperate.

"Matthew ate them all, or I would be happy to share," Celeste said.

"Fine. I'll wait until Erin falls asleep, and then I'll sneak downstairs for something. I just hope that she doesn't catch me. I don't want to make her feel bad. I turned her down when she asked me accompany her to hot yoga today, so I need to be on good behavior." He pushed delicate silver frames up from the bridge of his nose and then handed Celeste a large mailing envelope. "This came for you earlier. More college stuff, I imagine."

Celeste read the return address. Barton College. "How strange. I received correspondence from one of their students today."

"Based on the weight of this package, I'd say they're certainly interested in you." Her father winked. "As they should be. Don't forget we've got the trip down to Yale this weekend. Your mother is beside herself with excitement, as you can imagine."

"Probably excited about all the gnarly snacks she's going to pack," Matt murmured. "Glad I'm not going."

"Be nice, or I'm going to make you join us," Celeste snapped. "Our mother is dipping her culinary hand into new adventures. I applaud her. At least, theoretically."

"I'd love to join you for a family car trip, really, but I have two study groups and a paper to finalize." Matt stood. "Speaking of which, I should get going and do a little work tonight."

"I'll walk you out," Roger said.

"Congratulations again on your presentation, Celeste." Matt put a hand on her shoulder before walking away.

"Thank you, Matthew."

"You got it, kiddo. Call me if you need anything, okay? For real."

"I will."

Alone again, Celeste opened the envelope from Barton College. It wouldn't hurt to look. The liberal arts school appeared, at least in print form, similar to many others in the brochures she'd collected over the past few months, although it was certainly on the smaller side, with only twenty-five hundred students. Yet she spent a solid thirty minutes studying the course listings, reading about the history of the school, and admiring the full-color photos of the campus and students. Her own picture could be in a brochure, she thought. No one would know the difference. No one would be able to see from a photograph that she was not, in fact, like any of the other students.

Celeste grabbed for her phone. The search bar in the browser called to her, in the relentless way it often seemed to do. So she started to type what she felt obligated to. *Asper...* And then, as she always did, she deleted the letters.

*What is wrong with me?* she typed sarcastically.

Celeste practically snorted. The first result was some sort of "emotional intelligence test" which she would likely fail.

Later that night, she was propped up in bed with her laptop as she finished typing up her thoughts on Flaubert for her French class. An email arrived.

*PS—When I assured you that the event is on Saturday the 15th, I meant that the event is on Saturday the 22nd. Really. That's my final offer. Take it or leave it.*

*You must think I'm a nut bag. I'm not. But at this point, I'm wondering if you might need proof otherwise? I can send letters of reference that outline my delightful nature.*

*-Justin (Likely soon-to-be ex-student liaison to Barton College.)*

She smiled. He was quite something, this Justin Milano. And she did not find him to be a "nut bag." There was in fact, she thought, something rather sweet about his repeated emails. It seemed the decent thing to do to reply and alleviate some of his anxiety. She would just reframe things in a positive light.

*Dear Justin—*

*Thank you for the information about the meet-up on the 22nd. I will look into whether this date will work for me, as my days are very tightly scheduled with activities. I do very much appreciate Barton's interest in considering me as a potential student.*

*Please do not concern yourself with the number of*

*emails. You were clearly eager that I have all the adequate
information, and I am grateful for your thoroughness. It seems
to me that Barton would be impressed with your friendly style
and devotion to clarifying details, but you can rest assured
that I will not seek to elaborate on our communications should
anyone from the college feel moved to investigate, since I do not
wish to cause you any trouble. I feel sure that you will retain
your position.*

*Best wishes,*
*Celeste Watkins*

She sent the email and stared at the screen, rereading his messages. Celeste's stomach sank. Her message was ridiculously stiff and formal, even she could see that. His? Fine, maybe they could have been more professional, but it was easy to read the level of comfort he had with himself. A comfort she could not connect with.

Celeste did what she could to distract herself from the feeling of shame that was taking over. She reread a piece called "Politics and the English Language" by George Orwell. Then she read the more recent "Cyber Neologoliferation" by James Gleick, but she was less comforted than she would have thought by reading the article about lexicographers. Her agitation mounted.

Celeste slammed the laptop shut and drew the covers up over her head. She spent twenty minutes frozen, gripping the sheets. Then her panic rose, and her breathing escalated, until she eventually freed herself from suffocation by sitting bolt upright in the dark.

The night sky was bright from the moon's glow, so Celeste

lay back down and kept her focus on the view from her window. She would count stars, she decided. She would count and count and disappear. But when she searched for stars, there was only one to be seen. Even on this clear night.

"Of course," she whispered to herself. "Of course there is only one when I need a thousand."

###

At three a.m., she awoke. Her comforter, walls, shelves, rug, all were highlighted in the night. Celeste blinked and looked around. Something had disturbed her. Although she scanned the placement of nearly every item three times, organization prevailed. Nothing had randomly flown off a shelf, so what had woken her up?

She smoothed out the sheets and shut her eyes, but fifteen minutes later, she was still awake. She reached next to her bed and opened her laptop.

After she reread the emails from one Justin Milano of Barton College in far–away San Diego three times, she grew more unsettled. Celeste did not like the idea that this Justin might have any rumblings of discomfort regarding his earlier messages to her. In fact, it bothered her quite a bit. Celeste wrote a second reply to him.

*Justin-*

*I have been thinking about your mention of this Camptown shrimp dish, and I'm intrigued. The word Camptown can refer to a number of things, but I'm envisioning frontier towns and fly-by-night living structures.*

*Perhaps shrimp dishes were popular in those communities? Rustic cooking at its finest? Bayou bliss by the water?*

*And one, of course, thinks of the mid-1800s song, "Camptown Races," written by Trent Foster. While the lyrics are quite silly, I can see why it was so popular with minstrel troupes across the country. So upbeat and whimsical, don't you think?*

*-Celeste*

She sent the email and started another.

*Justin-*

*Sorry for another email, but I also realized that "Camptown" is a word often used in conjunction with discussing prostitutes who served in the U.S. Military during the Korean War.*

*I can't imagine that this shrimp dish is in honor of that reference. Unless "shrimp" in this context is some sort of inappropriate critique describing the men who frequented such services?*

*So now I am struggling with mixed feelings about the dish that is served at the restaurant where Barton will be holding their meet-up.*

*-Celeste*

She continued.

*Justin-*

*Please accept my sincerest apologies for all of these emails. Shall we blame restlessness over anxieties about college visits and applications for my inability to condense my thoughts? Or—as a more entertaining possibility and one that carries less shame with it— shall we simply blame the titillating name of the aforementioned seafood appetizer?*

*I cannot imagine that Barton might have imagined the degree of analysis one such as myself might put into this restaurant selection.*

*-Celeste*

And then one final email.

*Justin-*

*One last thought: My father once spent a month studying shrimp culture. And while his work was very much scientifically based, I always liked the idea that he was embedding himself in true cultural aspects of being a shrimp, as though there exists an entire social world that we did not know about. It amused me to think that there were shrimp out there holding photo exhibits at galleries and designing runway fashions. Or composing folk songs. Or drumming up new lingo for the teenage shrimp to latch onto.*

*-Celeste*

There. Celeste smiled and set the computer on the floor next to her bed.

And then gasped and clapped her hands over her mouth.

She may have made a grave miscalculation. Her joke about equating "men" and "shrimp" had meant to address the size of the men. Meaning their height. And perhaps it had read as belittling… well, another anatomical part.

Well, there was nothing to do about it now. And what did it matter? It's not as though she would ever meet Justin and have to face him after having made such a tremendous sexual faux pas. And if her multiple emails made him feel better, then it was all right.

She could now fall back asleep.

And in the morning, when she logged back on to her email, she would see this:

*Celeste-*

*Thank you. Thank you for all of that.*

*-Justin*

## CHAPTER 3
# COCONUTS

T HE DRAMA ROOM at school was often abandoned during Celeste's free period, and there were many days when she snuck in here to be alone. While the library could be a good choice for her, since she liked nothing more than to be surrounded by books, there were always other students there. Being alone held more appeal.

Today she was in the small room that held all of the costumes used for school productions. Celeste sat on the floor next to a garment rack while a vent blew boa tendrils from an elaborate robe of some sort over her arm. She had never gone to any of the school's shows, but she guessed that the costume was supposed to be for a king. Or a Vegas showgirl. In either case, she liked the tickle that danced on her forearm while she wrote down some thoughts in her American history notebook.

Her phone sounded with a text from Dallas.

**Dallas:** Did you read the book that I gave you? Hot romance, huh?

Celeste sighed. She truly loathed that the school collected and distributed cell phone numbers. Why was this Dallas girl paying attention to her anyway? It was most confusing. While it was seemingly kind, Celeste needed to put a stop to this, since it would inevitably lead to disaster, no matter how nice Dallas was. She tried to formulate a polite, but distant, text response and then decided that no response at all was the smarter method of shutting down a conversation. It had been nice to talk to Dallas the other week, but it simply didn't make sense to hope that they might become some sort of power duo.

High school was not fun, Celeste had to admit. It was actually quite disappointing. She knew how to manage it, but that did not mean it was enjoyable. Next year, when she would be on a university campus with access to all sorts of educational avenues, would be much better. Course catalogs and campus maps that identified academic buildings were her saving grace this year. She closed her eyes and let herself daydream about the hours she would spend investigating old books at the library and researching coursework for classes with elaborate and specific titles....

She missed Julie right now. Although Julie would be sorely disappointed in her if she knew the truth about Celeste's isolation. Her whole family would, but if Julie still lived near here, Celeste would not be able to trick her into believing everything was fine. Shielding them all from the truth was the only option, so she would continue smiling and bantering happily about her days when they asked.

Yes, she spoke to people at school, but that was virtually a requirement. She wasn't mute. The opposite, in fact. She talked too much, and evidently not in the right ways or about the right things. Dallas had just been very nice to her, but one independent classmate who hadn't been bored to tears by her philosophy analytics did not count. She deleted Dallas' text, but did not feel any sense of satisfaction. If Celeste had pink hair and a hyper masculine boyfriend named Troy, she, too, might enjoy the social aspects of high school. As it was, she did not. And so she made sure that she interacted as little as possible with her peers.

High school, she had determined, would be a wash. Constructing an environment in which she would move virtually undetected had been easier than she would have imagined, and it wasn't as though she had to fend off inquiries for social interaction at every turn. This Dallas bit was an exception.

It was a most strange experience, she thought, to move among crowds of students as she did, and yet not have any real friends.

But whether or not Celeste wanted friends was beside the point. It was best, she had learned, not to set herself up for failure.

Thank goodness that she had Matt. Matt, while not outwardly gallant and heroic, loved her with a ferocity and protectiveness that was quiet and subtle. Matt's wiring didn't make it easy for him to lavish affection with words or physical displays. And yet, what he gave her was more than enough. Having him still live nearby and often at the house eased the pain of his moving out. Which of course he had to do. Once he'd finished his undergraduate work, it made sense. She couldn't expect him to live across the hall from her for his entire life. It's not as though it was acceptable to have her brother move into the dorm room across from hers when she went to college next year. But she wouldn't need him then because she would finally be out of high school and in a mature educational environment. Where, exactly, she would end up was still undecided. But there were options.

She turned on her iPad. Reading more about colleges would be comforting now. She couldn't get enough of the course catalog, so she read about classes for a bit and then did a more general search to see what else she could learn about this legendary school. Celeste gasped when a webpage popped up.

"Oh no. No. No. No." She glared down at the words on the page. *Campus life.*

Details about parties, and campus events, and lifelong bonds stared back at her. She hurriedly clicked on links to other schools. Greek systems, drinking games… something dreadful sounding called "Springfest" that featured a full day of on-campus bands and student festivities! This was not right.

Celeste read on.

"I had three roommates my first year, and we're still the best of friends during our senior year" was one testimonial.

"Ugh, my freshman roomie sucked. Totally uptight and awful. Ruined my year. The school wouldn't let me change rooms" was another.

Oh dear God, what a perfectly terrifying thought: she would have a roommate next year. A stranger. Or a number of roommate strangers. Probably with actual social talents as well as intellectual abilities. And Celeste would likely be the "uptight" and "awful" roommate that got written about on campus review sites.

Panic set in. The plan had been to shield herself during high school and then soar off to college, where life would be fulfilling. Suddenly it became clear to Celeste how utterly stupid a plan this was. College was going to be worse than high school. She would be trapped on campus in repeated and forced social situations. Ones in which she would be expected to function appropriately. This was a tremendous problem.

She sat rigidly on the concrete floor and tapped her head against the painted-brick wall. What was she going to do? Her personality certainly hadn't won over crowds during high school, so there was no reason to think interpersonal relations would magically improve when at college. Why hadn't she thought of this until now? For a smart girl, she had done something incredibly stupid.

It felt as though the costume room was closing in on her, and she would be lost forever under a mountain of pirate hats, poodle skirts, and goblin masks. Celeste stared at a hideous grass skirt. It might just do to run off to an as-yet-undiscovered island. She would wear coconuts and spear fish and never be required to deal with human beings again. She would have a new title: *Celeste Watkins, intellectual deserted-island goddess.* However, one must have internet access, and a deserted island might not provide that. Not to mention that she had no means with which to locate an as-yet-undiscovered island. Such an exploration would presumably require a boat and an expert degree of nautical mapping skills, neither of which she had.

Then she had a thought: Who says that she couldn't just create a new identity? She still had time this year. There was no reason that she had to show up at college next fall with the same old stilted and stunted personality she currently had.

A personal reinvention would simply have to take place, and the clock was ticking.

## CHAPTER 4
# HOT ENOUGH FOR YOU?

"ARE YOU SURE that you want to do this?" Celeste's mother, Erin, pulled into the parking lot on Saturday morning and looked at her daughter. "Hot yoga is not for everyone." She tucked her short hair behind her ear, and Celeste had a full view of her mother's skeptical expression. While Celeste did prefer her mother's relatively new, closely cropped style to the long hair that she'd had for years, it did have its downside: there was no opportunity for flyaway hairs to obscure her face and hide her feelings.

"Hot yoga does not need to be for *everyone*. But it will be for me. I feel sure that I can become a yoga enthusiast."

"An enthusiast? I just thought you wanted to try a class with me. I guess we'll see if you like it." Erin gave Celeste a solid nod and smiled. "Let's do it."

"Yes. Let's do it," Celeste repeated more robotically than she cared to. Contractions were not easy these days. "We shall have a mother-daughter bonding experience."

"And we've got more coming up. Your father took you to Yale last weekend, so I get to take you to Princeton and U Penn in December. I'm looking forward to watching all of these schools battle it out for your acceptance."

They headed through the sharp October wind and into the warmth of the building. "I do believe that I am well prepared, yes? I have this yoga mat, a skidless towel that all of the online yoga sites say is quite the trend, and I spent the past few days hydrating sufficiently so that my body will not suffer when I sweat. Of course, I also have this decorative water bottle. My outfit is similar to yours, and I think that it is essential that I look the part as I delve into this new area of interest."

"I told you that they have mats at the studio that you can use, sweetheart."

"Erin!" Celeste shrieked. "What in the world would possess you to think that I would consider using a communal mat? I could catch some sort of repulsive fungal infection or worse! Hardly the way to launch my new identity."

"A new identity? What are you talking about?"

Celeste fidgeted with her gear. "It is nothing."

Erin eyed her daughter. "You don't need a new identity. And I believe they clean the mats thoroughly, but I'm glad you like the one we got you. And, for God's sake, would you please call me 'Mom'? It's unnerving when you use my first name."

Celeste shrugged as they entered the yoga room. She gasped. "Oh dear, it is quite warm in here."

"It *is* called *hot yoga* for a reason. But I've found it to be quite invigorating. I think you might like this experience."

Celeste followed her mother to a spot in the large room and mimicked how her mother set up her things. "Thank you for purchasing all of these lovely starter materials for my new adventure. I know the capri pants were expensive, but I read that low-quality ones can become see-through when saturated with one's sweat, and that would be humiliating. I believe that is a reasonable concern given that I am already sweating, and I have not yet begun any poses."

Erin lay back on her mat and closed her eyes. "That's normal. We get here twenty minutes early to adjust to the heat and let our bodies and minds prepare for class."

After swooping her long hair onto the top of her head and tying it into a puffy knot of curls, Celeste also spread out on her mat and shut her eyes. Despite worrying that—given how she was already drenched in sweat—performing actual yoga work might be problematic, she did her best to envision success. This class would put her in touch with an untapped side of herself, and she would be ignited with a new fire. Her mother might be dismissive of the entire notion of a new identity, but Celeste was not. Her determination to no longer be on the social-pariah end of the spectrum once she entered college was strong. So *she* would be strong. And she would be a yogist. Was "yogist" even a word? No, of course it wasn't. The hundred-and-five-degree temperature was affecting her in a most basic way. Celeste did not forget words. She was becoming a yogi. Or a yogini, which was a word that she thought to be beautiful and romantic. She inhaled and exhaled deeply, trying to convince herself that she was one with the oppressive heat.

*Celeste the yogini* had a wonderful sound to it. She envisioned herself organizing a yoga club while at college and the eagerness of students to sign up, a crowd around her as she answered questions about times, gave advice for first-timers, and assured everyone that they would all do very well. Leading yoga would propel her to social acceptance, she was sure.

But twenty minutes into the official start of the class, Celeste's hopes for a yogini lifestyle were diminishing. Hot yoga was despicable. Truly. It was difficult to know if her vision was blurred from the sweat that poured tirelessly into her eyes or from the dizziness that had overtaken her, but in either case, she was undeniably miserable. And hot. Oh Lord, it was hot. She understood from her reading that she was supposed to keep her pose steady and firm, her mind clear and content, and that perfection would come from deep relaxation into this process, but that was becoming increasingly difficult. And, if she recalled correctly, the goal was to reach for what was called *the infinite*." At this point, infinite sweat was the only success she'd achieved.

A glance in the mirror reflected that Celeste was shaking and not exactly demonstrating perfect pose. She peeked to see how her mother was doing. It didn't appear that Erin was anything but deeply involved in reaching for the sky and probably breathing in some sort of soothing, healing manner while the earth aligned around her or whatnot. This standing triangle pose, or "Trikanasana" pose as the instructor called it, was straining her body. And the name sounded horrifyingly reminiscent of one of the many bacteria she was probably being exposed to in this sweat lodge.

Celeste refocused. This was a poor attitude that she was entertaining, and she would allow herself to experience this opportunity to the fullest and find her true calling, and yoga really was the perfect calling for her... if it weren't for the never-ending, excruciating, stifling heat.

In an effort to combat the uncomfortable temperature, she would simply think about cold things, and those thoughts would trick her body into believing that her skin may not, in fact, dissolve at any moment. *Air conditioning, shade, the Bering Sea, industrial freezers, snowmen, salted-caramel ice cream, the nose on the neighbor's ever-snorting bulldog, the wind atop Mt. Everest...* Celeste would give anything to be clinging to the side of a Himalayan mountain right now, frostbite and potentially lost limbs be damned. And since her ambitions of becoming a yoga devotee were quickly evaporating, extreme mountain climber was a more likely new goal.

Celeste rolled onto her side, unable to tolerate hanging her head upside down for one minute longer. Total collapse was the only option right now.

"There's nothing wrong with taking a break," Erin whispered from her mat. "It's very smart to listen to your body. And this is only your first class."

And her last. Celeste let her eyes close as she lay incapacitated. When the lights dimmed for the last section of the class, she sighed with both relief and discouragement. Yoga was a failure. *She* was a failure.

*No,* she scolded herself. *No. I will not be defeated by an inability to perform acrobatics in a room that simulates a South American jungle experience. I will not give up on reinventing myself, because reinvention is my out. Or my way in.*

Facing this hot misery head-on was the only option. So she did just that.

After dropping her mother at their house, Celeste backed seamlessly into a parallel-parking spot on Mass Ave. in Somerville. "Spatial relations skills aren't for the meek," she stated assuredly. "And I am not meek."

Granted, she felt a tad meek after that rather demanding yoga class; but this was her new life and she would simply view the more difficult parts as divine challenges. The sweat had dried—mostly—from her skin, and she had to admit that although she had perhaps completed only a small fraction of the actual yoga poses, she had at least not up and died during class. That had to be considered an achievement. Part one of her yogini day was over. Now to find her new people.

A quick internet search had helped her locate the perfect post-yoga spot, a natural-foods cafe ten minutes outside of Harvard Square. Deciding it was a good move to present her new self properly, she carried her rolled-up yoga mat via the shoulder strap as well as her canvas tote bag. The yoga mat/tube caught on the doorjamb as she stepped inside the cafe, and while it may have taken two attempts before she was able to cross the threshold without ricocheting off the tube, she did make it in. Celeste was a bit taken aback at the shop's interior, given that she was not familiar with sitting on bean bags or inhaling musky incense in nearly unlit rooms. But this cafe, from what she ascertained online, was an appropriate place for upcoming yogini like her to socialize. And there were, she saw with delight, girls around her age, all wearing loose-fitting pants and tops and lolling about on floor cushions while awful music drifted through the room.

It was rather dark, so it took a few minutes for Celeste to locate a free bean bag, but she did and dropped clumsily into it, trying to control the grunt that erupted when she landed with a thud.

A woman in a long, patterned skirt approached her with a menu. Celeste was sure that the waitress' skirt was actually a wall tapestry that had been tied around her waist, and she made a mental note to locate and purchase such a tapestry skirt for herself. Also, long necklaces made with wood beads. "Welcome to The Harvester. Let me know when you're ready to order."

"The Harvester," Celeste felt, sounded a tad too much like the title of a horror movie that was set on a farm and less like a sexy yoga cafe, but that was okay. "Thank you so much. I'm delighted to be here, as I feel compelled to replenish both my body and soul after the draining hot yoga session I partook of this morning."

Tapestry lady shrugged. "Fabulous."

The menu was somewhat concerning, as Celeste was not familiar with drinks concocted of kale, wheat germ, and amino acids, and such, but she was open to new experiences. She placed her smoothie order with the waitress and smiled as she sat back in her lumpy bean bag chair. Although she had doubts about her choice, a drink dominated by sunflower-seed puree and elderberries, she assumed that the guava-tomato juice base would probably cover up any funny tastes. Maybe.

This would be her new (or first) hang-out spot. How exciting!

A thumping sound came from the next table, where a group of three college-age women in fashionable exercise outfits and numerous jingling bracelets were drinking brightly colored fruit shakes. One had clapped her hands on the table and gasped. "You cannot possibly be serious!" she was saying. In an alarming move, the girl turned in Celeste's direction. "Tell her."

Celeste looked around. "Me?" It was too soon for interaction such as this. She did not even have her beverage yet.

"Yes," the young woman said. "You look like you know what you're doing. Tell my friend that waxing is essential, or she's never going to hold onto, much less keep, a man."

"Oh. Yes. Yes, indeed." Celeste did not recognize her own voice. "Waxing is absolutely essential." Despite not knowing what waxing was, she felt it important to agree. "Totally."

"See? This chick knows what she's talking about. Legs, eyebrows, chin, the whole thing. Gone."

"The whole thing," Celeste agreed. "Very important. Wax. Everywhere."

"Brazilian, right? Tell her she's got to get a Brazilian if she's got any kind of self-esteem."

The girls at the table looked to Celeste for confirmation, so she nodded vigorously and ran a hand through her big curls. This was quite confusing. The girls did not seem like the earth-mother yoga types Celeste had been expecting to find at this place, but she would just roll with the crowd and take lessons in how one should act. "Oh, completely, yes. A Brazilian is a must."

Celeste was not sure what a Brazilian was, but she would have to get whatever this was. Where did one purchase a Brazilian? A South American specialty store? "I get them all the time. The more expensive, the better."

"Exactly!" the girl nearly shouted.

"If you insist," one of her friends said. "I suppose it'll make me less worried when I'm in Greece next month wearing that thong bikini."

"Yes," Celeste added. Her drink arrived, and she took a sip. Okay, it wasn't good. At all. But it was loaded with nutrition, and yoginis required nutrition. And, based on the taste, they probably also required diarrhea, vomiting, or a combination of the two. She valiantly took a giant swig. Rapid consumption might be the key to getting this down. "Brazilian is the only choice."

"Sure, it hurts when they do it, but you can't have any hair peeking out of a bathing suit. Or at naked yoga class. I can't think of anything more god-awful, can you?" The girl turned to Celeste, "Have you done the naked class in Medford yet? It's so freaking awesome. Freeing and fabulous."

"I… I have not. But I am… excited to hear about this," Celeste said with strained cheer. "I do so relish being naked… in group situations…"

Then the girl made a dramatic ripping sound. "So with waxing, they pull the hair out fast as a whip. and then it's over. Just yank it all out. It's the whole reason wax was invented."

The glass in Celeste's hand started to shake. "Wait, what?" She was getting an inkling about what waxing meant in this context.

The waxing enthusiast looked to Celeste. "I mean, if she thinks her boyfriend is going to stick around with an out of control situation going on down there, then she's got to get her head screwed on straight."

"Down… there?" This sounded more and more alarming.

"It's our job as women to keep up with feminine

maintenance, and this is just part of it. You hear me, girl? And a little decorative bejeweling never hurt either. Something special, yeah?"

That was it. Celeste set down her glass and climbed out of her sunken spot. She stood and chaotically threw her tote bag into the crook of her arm as her yoga mat waved awkwardly in front of her. "No, I do not hear you." She threw money onto the table and stormed a few feet past their table before whipping around. "I cannot believe I suggested that painfully extricating the entirety of one's pubic hair in any manner—not to mention such a barbaric one—is a requirement for garnering the commitment of a man. No, no, I refuse to advocate that a woman do anything uncomfortable to her body simply because men have the perverse cultural expectation that all women come to them hairless. Or worse, with assorted gems adorning their genitalia!"

The last thing Celeste heard before she flew out the door was, "Oh. My. God. Did she just say 'genitalia' in public?"

Celeste was now officially over this day. She would not be returning to hot yoga, nor would she continue on her path to becoming a yogini. Nor would she be wearing jingling bracelets and drinking repulsive beverages.

And a Brazilian wax was out of the question.

## CHAPTER 5
# IN WHICH WE ARE INTRODUCED TO A BOY

INSTEAD OF TAKING her usual turn, Celeste parked the car on Mt. Auburn Street, hid behind sunglasses, and walked the brick sidewalks aimlessly. Bordered by the college campus and the Charles River, Harvard Square was her comfort zone. She accepted a flyer from someone offering discounts on hair coloring and another from a guy with tight bright blue pants, which announced auditions for a lead singer for his band. She crumpled the papers into her pocket.

And so she walked and walked. She let her mind go numb because once in a while, it was okay to shut off. Instincts guided her until she found herself sitting on a bench facing the river. This was *her* bench. It was where she came for solace.

The location was a source of both never-ending pain and deep healing. It was where Finn died in a car accident in the dead of winter. She thought about it every day. Erin had been struggling with severe, blinding depression and had taken off in the car, probably totally unaware of what she was doing. Celeste had the devastating experience of walking home from a piano lesson and coming upon the accident. She saw the shattered glass strewn about the street and sidewalk, the crumpled hood, and most of all, her brother's body, lifeless on the icy snow. He'd been in the backseat without a seatbelt, having jumped into the car at the last minute to stop their mother from driving.

Being here in the spot where he died was always a safe place for her. She could connect with a time in her life when things felt easier. When she had been happy. She sighed. There was no way that she could do this, get through this year and then survive college.

Finn had never succumbed to a challenge. Quite the opposite. The desire to face challenges and go at something full force had defined him, He would be very displeased with her hopelessness. If she pretended that he was next to her, guiding her, encouraging her, pushing her hard, maybe she could navigate the rest of high school and then take on college.

She stopped herself. Celeste knew that she was now in dangerous territory. If she was at a point where she was reverting to imagining that her dead brother was standing next to her, then things were bad. Almost three years of carting around a life-size cardboard cutout of him had taught her a thing or two about dysfunctional coping. Flat Finn remained, thankfully, folded on his hinges, safely in the attic.

Clouds were beginning to infiltrate the blue sky, and the October wind off of the Charles made her shiver. Still, she watched crew rowers glide across the water and did not budge from her spot.

"Celeste?"

She startled. "Matthew! What are you doing here?"

He sat next to her. "Just came down here to walk on water. Perform a few other miraculous antics. You know, the usual."

"Of course. The wind is picking up, so I do hope the upcoming rough waters will not thwart your plans." Even Celeste could hear the lack of affect in her voice. She was tired.

"You don't sound right." Matt examined her. She tried to turn away, but he reached for her sunglasses and lifted them up. Matt waited until she met his look. This is what Celeste hated, the worried expression on his face and the clear concern that she was a disaster. Matt awkwardly rubbed his fingers under her eyes and over her cheeks.

"Matthew, stop that. I am perfectly fine." She hoped that her voice was convincing. "I'm probably just still sweating from yoga."

"I had no idea you were into yoga."

"Well, I am. Or I was. It may not pan out into a full-fledged lifestyle after all. And you cannot possibly keep up with all of my activities," she said hurriedly. "This is a busy time for me, both socially and academically. In fact, I should probably get going because I still have a busy day. It's got to be after four o'clock already." She stood. "Would you like a ride back to your apartment?"

Matt tipped his head to the side. His dirty blond hair blew into his eyes. She could see that being by this bench was emotional for him too. Both of them were quiet for a moment.

Finally Matt answered her. "Sure. But let me buy you a cup of hot chocolate first. Okay?"

"Were I five years old, a cup of hot chocolate might sound lovely."

"A different hot beverage then." Matt got up and shoved his hands into his pockets. "Let's hang out for a while."

She paused. It was hard to say no to her brother, and his presence was already helping her a bit. "I gladly accept your invitation."

They walked silently down JFK Street and into the weekend hubbub of the center of Harvard Square. She stopped them by the window of The Curious George Store. "I used to love those books..." she said.

"Pfft. I always thought the Man with the Yellow Hat was a condescending ass."

"Matty!" Celeste scolded him. "He was not! He was in charge of a mischievous monkey. He had a right to show the occasional spark of irritation. And more so, he was forever coming to George's rescue."

"If by 'in charge' you mean that he kidnapped a perfectly happy monkey from his doting parents and illegally took him from the jungle, and then tried to confine him to a zoo, sure he was a shining example of being in 'charge.' And what exactly does the Man do for work, huh? Something nefarious if you ask me. All that money? Fancy yellow cars? And what's up with coordinating his hat to his car? Or... his car to his hat? Which came first?" Matt shook his head. "So many questions."

Celeste swatted Matt on the arm. "You are hopeless."

"Seems to be the consensus."

They crossed the Brattle Street intersection as Celeste asked, "Why would you say such a thing? You are not hopeless. You are the opposite."

"Oh, nothing. Sorry. Ignore me." Matt slowed to look into the windows of The Coop.

She waited for him, taking in the diverse Harvard Square crowd. She did love how everyone, even she, seemed to fit in here. There were no rules, and there was a spot for the oddest of the odd. Take the homeless man who wore a plastic crown and rode through the mass of people on a unicycle while reciting Bible verses? Hardly anyone gave him a glance. Skaters, professors, hippies, business people... Everyone belonged, no matter what individuality or stereotype they embraced. Cambridge was home for her. How on earth was she going to leave here next year? Perhaps she should go to Harvard and stay right where she was. She could live at home, after all.

But just then a group of chattering, smiling students walked by her, one of them with a Harvard jacket on. And it hit her again: even at college, *even at Harvard,* there were social expectations that could not be avoided. College did not just take place in isolated classrooms.

The yoga thing clearly hadn't panned out, but something else would need to. Celeste was not about to turn up at an Ivy League school without making dramatic changes to herself.

"Hey," Matt said. "There's a tea shop around the corner on Church Street. I feel like we should have tea."

"I do not like tea."

"Me neither." He scooted through the crowd.

She quickened her pace to keep up with her brother. "Then why must we have tea?"

"Because you're clearly part British."

"I assume you are referencing my speech patterns." She sniffed and lifted up her chin. "That is not funny."

"It's a little bit funny, my Victorian sister."

"One cannot help one's tendencies."

"Then we shall have tea together, shall we not?"

"Fine. But I expect this place to have Shrewsbury cakes and rout drops. Perhaps even cocoa flummery."

"See? Told ya you'd like having tea!"

"I will not like it. I am guessing that I should prepare for a stale scone and a flavorless hot beverage, so I will instead rely on your companionship for enjoyment."

"Then you're definitely in trouble." They walked a few blocks, and then Matt held open the door to the tea shop. "After you, m'lady. I want to hear about your visit to Yale last weekend."

With her hands warming up as she cradled the tea cup, Celeste gave a short summary of Yale. It was... Yale. What was not to love? Beautiful campus delivering one of the top educations in the world, intense academic pressure, highly astute and brilliant professors. Things Celeste loved. Or should love.

"You don't make it sound very exciting."

"It was," she said dryly. She was having an inexplicably difficult time mustering enthusiasm. "I... I suppose that I do not want to get my hopes up should I be denied acceptance."

"Celeste? They *asked* you to come for an interview. You're getting in."

"There are other schools to consider. I am keeping a compare-and-contrast chart of different colleges. We shall see which one comes out on top. There's Dartmouth. Harvard... those. What are the others? I don't know. Those silly schools..." Her voice trailed off.

"What?" Matt leaned in. "Who are you, and what have you done with my sister?"

"Huh? Oh… oh dear." Celeste shook her head and smiled. "I am not sure what came over me. Really, all are highly desirable schools. I will be delighted to accept any one of them."

"Obviously Harvard is Harvard, but you don't want to stay at home. Trust me. Get out while you can." He winked. "Really, I don't know how you could find a better fit than Yale. And it's not too far, so I can come down and embarrass you in front of your friends." Matt nudged Celeste in the arm.

"Actually, I would adore having you visit, Matthew." She didn't know what else to say. Yale, Princeton, Cornell, U Penn… They were all blending into one collegiate blob. "Perhaps when you come to visit me, you will take the opportunity to extend your travels."

"And to where else, I dare ask, do you suggest I travel?"

"Why not explore our great country. The west coast, as a random suggestion. California has lovely weather, really, year round."

"Celeste…" Matt warned

"It is merely a suggestion. Los Angeles, I believe, is beckoning you."

"I sense that a Julie conversation is upon us, so let me just stop you right there."

"Julie and I still email each other," Celeste said, "And text. Why do *you* not do that with her?"

Matt did little to hide his exasperation. "You know we're not together. Therefore, we don't go around texting each other adorable things."

"I did not say that the communication exchanges had to be adorable."

He crossed his arms. "What exactly should we be talking about then? Just minor chit chat? The weather? I could say, 'It's cold and miserable here like it always is,' and then she could say, 'It's sunny and fantastic *here* like it always is.' Would that make you happy? Because it wouldn't make me happy."

"I did not mean to upset you, Matthew." Celeste did feel terrible now. She knew that Julie was a sore subject. Still, there was always the hope that they might recapture what they'd had together. She had very much liked Matt and Julie as a couple, and their separation still hit Celeste hard. "You could send her a picture of you in that T-shirt. It is very much what she calls 'geeky.'"

Matt glanced down at his shirt, and Celeste was pleased that he couldn't stop himself from smiling.

"See? She would find it amusing. *Never trust an atom. They make up everything.* It is quite funny. You two could engage in a friendly exchange."

"And then what? It's done, Celeste. It's been done for a long time."

"But I have concerns that you live alone and that you do not have a girlfriend. There has been no one since Julie, has there? Two years, Matthew. That is a long time."

He glared at her.

Celeste missed Julie, too. Julie who had swooped into their lives when Celeste had been thirteen. Julie who had captured their hearts and taught them to save themselves from the paralyzing, dysfunctional grief that had taken hold after Finn was killed. The pain nearly destroyed the family, but Julie's presence in their lives slowly undid many of the tight knots that kept them from moving forward. And in the process, Matt had fallen in love. Deeply in love. But now that was over.

"You are a grown up now, Matthew."

"Oh my God, I'm a what?" Matt gasped and flailed his hands around. "How did this happen? When? It's not fair!"

Celeste rolled her eyes. "You are terribly funny. I know that I made an obvious statement, but I hate to see you age and not have a great romance in your life."

"You hate to see me *age*? Are you aware that I'm not a hundred years old yet? I mean, soon, of course, but I have a little time left before I reach for my walker."

"I suppose you do. But the proverbial clock is ticking, and I say that as someone who has no affection for proverbial expressions."

"Celeste…" He sighed. "I don't want to talk about this. Please."

"I apologize. I do. We can go back to discussing my collegiate future."

Two mugs of tea later, brother and sister returned to the cold. It was getting dark now, and the street lights and neon signs lit up the street. Celeste tucked her arm into Matt's as they walked. "Matty?" she said softly.

"Yeah?"

"Thank you."

He looked as his feet as they walked. "Nothing to thank me for."

"That's not true." She leaned her head on his shoulder and squeezed his arm. "I suspect that to others, right now we may appear to be a romantically linked couple. But I enjoy looping my elbow with yours, so I do not mind."

"Don't be gross," he said with a laugh, "although this is the closest thing to a date that I've had in a while."

"At least you have had dates in your life. I have yet to experience even one."

"That will change, you know. I promise."

"No. I don't believe it will. It feels clear that romance will not be a part of my life. I don't hold that appeal."

"Celeste, stop it. Don't worry about dating right now. As your brother, I'll say that it grosses me out to admit this, but you're a beautiful girl and must have guys all over you. I bet you're just being picky. As you should. And, frankly, I don't think you should date until you're forty."

"No matter. I am fortunate to have such a solid, dynamic group of comrades. Truly. It really is special to be part of the so-called 'in crowd.'" She flinched. This was a particularly hideous lie, Celeste thought, but it reassured Matthew. "Yet, in terms of dating, if males are drawn to me for my appearance, they are soon discouraged by my other qualities. Eccentricities, of which I know I have many, do not hold universal sexual and romantic lure. I understand that."

Matt stopped them, and he looked her in the eye. "Listen to me. You don't need to give a crap about universal anything. You give a crap when you have love that defies boundaries. That's it."

"Is that what you had?"

He paused, clearly uncomfortable. "I thought so."

"But it was not enough. Not enough to make you try with everything you had."

"Stop."

"You did not. Or you would be with Julie. I know that you are fantastically in love with her. Still. But that does not, I gather, matter."

"That's different. Circumstances changed. She got that great job in Los Angeles with the UC–Davis study-abroad program. She had to go. I mean, she's in charge of creating programs in different countries and communicating with universities all over the world. It was an amazing position for her, and she earned it. And I had to stay here for M.I.T. "

"So there. You have proved the point. If you and Julie were not able to rise above simple challenges such as location, I decidedly cannot rise above what is clearly a more catastrophic set of problems."

"Location is not simple. And what about you is catastro—"

"Wait! California!" She stopped short and jerked Matt back.

"Huh?"

Celeste scanned the street. "I just remembered something."

And there, across the street from them, was Border Cafe. It was already five-thirty, past the start time of the Barton event. Not that she would have gone inside anyway. Church Street was bustling tonight as people headed for their favorite restaurants and bars, and a line was forming outside The Brattle Theatre. She moved her head to see past pedestrians. A young man in a bright blue hooded sweatshirt and black down vest stood out front, holding open the door for diners who were entering and exiting, and he did so with such style that

Celeste couldn't help but be intrigued. Each time he reached for the door handle, he simultaneously performed a dramatic bow, complete with a sweeping hand gesture, followed by a quick, full-body spin. The patrons were eating it up.

"It has a slightly tacky sign, does it not?" she murmured.

"What has a what?" Matt asked.

"That restaurant. I have never noticed it. I was invited to something there tonight, but I politely declined."

"You've lived here your entire life and never noticed Border Cafe? I've failed you as a brother, clearly. You want to grab dinner? I feel a craving for a margarita or nine."

"What? Now? No. No, certainly not." But she could not take her eyes off the boy who stood out front. He bounced on his toes a few times and then hopped in the air and landed by the door just in time to let out more customers, who he then saluted very properly and marched alongside with high knee-lifts as he escorted them to the next block. The three girls giggled in response to his antics as the boy dashed back to his post.

"Hello?" Matt waved his hands in front of her face. "Celeste? What are we doing? If we're not going in, then let's go. It's getting cold."

"Sure. Okay..." But she watched the boy. "Let's cross here." She dragged Matt across the street, causing a taxi to brake hard.

"No, that's fine. I don't mind if that taxi hits us. Really. Hospitals are fun on Saturday nights," Matt grumbled. "No one's ever there."

"They are indeed fun," she replied, only half paying attention.

As they slowly walked toward the restaurant, she made eye contact with the boy in the hoodie. He paused for a moment—just a moment—and tilted his head to side. She took in the way his soft brown hair did a sort of whooshing-off-his-face thing that she quite liked. As if on cue, he ran a hand haphazardly through it and started to smile at her, looking a bit hopeful. Hopeful as to what, Celeste did not know. Most likely that his boyish good looks would charm her and that he'd bring in more customers. He had short sideburns. Wide eyes of the lightest blue. And smooth pale skin that was flushed from the chill. There was energy and freedom and kindness about him. Celeste had to admit that if the Barton event weren't going on right now, she could be persuaded.

"Come on!" Matt yanked at her arm. "You can't just stop walking in the middle of an intersection."

She realized that they had crossed one street, rounded by the restaurant and were now stagnant in the crosswalk of Palmer Street, her eyes still glued to the boy. "Yes, this is unsafe. We should move." Matt tugged at her arm. "Yes, okay." Her voice was barely audible.

Then, in what Celeste found to be the smoothest of movements, the boy dropped to one knee, swept his arm across his body and gestured to the front door. She blushed and shook her head slightly. She turned her back to him and finished crossing the street.

But when safely on the corner across from the restaurant, Celeste dropped her arm from Matt's and looked back. She swept one foot behind her and lowered herself evenly in a perfect curtsy. It was not a voluntary move, but more as though her body had been invaded by someone with flirting skills.

She bounced up and rushed ahead of Matt, her palm pressed to her forehead in horror. "Damn it, Matthew!"

"Oh my God, what is going on? Did you just *curtsy* at someone?" Matt tried to turn his head to see behind them, but she put her hand flat on the side of his face and pushed him away.

"This is your fault! Why did you refer to me as *Victorian*? Look what I have done! How atrocious and... and... absurd!" She stormed ahead. "You should consider yourself fortunate that I am still willing to give you a ride."

"Will we be making the journey by horse and carriage or—"

"That is not amusing to me!"

Still, despite the moronic curtsy, Celeste felt a certain level of cheer at having seen the boy in the blue hoodie and black vest. The boy with the whooshy hair and cool sideburns.

The boy who got down on one knee for her, if only for a moment.

# CHAPTER 6
# THE SNOWY OWL

*Dear Celeste-*

*So sorry we didn't see you on Saturday! The Camptown shrimp were good, but it was missing something. I'm pretty sure it was Barton's most sought-after student. The lead recruiter for our school, Peter Fritz, spent the entire night adjusting his tie and scanning the room for you, even though nobody knows what you look like! Anyway, I'm back at school now, but I'll be part of some more events over Thanksgiving weekend and then winter break. The east coast is a hot spot for applicants, possibly because during the winter months we wave around giant pictures of sunny San Diego and throw sand and seashells. Of course, there was once an unfortunate incident with a seashell and someone's head and a possible laceration… Look, I don't have good aim, what can I say?*

*The school is sending out actual official emails and postcards for these events, so you won't have to rely on me for*

*information via six hundred separate emails! You'll miss them,*
*I bet, right? Yeah, I know, I know…*

*Really, Barton is such a great school, and we would love*
*to tell you more about it. I'm sure you're getting pursued by*
*all the big names. I get that. But I can't say enough about the*
*professors here, not to mention that the students are some of*
*the greatest people I've ever met. To be honest, I didn't have*
*that phenomenal of a time in high school, so maybe I notice*
*this more than others would, but campus culture is part of the*
*whole college experience. Very strong academics lured me in,*
*but it's the people who keep me here.*

*-Justin*

Celeste slumped deeper into the armchair and squirmed,
using her feet to pull the ottoman closer. This cushiony chair
was one of her favorite spots. Nestled into a funny nook below
one of the windows in her room, she often sat here, as she did
now, with a knitted blanket around her shoulders while she
worked. In warmer months, she would lift open the window
and allow spring and summer air to flow in. She loved the
smells during those times, when plants and flowers came to
life again. In the evenings, the jasmine released its scent and
flooded her room, and Celeste would close her eyes and in-
hale, drifting away in thought.

She pulled her blanket tighter around her shoulders. It
was interesting that Justin commented on his high school experience. She fidgeted for a moment and then typed.

*Justin-*

*I, too, am sorry that I was not able to attend the Barton "meet-up" and that I missed the now infamous Camptown shrimp. Please extend my apologies to Mr. Fritz, as well. I do hope the event was successful.*

*Yes, high school can be a challenging and cumbersome balancing act for many teens, what with all the social and academic pressures weighing down like multiple copies of Dickens novels stacked atop one's head. Even at private schools like mine, students can demonstrate remarkable levels of callousness and heartlessness.*

*While I must acknowledge being highly flattered by Barton's eagerness to meet me in person, I also must be fair in conveying that I have set my sights on, as you correctly guessed, Ivy League institutions. Barton does sound like a lovely school, though. I am curious; how does Barton know about me?*

*Best wishes,*

*Celeste*

This business of emailing back and forth with Justin felt markedly out of character, yet it also felt distinctly good. And there was, she knew, safety in these exchanges because she would never meet him or have to manage in-person communication. It was as though he did not actually exist in the real world, but rather retained a small and imaginary place in an alternate universe. She liked having him there.

*Celeste-*

*One of your teachers... I can't remember his name... something fishy sounding... I mean, not that he's a fishy-sounding person in terms of his behavior or character, but his actual name has something to do with fish. Do you know a Mr. Bass? Or Mr. Filet? No, that can't be right. Anyway, this teacher of yours went to Barton and must think you'd be a good match. But in any case, he talked to the dean about you, so we've been told to woo you. (BTW, our dean's name is, I swear on my life, Dr. Dean! So he's Dean Dean!) But I gather my wooing is not working all that well… Let's see… You'd love the west coast. Do you like farm-to-table restaurants? San Diego has a lot of those. I like this place called Blue Ribbon Rustic Kitchen in Hillcrest. They make a burrata that will BOWL. YOU. OVER. And we have deep blue harbors where you can go and watch boats or take a cheesy tourist boat ride (but it's fun to do once). Symphony, opera, theaters? No? How about sandcastle lessons? Seriously, I'm not making that up. Look it up on Yelp. I'm not very good with sandcastles because the patience required to position EVERY SINGLE STUPID GRAIN OF SAND is a bit much for me. Oh, so also, there's Point Loma, Sunset Cliffs National Park, anything in La Jolla… Speaking of La Jolla, there's the Salk Institute. You know, if you're into genetics, or microbiology, or diseases, or plants. Or the genetic microbiology of plant diseases. I'm pretty sure they do everything there. I think you can take a tour of the architecture, although I suppose that's not exciting unless you're one for architecture, as I am. Barton, by the way, has a fabulous architecture program. That's what I'm majoring in, in case I haven't mentioned that. Do you know what you want to major in? I could get you some more information on whatever programs you like.*

*I'm home in three weeks. Mr. Fritz would be on cloud nine if you agreed to come to the next event. It's Wednesday,*

*the night before Thanksgiving. Of course, I don't have the date
in front of me, as might not surprise you by now. You'll like
him. He drinks Bloody Marys with extra olives and wears a
watch on each wrist. (No, I don't know why, and I'm scared to
ask; but it's nevertheless super intriguing and funny.)*

*-Justin*

*Celeste-*

*I have to apologize for saying "on cloud nine." That was
a cliché and I hate clichés. There's no excuse. Ugh. Make no
bones about it, you can rake me over the coals for that and tell
me that the Barton ship has sailed, so I should go jump in a
lake.*

*-Justin*

The giggle that burst from her lips surprised her. And,
even more, the rush of happiness when another email immediately popped up in her inbox.

*Celeste-*

*Okay, one more thing. I have to show this to somebody,
and my roommate's out. I just made myself a cup of coffee,
and I have this mini milk-frother thing that, well, froths milk
obviously, so I put that on top of the coffee and then I drizzle
chocolate syrup over it. I make one in the morning and then
one usually late at night if I'm studying. Okay, but so I just
made this one and I stirred it up a little with these wooden
sticks I have (they're not really sticks as in branches, but just
super skinny, possibly anorexic, popsicle sticks that are sold as
stirrers), and so the chocolate smeared, and look! Do you see*

*what I see? I just drizzled away randomly. Swear. I didn't try
to make this happen.*

*Also, another out-of-nowhere question: Do you like
sushi? San Diego has excellent sushi. I'm sure Boston does,
too, but California sushi is so much better. (I may lose my
Massachusetts residency for saying that. Don't tell anyone. Go,
Red Sox!)*

*-Justin*

She felt quite sure that the last thing this boy needed was
caffeine, but below Justin's email, he'd attached a photo; an
overhead view of his coffee creation.

Celeste smiled. There was, undeniably, a chocolate owl
looking back at her. She opened the photo and enlarged it.
A snowy owl, she decided. It was really quite the creation, accident or not. Out of curiosity, she rotated the picture once by
ninety degrees.

*Justin-*

*There is much to address here, so I will use a numbered
list in order not to miss any points.*

1. *I very much like the coffee owl. I believe there are baristi
   who specialize in intentionally creating extraordinary
   designs in the foam of cappuccinos and such, and you
   have managed to do so without even trying. I think that
   is rather fantastic. You may find it interesting to learn
   that if you turn the owl on its side, your frothy image
   is no longer an owl, but becomes what I imagine Puck
   from A Midsummer Night's Dream to look like. But I feel*

*convinced that this owl's name is Clive. It suits him, do*
*you not agree?*

2. *Food. You have a strong interest in culinary explorations,*
   *I gather. I, too, enjoy the gastronomical world. My mother*
   *attempts a wide array of dishes, some with greater flavor*
   *success than others. I do not eat out often and have never*
   *tried sushi. I do hope that my mother does not attempt*
   *to serve sushi at home. I have visions of food poisoning*
   *passing before my eyes. As for farm-to-table restaurants,*
   *they sound lovely. My father grows tomatoes in the*
   *summer, but I have doubts that serving those in a salad*
   *constitutes true farm-to-table eating?*

3. *I have not had burrata, but Google tells me that this is a*
   *fresh mozzarella ball of sorts, filled with what is essentially*
   *mozzarella cream. It sounds rich and heavenly, and I*
   *should very much like to try it.*

4. *I cannot imagine that the Camptown shrimp dish's flavor*
   *was in any way altered because I was not there; however,*
   *I will trust that you felt that something was missing.*
   *Perhaps a new chef? A recipe tweak?*

5. *I, too, have a distaste for clichés, so that is something that*
   *we have in common.*

6. *Beverage notes: While I have never had a bloody Mary*
   *myself, even virgin style, I hear they are very good,*
   *particularly when made with fresh horseradish. Mr. Fritz*
   *clearly has a love for the spicy and piquant, does he not?*

7. *I am hesitant to firmly RSVP to this next Barton*
   *gathering, even though Mr. Fritz will be in attendance, as*
   *it is the night before the Thanksgiving holiday. I will see*
   *what arrangements can be made.*

Celeste paused in her writing.

> *To be direct with you, group social events often do not*
> *work out well for me. I find them difficult. In fact, most*
> *social events are seemingly impossible for me to navigate*
> *in a way that does not alienate others. I hope you*
> *understand.*
>
> 8. *San Diego sounds to be a very appealing city, and a*
>    *touristy boat ride and sandcastle building are attractive*
>    *lures.*
> 9. *Architecture must be a challenging and dynamic major. I*
>    *am undecided what to major in right now, although some*
>    *specialty in literature holds appeal for me.*

*Best wishes,*
*Celeste*

*Celeste-*

*I understand about group events. I don't want to make*
*you uncomfortable, but I'll make sure that you get an*
*invitation just in case you change your mind. Okay? Maybe*
*we could get together while I'm in town, and then it wouldn't*
*be a big group situation. Would you like that better?*

*I really enjoy emailing with you. Is that weird to say? I*
*hope not.*

*-Justin*

Words usually came easily to Celeste, but right now she

had none. She sat for a few moments, trying to decide how she felt and how to respond. This was unfamiliar territory for her.

She walked from her room and to the kitchen. Although she had teased Matt the other day about wanting to take her out for hot chocolate, a cup of rich hot cocoa seemed in order today. Although it hadn't snowed yet, it was certainly gloomy and cold enough out to set the mood for the upcoming winter. She heated milk on the stove and took sugar and dark unsweetened cocoa from the cabinet. It took a few minutes for the milk to come to a near boil, and as she whisked in the chocolate and sugar, a thought occurred to her. She abandoned the hot pot and scooped spoonfuls of sugar onto the counter until a solid circle of shimmering crystals formed. Then with the back of the spoon, she carefully swooped lines through the sugar.

Celeste took her cell from her back pocket and snapped a picture, which she then emailed to Justin.

Justin-

It's perhaps rudimentary, but here's my snowy owl for you.
-Celeste

The whoosh of the email echoed in the quiet kitchen, and Celeste noticed—with no small amount of shock—that her message contained two contractions.

"How odd," she said to the sugar owl. "How very, very odd."

## CHAPTER 7
# DON'T FLINCH

CELESTE BELTED OUT the final la la la's of the song as best she could, trying to keep her voice steady and clear. Auditioning for a band was nerve-wracking enough, so the expressionless stares from the three college boys in front of her were not helping. She replaced the microphone back on the stand and took an awkward bow.

It was hard, she was learning, to move easily in a skintight catsuit, but she had felt it appropriate to dress the part. Or what she guessed the part would look like. The costume selection from the school's drama department offered a finite selection from which to choose. She would return it, of course, since Celeste was not a thief, but she did feel slightly guilty about taking it without asking. The flyer that she'd taken from the rocker in Harvard Square didn't spell out too many details on song or fashion choices, and she didn't know much about "skate punk" music, so it had been up to her to package herself. The girl at the salon this morning had been all too enthusiastic about coloring Celeste's hair neon red, and even though she promised that it would wash out soon enough, Celeste was not yet comfortable with the red spiral curls that kept falling into her eyes. Now that the backing track was off, the room was eerily silent.

The lead guitarist of Flinch Noggins rubbed his lips together for a moment and shook some lint from his flannel shirt. "Huh. What did you say the name of that song was again?"

"The song is titled 'The Night They Drove Old Dixie Down.' It was originally performed by The Band, but was made most famous by the talented Joan Baez," she answered energetically. "You may have heard some of the Baez style in my performance, but I did try to put my own character into it." She brushed her hair from her face and waited for a reaction. "I thought it smart to showcase my abilities in a song that conveyed strong political and emotional themes because many bands are driven by raw passions. It is a song about the Civil War. When the southern states were experiencing defeat. We have all experienced defeat and suffering, have we not?" In fact, Celeste knew that she was experiencing both right at that moment because not only was it clear that she was not about to be the next member of Flinch Noggins, but this catsuit had embedded itself between her butt cheeks in a truly uncomfortable manner. "I did not realize that the term 'garage band' was so literal and that bands do, in fact, rehearse their performances in actual garages. How... inspiring." She glanced at the trash bins and the workbench piled with tools.

The drummer hit his sticks together and tapped his

combat boots on the concrete floor of the garage. "Here's the thing, Cecile…"

"Celeste," she corrected him. "Celeste Watkins."

"Okay, right, right. You've got a smokin' look. I mean, you're, like, seriously hot. But we're hardcore, man, and that was all Joni Mitchell and stuff."

She sighed. "Joan Baez. I do not know any of the popular skate punk songs, but I am a diligent worker and assure you that I could pick up your style very quickly."

The guitarist shook his head. "It wasn't even good Joni Mitchell, dude."

"Joan Baez!" she said with frustration. But it didn't matter. She walked stiffly to the dusty table by the door to gather her things. "Would one of you gentlemen mind lifting my bag for me? I have concerns about attempting to bend over in this outfit, lest I tear the seams. Or break a rib."

All three band members shot out of their seats and rushed to her side. The bass player reached her first and gently put her bag over her shoulder. "You don't seem like much of a skater chick. You know, with the weird song and the talking and all. You don't really fit in here."

"I just thought… maybe I could." She took a few perilous steps forward on her spiked-heel vinyl boots. "I do want to thank you for allowing me this opportunity. Goodbye. I wish the Flinch Noggins great success. I am sure you will find a suitable lead singer in no time. I am terrifically sorry for having wasted your time today. This was indeed an egregious error on my part."

Celeste hobbled out of the garage and made her way to the car. She fumbled with her keys in the cold November air.

Tomorrow was Thanksgiving, yet she was not feeling very thankful right now.

"Hey, Celeste! Wait up!" The drummer bounded over and leaned against the car. "You all right?"

"Did I leave something behind?" she asked.

"No," he said. "I just wanted to make sure you're okay. You looked kinda bummed back there."

"I am just fine. I must apologize again. I should not have come."

"Nah, don't say that. You did your own thing. I admire that. I'm sorry this didn't work out. I'm Zeke, by the way. I don't know if we even told you our names." The drummer finished securing his long hair into an elastic and held out a hand. She put hers into his and met his look. His brown eyes were friendly, and she found this disarming, especially since the band was clearly unhappy with her performance. "Don't be discouraged," he said.

"The audition process is just a process. It is not, I know, a guarantee of acceptance."

"Look, you did a nice job, although this Joan Baez is not really our thing. She must be a cool chick, though, since you like her." His breath was white in the night air. "I'm not sure what's going on with this outfit, 'cause it doesn't seem very you—Hey, wait a minute! I know you!"

"You do?"

"You're in my chem class! Oh my God, I didn't even recognize you!" He laughed and clapped his hands together. "Cool switchover, man!"

"You are in my class?" Oh no, this was not good. "I thought you were all in college?"

"Aww, the other guys are, and they don't like to advertise that one of us isn't, you know? They don't want a high school kid in their sick band." He winked.

"Oh," she said nodding. "Sick. Very much so. Yes, of course."

"At the rate I'm going, I don't even know if I'll get into college, but whatever. I'll just hope the band takes off."

"I see. I am sure you will do just fine. The good news is that anyone who auditions after me will look even better than they might have otherwise." She forced a smile.

"You're being too hard on yourself." Zeke crossed his arms. "I'm glad you tried out, and you should be, too. I didn't know you had this side of you. You're so studious at school. Like, totally in another league. But I guess we have something in common, huh? I feel kinda honored that you tried out, man."

"That is a gracious attitude despite its being clear that I do not belong here. I do not have the talent that you have. This is not really who I am."

"It must be some part of you." He nudged her softly with his elbow. "Listen, it's freezing out here, so I gotta go back in. But I hope you at least had a little fun?"

"It was an experience."

"Cool. I'll see you after break. Have a good Thanksgiving!" Zeke ran back to the garage.

It took ten minutes for the car to warm up nicely and to stop shivering. As she drove home, Celeste understood something important: Zeke had been nice to her. Really, genuinely nice. Maybe Dallas' effort to reach out had been sincere after all. And maybe Celeste should have replied to her text. Maybe it was not too late? It was a risk she would take.

> **Celeste:** Dallas, thank you for recommending that romantic story to me. I did read it, and I enjoyed it immensely.

A white lie was allowed on occasion.

So between Zeke and Dallas, there were now two people at her school who were speaking to her. Two was a rather small number, but it was better than none. Not enough reason to get overly giddy, but it was something. So despite her underlying sense of discouragement, she did feel slightly happy this evening.

Until she pulled up to her house off Brattle Street in Cambridge and saw her parents' cars. And another unfamiliar car. What? The plan was to get home before her family did so that she would have time to shower and scrub her hair back to its natural color and then change into regular clothes. How was she going to explain this unexpected radical new look? Her good mood evaporated. She was, in fact, quite angry. And the catsuit wedgie had reached new depths.

Celeste got out of the car and slammed the door. Then she thought better of making any noise. If she were lucky, she might be able to sneak in the house and up the stairs to the bathroom where she could lather the shocking red out of her hair. She walked slowly up the steps to the porch. Coming home usually comforted her. It was a safe place, away from so many troubling situations. She wanted nothing more than to skirt inside undetected and reclaim some normality.

Even though the door shut relatively quietly behind her, her father must have heard something because his head popped into the hallway from the kitchen. "Ah, Celeste, you're home. Wonderful. Someone is here—Oh, God. Celeste? Erin, come here. Something is going on."

"What in the world is the problem, Roger?"

Celeste widened her eyes, silently begging her father to let her go up the stairs. Standing in front of him in this body-hugging catsuit was most embarrassing.

"Uh, I think Celeste wants to change first. Before she meets our *guest*," he said pointedly.

A guest? What guest?

Her dad tipped his head toward the staircase and Celeste clopped across the wood floor, rushing as fast as she could in the impossibly high shoes. But just when she grabbed the railing, Erin's voice raised another octave. "Celeste! Please come say hello."

"As you wish," she barked back. "I would be happy to meet this guest of ours! What a goddamn smashing delight!" With a toss of her hair, she lifted her head high and walked confidently, if not steadily, past her still-stunned father and into the kitchen.

"Language," he warned in a whisper.

"Good evening." Celeste waited for the reaction.

"Holy…. Ha ha!" Fantastic. Matt was here too. And not doing a smooth job of acting normally. "This is the best day ever." He scooted his chair closer to the kitchen table and rested his chin in his hands, taking position to watch the scene unfold. "Hi, sister of mine. How was your day?"

Celeste glared at him. The smile plastered on his face was entirely unamusing.

Erin cleared her throat and swooped to Celeste's side. If there was one thing Erin was good at, it was pretending nothing was amiss when everything was amiss. There was a slight shake in her words, but otherwise she sounded remarkably cheery. "Aren't you colorful today?" Her fingers gripped Celeste's arms just a little too tightly as she pivoted Celeste around to face the small love seat. "You have a visitor."

There in front of her was a boy.

And she had seen him once before.

In front of Border Café.

Dear God, what was he doing in her kitchen? And on today of all days? She was finding it suddenly hard to breathe. Especially with his big blue eyes twinkling up at her, and his thick hair all messily pushed back from his face.

"This is Justin Milano," Erin said.

She gathered whatever poise she could and extended her hand. "It is a pleasure to—Wait, what?" Celeste turned to her mother. "This is who?"

# ONE AND THE SAME

## CHAPTER 8

"JUSTIN MILANO. ALL the way from Barton College in San Diego. He's home to spend Thanksgiving with his family."

"And so he came here?" Celeste whispered.

Justin stood and shook her limp hand. "Hey, it's really nice to meet you finally. You were on the school's contact list, so I just gave a call earlier; but you weren't here, so I talked to your mom for a while. I mentioned your fishy teacher, Mr. Gil and how he'd gone to Barton, and she said how awesome Mr. Gil is, and then she said that you were out, but that I should come on over anyway. Hope you don't mind?" He then tucked his hands into the back pockets of his jeans and lifted up and down on his toes. "I told your mother about how much Barton was interested in your attending, and how we'd emailed a bunch, and your mom had lots of questions about the school." Justin took a quick breath. "This is a great area you guys live in. I love Cambridge and used to walk up and down by the river and explore all the old houses on the side streets. Really charming houses with such style. Did Celeste tell you that I'm an architecture major? I guess I've always been interested in buildings. I love it all. Doors, eaves, porches, roofs. It's the little things, not just the main structure of a house. The character, the feel." He swayed side to side. "Oh, so, anyway, it's nice to finally meet you. I said that already, didn't I? Sorry."

"That's perfectly all right. I'm going to open some sparkling water. Would you like some, Justin?" Erin asked.

"That would be very nice, thank you."

"Celeste? For you also? Why don't you sit down with Justin? Dinner should be ready soon, and then perhaps you can tell us about your day."

"Yes," Matt piped in excitedly. "We'd *love* to hear about your day."

Celeste swallowed hard and then sat down next to Justin. Who was gorgeous. The weight of her family's stares could not be ignored. Whether they came solely from her outrageous look or because she was sitting next to a boy, she wasn't sure. Both were humiliating. She looked straight ahead and focused on the boiling pot of water on the stove. "My parents and brother are a bit taken aback by my appearance right now."

"Ah, I see. Well, I guess this isn't exactly what I thought you'd be like, but it's certainly a striking statement. Really, I mean, the hair is wild."

"I am returning from an audition," she explained.

Matt snickered. "An audition for something legal or illegal?"

She glared at him. "Legal, of course. A local band was looking for new talent, so I performed to the best of my abilities."

"I didn't realize that you sang," Roger said. He, too, seemed on the verge of giggling, yet Celeste found nothing funny about this situation. "How did this audition go?"

"Very well. The band is most interested in having me join as the lead singer, but I have to evaluate my commitments."

"Really?" Erin handed glasses with water and lime slices to Justin and her. "You know, I used to sing with a small ensemble in college."

Matt nearly jumped out of his seat. "Mother-daughter duets tonight, I beg of you!"

"Shut up," Celeste snapped.

"Just an idea, just an idea." He waved his hands innocently.

"Dinner will be ready soon," Erin said. "Homemade spinach pasta with pesto. Green beans on the side. And salad. I'm trying out a theory that monochromatic meals deliver a certain pleasurable sensory experience. Roger and Matt, would you help me while Celeste entertains her guest? And, Justin, I look forward to hearing more about Barton. I admit I know very little, although I do know that it has a remarkable reputation. One of those schools that I believe is undeservedly under the radar. We're so happy you're here."

The open kitchen allowed her family a perfect view of the loveseat while they finished cooking. She sat stiffly and stared straight ahead as she tried to identify a way out of all of this.

Justin leaned in and spoke softly. "I'm sorry. I hope you don't mind, but your parents invited me to stay for dinner. I don't have to if this is too weird."

The top of his arm touched hers. Celeste's entire body felt flush. She had no idea why. It must be the embarrassment of being caught in this ludicrous getup. It was possible that she might now overheat in this vinyl catsuit and simply dissolve into nothing right in front of him. It was not a totally undesirable concept.

This situation was unfair. She'd had no warning whatsoever that she would be meeting the person she had been emailing and with whom she had been exchanging snowy owls. The plan had been... Well, there hadn't exactly been a plan per se, but she certainly had never intended to find herself face to face with Justin. Nor with the boy who got down on one knee for her. Nor that those two would turn out to be one and the same person.

And now he was staying for dinner, and she was dressed in a highly inappropriate manner.

"We are overjoyed to have you as our dinner companion," Celeste said. "If you would please excuse me, however, for a few moments so that I might change into more fitting dinner attire? Well, or less fitting. Looser, you see. Proper attire is what I mean. I appreciate your understanding."

"Of course."

Celeste tried to stand, but her body was nearly crippled by the catsuit material that fought her attempts to get up from her sunken position on the loveseat. She tried using her hands to push off, again to no avail.

Without saying a word, Justin moved from his seat and took her by the hands, smoothly pulling her to stand. There were only inches between them, and Celeste could not bring herself to look him in the eye. In her boots, she was a bit taller than him, so she looked down and found herself gazing at his shoulder. And the way his simple T-shirt fell over his chest. He was on the thin side and had an average build, without the bulging muscles or tattoos she'd just read about in Dallas's romance book, but she found his physique to be entirely flawless.

"Wow," he said slowly. "Wow."

She did not know what he meant by this, but she didn't get time to wonder for long, because the step to the side that she took to put distance between them caused her to stumble. Justin's arms were under hers before she even got close to hitting the ground.

Well, there. Now her humiliation was complete. Yes, perhaps vomiting or something else having to do with body fluids could take this one step further, so she should perhaps be thankful for the little saving graces. At least now she had something to say at the Thanksgiving table tomorrow when they listed what they were grateful for. Wonderful.

"You okay?" he asked as he lifted her back onto her feet.

This time, she couldn't stop herself from looking up at him.

"I am," she said breathlessly. "Thank you."

She waited for him to drop his arms, but he didn't, even as she trembled. "I know you... I remember," he said.

Neither of them moved.

A shattering plate sounded loudly, immediately followed by the hiss of water boiling over onto the stove.

"Roger! The pasta!" Erin yelled. "And, Matthew, please clean up that dish that you dropped. What is wrong with you two? Snap out of it."

Witnesses, Celeste remembered. There were witnesses to whatever strange occurrence had just transpired. "I... I must change outfits now. I shall be back soon."

She made it to the hall and out of sight without incident,

for which she was grateful. Her boots came off after ample tugging, and only then did she attempt the flight of stairs to her room. Stripping off the catsuit took a few minutes, but it felt heavenly to be out of that horrid thing. She didn't have time to shower, so the silly neon red hair would have to stay. Putting on a hat would just make it look as though she was trying to hide the color. Plus, Celeste was not the Fedora or cowboy hat—or any hat—sort of a girl. A low ponytail at the nape of her neck would have to do. Loose jeans and a taupe open cardigan over a plain shirt helped her mood slightly, although she was still noticeably shaky.

"Stop it," she ordered herself. This silly physiological reaction was unnecessary. So what if he knew that she was the girl who curtsied to his bow? So what if she'd enjoyed his debonair performance outside Border Cafe? She would salvage this situation by simply going downstairs, pretending that her hair was back to normal, and conduct herself like the smart young woman that she was. He was a Barton College student liaison here to inform her and her family about the school and encourage her to apply. That's all. She would listen and nod. Then she would never have to see him again, and this entire fiasco could be put in the past.

After dinner, she would thank him for staying to eat a monochromatic meal with them, make it very clear that there was no need to continue communication because she was not going to apply to Barton, and then she would send him on his way before things got even more out of hand. And she would never walk down Church Street past Border Cafe again.

For some reason, the idea of eliminating Justin from her world made her sad, but she was resigned that it needed to happen.

# CHAPTER 9
## BLUR

CELESTE WAS NEVER going to forgive her family for abandoning her after dinner and leaving her alone with Justin. She was quite sure that Matt did not have any schoolwork that had to be done on the night before Thanksgiving "come hell or dead turkeys," and her parents' last-minute trip to the grocery store seemed highly suspicious. There was no plausible reason for them to run off like this, but she was now stuck with Justin. As much as she wanted him gone, she couldn't just throw him out as good manners should always prevail.

What was he still doing here anyway? Dinner was over; he'd given a great Barton College spiel and answered the six hundred questions that her parents asked, so it was time to leave. Perhaps he was inclined to give a more personal plea one on one?

Celeste crossed her legs, sat back in the living room arm chair, and clenched her hands together. Justin was surveying the bookshelves. She watched him, watched the way he slid his hands from his pockets to his hair, watched the way he never stopped moving, and watched how his expressions were animated and ever-changing each time he turned around to ask her about something that caught his attention. First-edition books, a pressed leaf in a shadow box, an award her mother received for her charitable work.

She also noticed, with a certain level of discomfort, that each time he walked past her spot, she was eye level with the top of his jeans. Celeste was not one for noticing boys and their backsides, but it was nearly impossible not to be cognizant of his, since it was right there in front of her. Maybe it was because she didn't have a lot of experience assessing male body structures that Celeste found the way his jeans fell over the curve of his—

She turned her head away. What was wrong with her? One should not leer lasciviously at a student liaison. Or at anyone, for that matter. He really needed to leave. Immediately.

"How long are you home for?" she asked.

Justin spun around. "I go back on Sunday. It's pretty much a whole day of travel to get to San Diego from Boston. You know, getting to the airport early, then I have a layover in Denver, and all that. I don't mind airports, though. Lots of good people watching." He grinned. "I like checking out other people, you know?"

It took her a moment to reply. "I do know. Yes. That is a more recent interest of mine."

He bounded over to the couch and lay half on his side, resting his elbow on the arm and holding his head in his hand. "Do you like airports? Traveling?"

"Oh. I have never been on an airplane. I know that must sound incredibly odd."

He raised his eyebrows. "Never?"

"No, never. There has been no occasion to do so as of yet. When we go on vacation, we stay in New England. Driving is simpler."

"Yeah? I get that. Airports pretty much rock my world. I once got stuck at O'Hare for nineteen hours, but I really didn't mind because it's a big enough airport that I camped out in different concourses for hours at a time and went into every store there. Also, I had a really good fake ID, and so after I'd used a Sharpie to map out the entire airport on napkins I went to a bar and drank a bunch of Old Fashioneds. My dad loves those, and I thought it'd be funny. But then I drank too much and fell asleep and missed my flight, so that added on another five hours. Also, I blew my nose with the airport-map napkins and got black ink all over my face and freaked out my seat mate with my crazy face when I finally did get on the airplane. So you've never been abroad?"

She blinked. "I have not."

"What're you doing tomorrow?" he asked. "For Thanksgiving."

"Just dinner here. With Matthew and my parents. We do not make a big fuss over holidays. We are a very small family." The way he had his eyes fixed on her was unnerving. "And you?"

"We're going to my cousin's house in Harvard. Hey, speaking of Harvard, I assume you're applying there? I applied, mostly for kicks. Didn't get in of course, but I like to think it was their loss. Worked out fine in the end, but I won't say that my self-esteem didn't take a little hit. I kind of set myself up for that because it was a big reach school for me. In the end, it's best for apple picking; that's what I've decided."

"I do not believe that an apple course is offered at Harvard. Or maybe—"

"Sorry, sorry. I mean, Harvard, Mass has great apple picking in the fall. Lots of orchards. When I hear the word 'Harvard,' I've decided to think of picking apples instead of in-your-face rejection." Justin sat up and leaned his elbows on his knees. He looked down. "I'm so sorry. It must be impossible to keep up with me. I don't know why I forget that."

Celeste adjusted the sleeves on her cardigan and set her hands in her lap. "I like apple picking very much. And while I do not have much knowledge of airports, you make them sound very entertaining." She took a breath. "Or maybe they would only be entertaining with you. I cannot say for certain."

He looked up and gave a half smile. "Hey, Celeste?"

She didn't understand the look he was giving her, but still, she couldn't *not* smile back at him. "Hey, Justin?"

"I was wondering if—" His eyes darted to the side. "Holy crap, is that the time? God, I've really got to go." Justin stood up and patted his pockets. "Keys? I think they're in my jacket. Your dad put it someplace. No, wait, my keys are right here. But my phone? I'm totally supposed to be helping with food prep. I gotta run. I could stay here and talk to you all night. Oh, there's my phone. With my keys, of course." He rolled his eyes at himself. "Anyhow... I really had a good time tonight."

Celeste retrieved his coat from the front hall closet. "Thank you so much for coming by and telling us about the positives Barton has to offer. It was very generous of you considering that your schedule must be tight on this short trip home."

"I landed earlier today, went to my parents', and then called your house. Priorities, right?" The way his eyes glistened and his face lit up was nearly too much for her. She had to get him out of here. She had no idea what she was feeling right now, and that was very disconcerting.

She ushered him aside as she opened the front door. "Good night and happy holidays."

He took his phone from his pocket and handed it to her. "Punch in your number for me, okay? Do you mind? I can just text you, and then you'll have mine."

"Here is my number, should you need it." She couldn't imagine *why* he might need her phone number, but she did as he asked to avoid prolonging his departure. "Okay, then." She handed him back his phone. "Good night."

"Good night, Celeste." He walked backwards past the threshold and onto the porch. "Okay, bye." Justin moved from side to side. "I'll call you or text you or something, yeah?"

"Sure."

He took another few steps back. "Happy Thanksgiving."

Was he never going to leave? "Yes, happy Thanksgiving to you and your family."

"Oh, yeah, I meant to say a happy Thanksgiving to your family also. Not just to you. But mostly to you, because, well…"

She eyed the staircase behind him. "Justin, please be careful because—"

"It's called *muddling*. Did you know that? You probably did. When they mix sugar and bitters together for an Old Fashioned. I can't say as I recommend that drink, or any drinks. It's why there's a legal drinking age—"

Justin took yet another step back, and Celeste let out a gasp. She rushed forward as he tripped down the flight of steps that led to the front walk, stumbling over his feet, but somehow managing to land upright.

"I'm okay!" he shouted. "See? Ta da!" He raised his hands and shook his palms. "Don't look so worried. I do worse all the time."

Paralyzed at the top of the flight, she looked down. She had no idea if she was supposed to assess him for injuries or trust that he was all right. She didn't want to hover over him or embarrass him.

"I have never tasted bitters," she said calmly. "Or bourbon for that matter. Is that what an Old Fashioned is made of?" The way he looked up at her with relief and gratitude nearly knocked her breath from her body. "You are sure that you are all right? You have not twisted an ankle, have you?"

"Bourbon or whiskey. Either can be used, and both are decently disgusting if you ask me. I do sneak a gin and tonic now and then, but I'm not a drinker. Just so you know. And I have not twisted my ankle," he said with a nod. "I assure you."

"Then I must commend you on a most exquisitely handled descent," she said. "You have shown fine recovery skills."

Justin tucked his hands into his pockets. She noticed that he did this a lot. Well, in the few hours that she'd been around him. He was prone to looking charmingly bashful. Justin sighed and rubbed his hands over his eyes. "Oh, God, you must think I'm… something. I know, I know, I'm kind of a hot mess, huh?"

"I think," she said carefully, "that it was very nice to meet you, Justin Milano."

He nodded and started to turn away. "I'm not going to walk backwards this time, okay?"

"Yes, okay."

He walked to his car, opened the door, and looked back. "Hey, Celeste?"

"Hey, Justin?" She bit her lip.

And with startling grace—especially because he had just toppled down the stairs—he got down on one knee and swept his hand from one side to the other. "Bye."

Because she was unable to think clearly, and because she was not in control of her body, she took a step back and recreated her formal curtsy. "Bye."

Watching him drive away filled her with massive relief. He was gone. This insane night was over. But as Justin's car rounded the corner, other feelings crept in. Sadness? It made no sense. Of course he had to leave. He had Thanksgiving preparations to make. She had red dye to wash from her hair. And then she had her senior year to complete, and college to attend. And a new identity to formulate. She was very busy.

But when Celeste finally made it upstairs, she did not go directly to the shower to wash her hair. Instead, she found herself making a phone call.

"Hey, you! I was just thinking about you and was going to call. My plane landed a few hours ago, and I'm just getting settled. What's going on, sweet pea? How are you?"

"There is no time for pleasantries, Julie. Something has happened," Celeste whispered into the phone. "Something very complex."

"I see. Then let's hear it. What complexity has occurred?" Julie was as steady as ever. Just the sound and familiarity of her voice was exactly what Celeste needed. It brought her back to the days when Julie lived down the hall. When Julie took care of her and brought her a new life in so many ways. Having a friend six years her senior was helpful, since Celeste needed all the worldly wisdom she could get.

"A boy was at the house. I did not invite him, but nonetheless he was here. First I saw him in Harvard Square, and he bowed and I curtsied, and then he appeared at the house tonight unscheduled, and I stumbled and he caught me, and then he stumbled, but I did not catch him. Not because I am heartless, but because I was not in the position to catch him. Physically, that is. Although I suppose emotionally, as well. However, he is quite self-sufficient. I am humiliated, given that I failed to present myself properly, and certainly not as top-notch collegiate material, which was, of course, the purpose of his visit to the house. I feel sure that my red hair and figure-hugging catsuit did not give me the studious air I would have opted for." Celeste threw herself onto her bed and put a hand over her eyes. "I am unclear what has happened tonight. A myriad of emotions is overtaking me."

"Celeste?"

"Yes, Julie."

"You have red hair and are… dressing differently?"

"There was a failed attempt at becoming lead singer for

a band. Never mind that right now. There are more pressing matters that require your attention."

"Take a breath."

"But I curtsied, and he got down on one knee! What is that supposed to mean?"

"Wait, what? Did someone propose to you?"

"No, of course not. That is an alarming presumption."

Julie's giggle was not well suppressed. "Okay, then. Start from the beginning."

"His name is Justin Milano, and he is a student liaison for Barton College. They are courting me."

"The college is courting you or Justin is courting you?"

Celeste let out a loud sigh. "The college! Focus, please."

"Yes, ma'am. Continue. Slowly, please, and give me details in chronological order."

"Yes, that is a smart idea. I knew that you would be good at managing this situation. Here is what has transpired so far. I should not say *so far*. It is over. If I say *so far*, then it leads one to assume there will be more incidents that will transpire, and there will not. But I will tell you the details of these past, never-to-be-repeated-or-added-to events."

"Oh my God, you're killing me. Tell me now!"

Celeste started with the emails and narrated all of the events leading up to Justin's tumble down the stairs and subsequent departure. Julie needed to have all of the facts in order to assess the damage properly.

"This is all most awkward. Yet, Julie? I feel exhilarated. I am experiencing strange sensations."

"Is there a chance—you know, just maybe—that you have a crush?"

"A what? I do not have *crushes*. I have college to prepare for and dye to wash out of my hair. And… and… college!"

"Okay," Julie said calmly. "It was just a thought. Although even if you aren't interested, it sounds to me as if he may like you."

"No. That is not the case."

"If you say so."

"I do say so. I am agitated and must take a shower now. Thank you for helping me put this situation to bed. Er, not *to bed*. One should not reference a bed when speaking about Justin. That would be highly inappropriate. And a cliché. We have put the matter to rest. There. It is done. I have externalized the chaotic events of the day, and now I can return to my normal stasis. Good night, Julie. Thank you for your guidance."

"I didn't exactly—"

"Good night!"

She took a thirty minute shower and shampooed her hair repeatedly, which did not seem to do much to remove the dye and then wrapped it in a towel as she stood on the floor of the shower. She reached for her oversized robe and tried to relax into the familiar comfort of the thick terrycloth. The day had officially been washed away, and she could move on. Except that when she got back to her room, she heard the sound of a text coming through.

> **Justin:** Friday night? You, me, and Mr. "I Wear Two Watches" Fritz? Appetizers? Anywhere you want!

Celeste pulled the robe tighter around her and threw the phone into her pocket. She flinched when the sound of two more texts came through the fabric.

> **Justin:** Oh, it's Justin, by the way. You might not have my number in your phone yet.
> **Justin:** I could pick you up. 7 pm?

This was not part of the plan. Perhaps it had been an unrealistic expectation that she could vanquish him and pretend he didn't exist. She had to admit that there was a part of her that felt uncharacteristically comfortable corresponding with him. Communicating in person, however, was an entirely different story. Justin didn't really know anything about her, and the way that she had presented herself tonight in that getup certainly hadn't given an accurate picture of who she really was. If she were, for some reason, to agree to meet with this Mr. Fritz, she would strongly prefer that it happen in a more formal environment.

Her phone went crazy.

> **Justin:** I know where you live.
> **Justin:** Wait, I didn't mean that in a creepy way...
> **Justin:** Hello? Oh gawd... Did I freak you out?
> **Justin:** I just meant that I would know where to pick

you up. And it's not like I'd show up in a van with the
windows all blacked out. That'd be super creepy.

**Justin:** I drive a Prius.

**Justin:** Nobody gets abducted in a Prius, right?

Celeste laughed and clapped a hand over her mouth. Then
she sighed. She would have to reply.

**Celeste:** I am not sure that is a good idea.

**Celeste:** This meeting with Mr. Fritz, that is. Clearly
abduction would not be a good idea.

He wrote back immediately.

**Justin:** But you'll think about it?

Celeste squirmed.

**Celeste:** I will think about it.

That should put him off for now. He would forget about
her by then anyway. That's what she wanted. Or what she
*should* want. It had taken years to perfect her tunnel vision;
she saw her parents, Matt, and Julie clearly, while everyone
else in the world took on a hazy blur.

Justin should be a blur.

# CHAPTER 10
# PUSH

JUSTIN DIDN'T FORGET about her. Celeste woke to a text from him.

> **Justin:** Happy Thanksgiving, Miss Celeste! This is my best effort at a coffee turkey.

She shook her head. Justin had attached another chocolate sauce drawing in the froth of his coffee. His was an utterly wild personality, she decided. She thought about what to write for a moment, since she absolutely had to reply. If one is sent a holiday greeting, one must reciprocate.

> **Celeste:** Happy Thanksgiving, Mr. Justin. I believe your turkey has a degenerative disease. He does not look well. Where are his feathers?
>
> **Justin:** Of course he doesn't look well. He knows death is imminent, but not from a degenerative disease... He saw me sharpening my axe.

**Celeste:** Did he drop all of his feathers due to fear?

**Justin:** I pre-pluck. Also, he is not as ugly as depicted here. My drawing skills may be limited. (Don't tell my architecture professors!)

What was she doing? Celeste had made the decision to distance herself from him and end their exchanges. She had to stop this nonsense. So she blocked him out of her thoughts and went about her holiday.

Frankly, Thanksgiving at the Watkins house often seemed freakishly more like Groundhog Day, in that they ate the same meal every year, played the same game of Scrabble (literally every year Matt managed to get a triple-word score with W-O-L-V-E-R-I-N-E which they all let him play, although technically it probably wasn't allowed), and then they all crashed early after overeating. It was a nice enough day, just not particularly exciting.

By Friday morning, Celeste's hair had paled to an unattractive, muted pink. She stared in the mirror. "I have been deceived. Viciously deceived. The stylist lied to me about the ease with which one could remove neon red dye from one's hair, and I do not recall a conversation about various pink stages." She stomped her foot in frustration and squeezed her eyes shut. "I would like to return to my normal state, please!" she shouted. "I have learned a valuable lesson about going to extreme measures in searching for a new identity, and I have given up on that quest. There is no need for discoloration at this time." She opened her eyes and frowned. Evidently screaming and begging were not going to fix this. Eleven shampoos in two days. She would just keep at it and hope for the best by the time school rolled around on Monday. And maybe by then she would be able to break this habit of talking to her reflection. There: two goals for the long weekend.

She heard a text alert. Her heart flew to her throat. Celeste peeked at her phone.

> **Justin:** I'm picking you up tonight. You can't say no! I have to suffer through a group event this afternoon, and I know you won't go to that, so you would give me something to look forward to if you went shrimping with me later!

This was, without question, the first time someone had indicated that being with Celeste would be a *reward* rather than some sort of irritation. She didn't understand why he would want this. Justin was the one with all of the entertaining qualities, not her. Replying to this text felt impossible.

> **Justin:** Please?
> **Celeste:** I have pink hair. If it were a wall paint color, it would be called "Faded Bubblegum" and no one would select it for decor.
> **Justin:** I loved faded bubblegum. It's a rare and valued shade. Maybe I'll dye mine to match.
> **Justin:** We don't have to meet with Mr. Fritz. Is that better?
> **Justin:** And I'll take you for Camptown shrimp. NOW YOU CAN'T SAY NO EVEN IF YOU WANTED TO! #savejustin #shrimpforever

Celeste laughed. She had never seen any value in hashtags,

but maybe that could change. Justin was going to rather extreme measures to entice her to attend Barton. And it did sound as though he would like a respite from his school liaison duties.

> **Celeste:** You have convinced me. I accept. Thank you for the invitation.
>
> **Justin:** Yippeeeeeeee! I'll tell Mr. Fritz that I need to duck out early from this horrible event. You've saved me!
>
> **Celeste:** Shall I meet you at Border Cafe then for celebratory shrimp?
>
> **Justin:** Absolutely not!

Celeste felt her stomach drop. She had again misunderstood a communication with someone.

> **Justin:** You're the one saving me, and I'm not letting my woman of salvation travel around the dangerous streets unaccompanied. #chivalryaintdeadbaby #sendhelp #sendshrimp #hashtagsgoneinsane #hashtagsdonotbelonginatext #whatever I'll pick you up at 7, okay?
>
> **Celeste:** If you like. Thank you for the ride. That is very considerate of you.
>
> **Justin:** You betcha. Catch you later?
>
> **Celeste:** Yes.
>
> **Justin:** #idontactuallylikehashtagsijustcantstop
>
> **Justin:** Okay, see you tonight. Really going this time.
>
> **Justin:** Signing off.
>
> **Justin:** I'm sure your hair looks awesome. Don't worry.

**Justin:** I understand, though. My aunt worries all the time that someone might see a gray hair if she hasn't had time to get it colored, and then the world would implode. Or explode. One of those. Whichever is more dramatic.

So... she would meet with Justin for one last Barton discussion over the now–infamous Camptown shrimp.

At six forty-five that night, Celeste sat poised formally on the piano bench in the music room, just off of the front hall. It was the first time she was wearing her snow-white pea coat. As much as she loved it, there had never been an occasion to wear such a stylish coat, but there seemed no reason not to go out in it tonight. She pulled on her matching white gloves and hat, both with fake-fur borders. After the disastrous first meeting with this college representative, Celeste was determined to make a more studious, appropriate impression. It was her hope that the white ensemble would eradicate any memories of her in that ridiculous audition outfit. Although she wouldn't attend Barton College, it remained important to her that she come across as pulled together. Muted pink hair and all.

From her seat, she could keep an eye out for Justin through the large window, and she could also hide from her parents, both of whom seemed omnipresent this evening. Celeste did not desire to be hovered over in any manner, and both Erin and Roger had been suffocating her for the past few hours.

"Still not here yet?" her father asked as he came into the room.

"It is not yet seven," Celeste said with exasperation. "He was not here at six twenty, and he was not here at six thirty-four, as neither of those times were the agreed-upon time. Stop asking."

"Sorry, sorry. Just checking." He stepped fully into the room and moved to sit next to her on the bench. "Scoot over, kiddo."

She obliged and made space for her father in front of the piano.

"You haven't played in a while, have you?" he asked as he hit a few keys.

"I have not."

"Play a little something now? I miss the sound of your music." Roger leafed through assorted sheets of music. "You used to love playing."

"I do not love it anymore."

Erin's voice rang from the hall. "Is he here? I thought I heard a car?"

Roger jumped from his spot and peered through the blinds. "What kind of car does he drive? Why isn't our porch light on? Quick, Erin, turn it on!"

Celeste slammed her hands down on the piano keys, punctuating each of her words. "That. Is. Enough," she said sternly. "It is unclear to me why a college admissions liaison warrants such hysteria, but I shall wait peacefully for my ride." She glared at her parents. "Please?"

Erin squinted. "Hair's still pink, huh? That's okay. Don't worry about it."

"My hair color is of no consequence when it comes to collegiate admittance," Celeste stated. "I shall wait outside."

"I don't think Justin is taking you out for collegiate—" Roger started.

"Good night!" Erin cut him off, grabbed him by the arm, and pulled him from the room. "Have fun!"

"But then we can't see when… Oh, fine… Have fun!" he called when he was out of sight.

It was Celeste's understanding that girls of her age were to be filled with the utmost annoyance and disdain for their parents. Her parents' behavior tonight was indeed making her understand why. Their frenetic energy was not helpful right now because—as much as she was not overtly making a big deal out of this situation—she felt very uncomfortable and edgy. She was not in the habit of dining out socially, especially on a busy Friday night, and certainly not with someone her own age. And especially not with a boy.

Well, it didn't matter that he was male, she reasoned. College liaisons might as well be genderless. Although Justin probably wouldn't appreciate that thought. He likely worked at achieving his mesmerizing masculine look, what with the fashionably swept hair, appealing physique, shirts that gripped his biceps quite wonderfully without being too tight or showy, but just naturally draped in such a way that…. Celeste shook her head and ordered herself to knock it off. The hair dye must have seeped into her brain and was causing neurons to misfire or something.

Headlights pulled up to the house, and Celeste flew out the front door before her parents could swoop in again. This was essentially a business dinner, she reminded herself., and she would treat it as such.

Justin was out of the car and standing by the passenger door when she reached the end of the walkway.

"Look at you, blondie." Justin opened the door, but kept

his eyes on her. "It's hardly pink at all. I didn't know you were blonde. I thought maybe a brunette. Dark brown. Like, a chestnut color. But now that I see the blond, I can't imagine anything else. Okay, maybe the bright red, which was cool, too." Without warning, Justin stepped in and put his arms around her in a quick hug.

Celeste did not know what to do. His arms were over hers, pinning them against her body, so she couldn't exactly hug him back. Not that she would. They did not have a hugging relationship. Maybe Barton College was an exceptionally touchy-feely, new-age school where students and staff all hugged each other constantly. There had been nothing about this in the brochures.

"You are kind, but my hair is very much in the pink family. still."

"I don't care. It looks good." He moved back and rested his hand on the top of the car window. "Ready to eat? I'm starved. The recruiting event tonight turned out to be filled with alumni, and they had it at some stuffy lounge that looked like an eccentric billionaire's study. The appetizers looked about as appetizing as—Oh, see what I did there? Anyway, the point is that the food was boring and I haven't eaten—Sorry, I'm rambling." Justin stopped himself and took a long, slow breath. "Hi. How are you?"

Celeste slid into the seat of the Prius and smiled. In that moment, she didn't care if her parents were staring through the window at them. She was not nervous anymore.

# CHAPTER 11
# #ITSNOTADATE

JUSTIN GULPED DOWN half a glass of ice water. "Told you they were spicy. Whaddya think?"

"I think that the Camptown shrimp very strongly exceeded their already glowing reputation." Celeste rested her elbows on the table and put her chin in her hands. "And I'm surprised that you hadn't mentioned the crusty bread that is served alongside. I do believe that I am drunk on a flavor rush, if that is possible."

"Good." He leaned back in his chair. "I like girls who eat, and we went through three orders. Seriously, there's nothing more annoying than taking a girl out and having her suck on ice cubes all night."

"I do not suck on ice cubes."

They had spent most of the past forty minutes discussing... well, given Justin's propensity for changing topics at the flip of a dime, discussing everything under the sun. His energy, his bounciness, reminded her quite a bit of Tigger from Winnie the Pooh. He did everything quickly: speaking, inhaling his food, and gesturing constantly with his hands. She never knew into which direction he might take the conversation or when one topic would remind him of another. And then another. And yet, even in the throes of his animated and ever-changing dialogue, he never took his eyes off of her. It was rather enjoyable. He did, she assumed, do this with everyone, and his charming style probably garnered him a sizable fan club.

"So I have an idea," Justin leaned in and whispered, forcing her to lean in even more to be heard.

"What's that?" She forced herself to meet and hold his look, despite this being quite nerve-wracking and unusual.

"You still hungry?"

"Would you like to order an entree?"

"I don't know Harvard Square well at all," he said. "How about you show me all the cool insider places to eat here? You must know every good spot, right? Let's start with pizza."

"Pizza," she said transfixed. It was not her fault, she thought, that his half-smile with its mischievous edge captured her and made it impossible to look away from him. She'd assumed that he would be returning her home after their shrimp tasting, but perhaps it was over pizza that he would give the final hard Barton sell. "Pizza," she repeated. "Yes, that is an excellent idea. If you would like, I can suggest Pinocchio's, an establishment that has been here for years. It's in a picturesque nook off of JFK Street."

"Why's it called Pinocchio's? Are they all liars there?"

She smiled. "No. The owners want to be real boys."

"Maybe that's just what they told you." He winked. "But you can't trust them because they're lying."

"What is not a lie is that the pizza is lovely, and so we shall ignore any fibs they should throw our way. It is a small place, mostly specializing in take-out orders, so do not have high hopes for fine dining."

"Let's do it." Justin pulled back quickly from his close position, knocking over a glass and sending water and ice cubs across the table. "Oh God, again? I do this all the time."

Celeste reached for all available napkins. "It is not a problem."

Justin shook his head as he frantically helped to mop up what they could. "Seriously. You can't take me anywhere. I'm such an embarrassment. Did I get you? You're probably soaked."

"I'm completely dry. It was an accident, so please do not fret over this. One does not cry over spilt milk, and so one certainly does not feel even the slightest pang of remorse over spilt water."

"You're too nice. I'm a complete klutz. Really, I shouldn't be let out in public."

"Justin?" He looked at her, both of them with soggy napkins in their hands, and Celeste smiled softly. Justin looked near frantic.

Then very deliberately and very calmly, she tipped over her own water glass. "There. Now we can go have pizza."

He looked down at the table, stunned, and shook his head. "You are remarkable," he said.

And so they had pizza. Celeste ate her slice and watched as Justin gobbled gooey cheese. In between bites, he managed to eke out, "If loving food made by liars is wrong, I don't want to be right." He ate three slices, and she two. It was amazing that he was not sick, given how fast he ate. They tossed their trash and without thinking anything of it, Celeste brushed a paper napkin over a spot of sauce that had fallen on his shirt.

"*Of course* I have food all over me." He rolled his eyes.

"It's just a spot. In the shape of a marionette, by good fortune."

She pulled her hand away. How odd that she'd made a presumptive move such as this. It was not her place to do this. But then she noticed that she was using her fingertips to brush off a smattering of crust crumbs that had somehow flown onto his shoulder. "It means that you enjoyed your food. And that I picked a good place."

"You're sweet." Justin held open the door for her. "So pick another place."

Celeste pulled on her gloves. It was quite bitter out tonight. "You're still hungry?" She struggled to put on her hat while wearing gloves, but Justin wordlessly took her hat in his hands and eased it onto her head.

"Of course I'm still hungry. Thanksgiving was like training day. Besides, as great as the food is in San Diego, I mostly eat on campus. Stupid dining plans. I have to stock up on good eating now so that I can get through until Christmas break. Campus food everywhere sucks, so that's why I work part-time as a student liaison. Extra money for real food."

Ah, yes, here was the confirmation that Justin was only doing his job. Was it wrong that she wanted to delay the end of the night? That she had been relieved each time he hadn't mentioned courses, or well-published professors, or all the many accomplishments of Barton graduates? Because she had been. But now it was a matter of waiting for his spiel, signaling the start of the end of their night.

"So where are you going to take me next?" he asked excitedly. "God, it's cold. I'm not used to this at all anymore." He shivered even in his down coat.

"Hot cider then? At Algiers?" she suggested.

"Okay, where's that?"

She started back towards Brattle Street. "You've never been to Algiers? It's practically an institution here. Dark and worldly," she hollered through a cold gust that blew their way. "Been here for years, by the Brattle Theatre. The service is dreadful, but that is part of the tradition. You must try the hummus and baba ganoush. Or, if you are still quite hungry, the lamb sandwich."

Justin pressed his shoulder to hers as they walked. "Cider first, for sure. Then everything else you mentioned."

After running together through the night's plummeting temperatures, they were soon nestled in a dimly lit corner of the Algiers cafe, surrounded by dark wood and scholarly customers, and both blowing into steaming cups.

"Where are we going after this?" Justin took a small sip of the scalding cider.

"It is your belief that you will be hungry still after eating all that we ordered here?"

"That is my exact belief."

She thought for a moment. "I have a plan that will, without question, satiate your desires."

"Well, now I can't *wait* to hear—" Justin used his body to turn his chair more in her direction, shaking the table and nearly toppling their ciders. Celeste giggled, and Justin grinned sheepishly. "I know. You can't be surprised by this point. So tell me this dastardly plan you have."

"It is not dastardly, just practical. If you want another true Harvard Square experience, then I will take you to a place that my brother and I love, Mrs. Bartley's, and we will order you an Upstairs on the Square burger, which is a tribute to the now-defunct restaurant of the same name."

"And what makes this burger so special? Why is it better than McDonald's?"

"Because McDonald's is disgusting. and we do not eat there. We eat at Mrs. Bartley's. The burger I have selected for you comes with no roll, but is instead served on spinach, then topped with chopped egg, bacon, walnuts, tomatoes, red onion, and a lemon vinaigrette."

Justin wrinkled his nose and shivered. "I can't say that sounds good."

"I didn't say it would be good. I said it would be an experience. But by ordering that burger, you get a double-dose of Harvard Square in one dish. I'd advise the addition of blue cheese."

"Then I will take your advice. I trust you."

"The alternative is that we go to Ben and Jerry's and order a Vermonster. That is a twenty-scoop sundae with many candy toppings, and sauces, and such; and considering that you and I are both still shivering, ice cream holds little appeal now, correct?"

"Yeah," Justin agreed. "How about we do that in the summer?" He smiled. "I'm home all winter break, too. You know, some people pack up and do holidays in St. Bart's or something, but we just stay in Needham and freeze." A server set down a bowl of hummus on the table, and as Justin reached for a slice of pita, he swiped his hand in such a way that his fork sailed off the table, clanging as it landed on the floor. The server flashed him a look, and Justin muttered an apology. "See? I'm forever annoying people."

"I do not find you annoying," Celeste offered. "I quite like your exuberance."

He took sugar packets from the table and began rolling and unrolling them. "Yeah, I'm sure."

"I do." She didn't like the disheartened aura that took hold of him.

"I interrupt people; I fall down; I have irritating attention issues. People think that I don't care about them because I forget to ask questions or stop listening to what they say. I've lost a million friends because of that kind of nonsense. Well, and I spill stuff. As you may, you know, have noticed." He forced a smile. "I've driven every teacher I've ever had to the brink of frustration. I nearly failed a handful of classes in junior high... Whatever. You don't want to hear this. Sorry."

"You are not annoying, Justin." Intuitively, she put her hand atop his. "You're not."

"I don't know how you can say that."

"I would not lie to you. There are occasions to tell white lies, but this is not—"

"Celeste, you're sweet, but I'm bothersome. There's no way around it."

"You do not bother me."

"Why?"

"Why what?"

"Why don't I bother you with all my... stuff?"

Celeste was confused. "Why would you being who you are bother me?"

"You say that now. Try spending any length of time around me, and you'll think differently. I wear everyone down, trust me."

"You have created an unfair situation. You just asked me to trust you," she said.

"And?"

"And you will not trust me when I say that I do not find you bothersome. That is not right."

He laughed. "You were on the debate team, right? I think the dean told me that. Dean Dean, remember? Anyway, you may be telling the truth right now, but you also may change your mind. I won't hold that against you when it happens."

Celeste thought for a moment. She took the wrinkled sugar packets from his hand and gave him fresh ones from the ceramic holder. "Another possibility is that young Dean grew up passionately trying to prove himself in various non-dean careers, but destiny intervened and he was unable to fight fate, accepting a job as dean at Barton College, where he has now become a topic of amused conversation for students and staff." She took a sip of her cider and then licked a dollop of whipped cream with her tongue. "And I won't change my mind."

"I can be very hard to tolerate."

"Okay."

"I could drive you crazy. I have eccentricities."

Celeste waited him out.

"I work really hard to manage them," he said.

She nodded.

"Anyway, that's enough of that. I don't want to ruin this nice hummus section of the evening. Did we get baba ganoush, too? I love that stuff. Eggplant is not really my thing, but…"

Celeste tore apart a piece of pita bread and watched and listened as Justin talked. When he paused for air, she bravely asked what she'd been avoiding. "Justin, I have a question for you."

"Yeah? Shoot."

"Tonight, why have you not asked me about attending Barton? Or regaled me with all of the educational attractions?"

"I'm sorry. I got all caught up in my crap, and you've been so patient and nice about it all. I didn't realize that you had more questions. Shoot. I'm ready."

In that moment, it became clear that this night was not about Justin's pitching Barton. She didn't know what it was about, but that was okay. In fact, it was lovely.

"Actually, no. I do not have questions." Celeste smiled.

After another stop for burgers, followed by coffee at Starbucks (which was very good, but noticeably absent of snowy owl foam images), Justin drove her home.

Their drive was quiet, neither of them saying a word. Silence between two people could be unbearable or it could be comforting, and this was comforting. The confines of the car created a shelter where it was just the two of them and where Celeste felt safe. Protected. It was unexpected, but undeniable. Watching Justin drive was mesmerizing, the way he maneuvered traffic and crowded streets with an ease that was such a contrast to the parts of him that were more touched with chaos. She liked the relaxed, thoughtful look on his face as he drove. Celeste looked out of the window at the dark sky as music filled the car. She didn't know the song, but the lyrics resonated. Perhaps too deeply.

"I am unfamiliar with this musical selection, Justin. What are we listening to?"

"This? It's 'Shine.' David Gray. I love his stuff, and this is one of my favorites. I guess it's kind of a sad song, but it's hopeful, too. I think he's saying that love is complicated, that *life* is complicated. There are hard paths we go down, but there can be determination to survive and thrive in the face of adversity. We make choices. I don't know… That's the thing about music. You get to make it mean whatever you need it to mean. But anything that has to do with rising from the ashes always gets me." He pulled up in front of her house. "We all have to overcome something, right?"

She nodded. "We do."

The car was cozy and perfect, and she didn't want to leave; a degree of melancholy took over when Justin turned off the ignition and got out. Celeste undid her buckle and reached for the door handle, but he had rounded the car and opened the door for her before she could. The air was bitter, even more so than it felt just ten minutes earlier in Harvard Square. As she stood, she said, "Thank you so much for the Barton information that you've given me over this holiday weekend, and of course for this evening. Please extend my gratitude to the admissions staff as well. I am highly appreciative and humbled by all of the attention. I will give the school the same thorough consideration that they have given me." Celeste winced as he shut the car door.

"Oh. Yeah, absolutely. I'll, uh, I'll walk you to the door."

"That is very gallant of you. Thank you." She led the way up her front steps, walking as slowly as possible. By the door, under the porch light, they both stopped. She looked at him. His expression was hard to read, but he kept his eyes on her. There was more silence between them, and she had no idea what to do with it. Celeste tried unsuccessfully to retrieve the key from her jacket pocket without taking off her white mittens.

"I'll get it for you." Justin slipped his hand into her pocket and fumbled for the key. Being so close to this boy felt divine, and the touch of his hand brushing against her waist, even through fabric, made her wonderfully dizzy. It was Celeste's hope that he never found the house key and that they remained stranded on this porch for all of eternity. Alas, that was not the case. "Want me to unlock the door for you?" he asked.

His eyes were such a spectacular steel gray in this light. And his hair had so many tones to it. The all-over light brown, but then some much lighter strands and a few dark streaks that ran from his temple...

"Celeste?"

"Yes, thank you." She snapped back to reality. "It is fantastically cold this evening, is it not?"

Justin jiggled the key in just the right manner such that it opened with little fuss. He pushed on the door and handed her the key as he stepped aside so that she could pass in front of him. He dug his hands into his pockets. "I should... I should get going. I've kept you out late enough."

She turned in the entryway. "I had a very enjoyable evening. Thank you for your time." Well, he had hugged her at the beginning of the night, so it seemed only right that she do the same. She focused on the top button of his jacket, which was easier than looking at him, and reached her arms over his shoulders. Celeste leaned in and touched her body to his.

This was to be a brief, friendly hug.

But then she found her cheek resting on his shoulder, and she could smell the hint of aftershave. His arms circled around her body. Celeste closed her eyes and tightened her arms around him. He squeezed back.

When she finally took a step away, she said, "So. Again, thank you for the evening. It was a pleasure to meet you, Justin. I do hope that the rest of your holiday vacation is amiable."

He smiled. "Goodnight, Celeste."

"Goodnight, Justin." She shut the door and immediately rushed into the dark piano room. She leaned against the wall next to the window and caught her breath. Then she waited a moment before rolling to the side and peeking through the shade. She needed to watch as he left her.

Well, not *left her*. That was a bit dramatic, not to mention utterly unreasonable. He wasn't leaving her; he was going home. And then back to California. Where he belonged. Justin made it back to his car all too quickly. In the movies, the boy always looked back, but Celeste didn't know if this was a case in which the boy should look back or not. She didn't understand what this night meant, what Justin meant. But she wanted him to look back.

He didn't, though.

What he did do was reach the driver's side door and throw a hand up in the air, punching the night sky twice. And under the fuzzy light from the moon, she could see him smile.

# CHAPTER 12
# THE UPRISING

DECEMBER. SNOW AND ice setting in. Night skies taking over in the afternoon. If it weren't for Justin, Celeste would be on the verge of buying one of those anti-seasonal-depression lights. His constant correspondence lifted her spirits more than she could have imagined. There was truly something to be said for waking up to one of his late-night emails or getting a mid-morning text with a picture of his coffee froth.

Today she was between classes when his text came through. A picture of particularly swirly chocolate lines greeted her.

> **Justin:** Frothy Saucy Rorschach Test starts now.
>
> **Celeste:** Am I to understand that you intend to read into my psyche based on what image I see in this photograph?
>
> **Justin:** Yes! C'mon! Play along.

**Celeste:** If you insist. I believe this experiment is as valid as reading tea leaves, but I will comply.

**Justin:** You have thirty seconds to answer. Don't overthink this. Tell me what you see.

**Celeste:** If you are waving your hands in some sort of eerie, mystical way...

**Justin:** Sorry, sorry. Proceed.

**Celeste:** I see a gnome on a surfboard.

**Celeste:** Or possibly hieroglyphics that translate to read, "Wandering leads one to the church of alpine sheep."

**Justin:** Fabulous! Based on your interpretations of this image, I decree that you are a woman with unusual religious beliefs who has a latent desire to engage in water activities with ceramic figurines.

**Justin:** Gotta hop in the shower before class.

**Justin:** Miss you.

The impulse to scream out and wave her phone to those around her was strong, but instead Celeste bit her lip to keep from smiling. She was sure that no one in her chemistry class was interested in the fact that some boy said he missed her. To Celeste, however, this was a monumental occasion. She read the two words that were so simple and so yet moving. *Miss you.* She found her seat in the classroom. Replying made her both uncomfortable and exhilarated.

**Celeste:** I miss you, too. Have a nice day at school.

"Celeste, put your phone away, or I'll take it." Her teacher frowned and then turned to the blackboard. "Everyone settle down. Class is starting."

Zeke, the drummer from the band of her failed audition, Flinch Noggins, tiptoed into the room and slid into the seat in front of her without their teacher noticing. He reached a hand over his shoulder and held his palm up to Celeste. For the second time that day, she fought a smile and lightly tapped her hand to his. That was, she knew, not a bitch slap. It didn't seem to fit in with Matt's description of a high-five, though, so she would have to ask him about this hand-to-hand maneuver. Whatever it was, she had pulled it off.

Her concentration was shot today, which she found odd. Focusing on class material, losing herself in it, was her strength. But today there were social distractions, which for Celeste were unfamiliar and overtook even the most challenging and fun of chemical equations. It was all right. She could let her mind drift for one class if she wanted to.

And she did. She wanted to think about Justin and his emails and his spilling things. The way his pale blue/gray eyes were perfectly framed by his light brown eyebrows. She liked his eyebrows, which seemed stupid. One does not obsess about another's eyebrows. But he did have nice ones. And his hands. Maybe it was because he gestured constantly that night in Harvard Square, but she'd ended up watching his hands closely. There was grace, she felt, in the way he moved them. The way he moved his whole body, really.

Celeste snapped out of her daydreaming when a new fact became utterly clear. Julie was right: she had a crush.

This was a first.

A joyous and devastating first.

Justin was a college student, presumably surrounded by outgoing, social, and fun girls at school. Celeste was not in a league to compete with them. Realistically, he was simply an incredibly nice guy who liked her on a friend level, and that was more than she'd had in ages—and never before with a boy. Therefore, long-distance texts and emails could continue in their current form. Who knew if she'd even see him again?

It was, she acknowledged, probably better that they remain online friends. Very little risk with decent odds for continuation.

But, oh, she wanted to see him again. To watch the way he moved.

The bell sounded loudly, and she jumped in her seat.

Celeste rushed to her locker. It was lunch period, and she wanted very much to finish reading her book. It was one of those days when she was more grateful for e-readers than she could say. Not that she should be embarrassed that she was reading *Gone with the Wind*, but since she was often found reading literary classics in tattered old bindings, being found reading what was arguably closer to a soap opera felt uncomfortable. But the story was so romantic. Scarlet was out of her mind, Celeste had decided. Celeste found Ashley to be an utter drip, and she did not support Scarlet's many outrageous choices and behaviors, yet she couldn't put the story down. The fiery passion, Scarlett's dedication to getting what she wanted, the dramatic backdrop of the Civil War? It was impossible not to be lured in.

Celeste shoved her bag unceremoniously into her locker and grabbed her lunch card and tablet. If she hurried, she could grab the small table by the exit and keep her back to the room. Abandoning the drama room was a recent change, but she believed it a necessary one. Hiding in a costume closet was borderline bizarre, and frankly she felt to blame for the whole singing audition fiasco. Besides, the cafeteria had actual windows, and therefore sunlight, and one needed a daily dose of vitamin D.

After reading for only five minutes, though, she found herself unable to shut out the conversation from the next table.

"How the hell do I know how to fill out these damn college applications? I don't know what they want." Someone let out a grumbling noise and dramatic sigh.

"Right? This personal essay bull is impossible. I've got three weeks to get all of these in. I'm drowning," another person said.

"What if I don't get in anywhere? Am I going to have to spend another year at home? Oh God, kill me."

All of her applications had been completed in full months ago. They'd all even been done in time for early decision deadlines had she wanted an early acceptance, but considering that she still had no clue which school she would choose, she had simply submitted them for regular decision. Her visits to UPenn and Princeton this month with Erin had been lovely. Or they should have been lovely. She couldn't lie to herself; she was shockingly uninspired. Maybe it was just going to be impossible to imagine herself at any college. She would select a college to attend when the time was right.

The unhappy mumblings from the next table continued. Celeste couldn't help herself. She backed up her chair and walked the few steps to where three miserable looking girls, including Dallas, sat, their food untouched.

"Hello," Celeste said. She hadn't spoken to Dallas much. Or at all. But she was standing here now, and she couldn't very well run off all scatterbrained and the like.. "I am terribly sorry to interrupt you, but overhearing your plight was unavoidable given our close proximity. I might be able to help if you have interest."

"Hey, Celeste." Dallas gave her a weak smile. "This is Leighann and Jennifer. What do you mean you could help?"

"I have spent the past five years preparing to apply to colleges, and I have done extensive research on strategies to successfully master the art of submitting applications. If you would like, I could assist you." Celeste's heart was pounding, and her voice was trembling in the most appalling way; but she couldn't let any visceral reactions stop her. She was in the midst of initiating an interaction with her peers—really for the first time in years—and she had absolutely no idea what had propelled her to such foolishness. "The application process is intimidating, even belittling at times, and I could certainly consult should you be interested."

"Dude, seriously?" Dallas' eyes widened, and she nudged the girl on her right. "Leighann, is this a dream or what? For real, Celeste, we were just talking last night about how we totally need an application coach or something. And here you are!"

Leighann clasped a hand to her chest. "Really? You'll help? My parents are no good at this stuff, and the guidance counselor here keeps telling me the same thing over and over. To just be myself, be honest, blah, blah. That's not going to help me get in anywhere. It's almost winter break, and the clock is ticking."

Jennifer pulled out a free chair and motioned for Celeste to sit, and she did, albeit nervously. "I've been in that guidance office a zillion times, and it's not helping. I'm afraid I bombed my campus interviews, too. I don't know what they want from me."

The desperation on Jennifer's face angered Celeste. How could their expensive private school have been failing all of these students so terrifically? The assumption was likely that decent grades from this well-respected high school would automatically result in acceptance at one good school or another.

Before she could gather her thoughts, a hand tapped her on the shoulder.

"Celeste! What's up?"

She turned to the right to see Zeke shooting past her. "Zeke!" she called. "Wait!"

He backed up. "What's going on?"

"You may be interested in this conversation given what we spoke about last month. I was in the process of offering to assist the young women at this table with their college applications. If you have not had occasion to previously converse, please make the acquaintance of Dallas, Leighann, and Jennifer. Would you care to join in?"

"Hey, ladies." Zeke rifled through his backpack and retrieved a messy stack of papers. "These are my attempts at an essay. They're all horrible, I know. And my extracurriculars don't sound great. *Drummer in going-nowhere band* doesn't exactly have a good ring to it."

"I would be happy to take a look at what you have written

and make suggestions." Celeste adjusted her seat. "Deadlines are fast approaching, so perhaps we could meet after school every day this week? Essentially, once we have packaged each of you properly with the right essays and such, then applying to multiple schools becomes simple."

"Do you know anything about applying for scholarships and financial aid?" Zeke asked. "I don't understand any of the paperwork. They make it so confusing."

"I could certainly review all of the information and help you. That is not a problem." She would have to do a lot of research into both of these, but she enjoyed that.

"Okay, so where should we meet?" Leighann asked. "There's the school library, I guess."

"God, I'm so sick of being in school," Dallas said. "Where else? I don't know. A cafe?"

"Ugh, too noisy." Jennifer blew bangs out of her eyes.

"There my band's practice space," Zeke offered. "Although it is a garage."

"You're in a band?" Dallas perked up. "Rad, man."

Zeke adjusted his messenger bag and smiled. "We do all right."

"We could work at my house," Celeste said quickly. "Tonight. There is plenty of room for us there, and it might be more comfortable than the library or a garage, although both serve purposes for other occasions."

"Perfect." Dallas smiled. "This is awesome of you, Celeste. How about we come over at, like, six?"

"I'll bring soda," Leighann said. "And if I can ask my

friend Amber, then I'll have her bring these double-chocolate cookies that she makes. They're killer."

"Certainly. Amber is welcome to attend. Any and all are welcome."

Celeste was having people to her house. A number of people. She was exhilarated and terrified at the thought. But mostly exhilarated. "It is Monday, and I feel confident that if we work every evening, by Friday night you will all have completed your applications, and colleges will be rioting to secure your acceptance." She brushed a stray hair back to her ponytail and waited nervously.

"Cool. Text us your address, and we'll see you tonight," Zeke said. "I'll bring pizza. Anything else you want?"

"Laptops will do for tonight." Celeste paused. "I very much like bacon on my pizza, if no one objects."

"You got it," Zeke said as he rose from the table. "What's your favorite place?"

"Pinocchio's is quite good, if you do not mind."

"Anything for Coach Watkins. I have to get to French early. Later."

"I'll join you," Leighann said. "I can't conjugate the future perfect to save my life. Thanks again, Celeste. You rock for doing this."

Celeste waved tentatively as they walked away. What an extraordinary exchange she'd just had.

Dallas watched Zeke as he left the room and then turned back to Celeste. "How come you never talked to me again after I gave you that book?" she asked directly. "I only got one dry text from you."

Celeste was taken aback. "I apologize."

Dallas crossed her arms. "It's okay if you didn't want to be friends. I get it."

Celeste shook her head. "That's not it at all." She slowly sat down, thinking about how to respond. "I was not sure that your reaching out to me was sincere."

"Well, it was."

"Again, I apologize."

Dallas examined her long nails which were painted deep burgundy, each with a small diamond-like gem at the tips. "So if I lend you another book, then you'll text me back from now on? And you'll *return* the book?"

"Yes," Celeste said as she blushed. "How awful of me to have held on to the book. I am very embarrassed. Perhaps I might offer you a book recommendation. As a sign of my regret and my inclination toward friendship."

"Yeah? What book?"

"Have you read Margaret Mitchell?"

Dallas shook her head.

Celeste smiled. "Then I have a particularly epic saga that you will enjoy immensely. I shall pass on my original paperback to you this evening."

"I could use a good romance. I broke up with Troy a few weeks ago."

"I did not know that."

"If you'd been talking to me, then you would have." Dallas winked. "But now you know."

"I am sorry to hear that. You seemed to like him quite a

bit. We will keep you so very busy this week that you will not notice any lingering heartache."

"Cool beans." Dallas walked a few feet away and then turned back. "I'm really psyched we're going to hang out."

"I, too, am psyched," Celeste said. "Cool beans, indeed."

She returned to her table. Although she was alone now, she did not feel lonely. It wasn't clear to her exactly *what* she felt. But she was calm. Steady.

Or so she thought until it took three tries for her to type in the correct login password on her tablet. She made herself focus. A lesson plan of sorts was required here. Staring at a blinking cursor for five minutes put her into a trance-like state. What was she going to do? Hand out copies of an outline? Her peers would be bored. They'd all seen enough dry preparatory material to last a lifetime. Real-world guidance was what was needed. Perhaps she could provide a sample application and walk them through from start to finish.

Celeste wiggled her toes as she opened a browser. For instance, she could fill out another application online tonight. Like, say, the Barton College application. Just as an example. As a random school. It could be any application. She may as well use the Barton one. Her fingers trembled as she created a username and password, which she thought was plain silly, because she was nothing if not highly competent at filling out applications for higher learning. And it wasn't as though she would be required to hit a button to actually submit the application.

There was no need to take it that far.

◼ ◼ ◼

That night, sixteen people showed up at her house. People brought people who brought people. When Celeste said that "any and all are welcome," it never occurred to her that the group would grow to such a number. It was a good thing that the living room was large enough to accommodate everyone who was now sprawled out on the couch, two arm chairs, and the floor. Erin and Roger appeared to be as surprised as Celeste was each time the doorbell rang.

"Why haven't you had any of your friends over before?" her father asked. "We've wanted to meet your comrades for so long."

"I… I am a private person," Celeste stammered under her breath. "What is more important right now is that we do not appear to have sufficient food and drink for our guests. This is quickly becoming a disaster. Only a few people brought what I believe are called 'munchies,' and we are perilously low before the instruction has even started."

"Your parents are here to rescue you. Erin and I will run to the supermarket for snacks, and we'll pick up more pizza too."

"Thank you. That is most kind. Perhaps some paper plates and cups, too?" Celeste clenched her hands and shook them out. "I should get started."

"This is lovely." Erin made a cheering gesture that caused Celeste to roll her eyes. "Young people gathering together for a common cause. It's like an anti-war group from the sixties. Oh, there's the door again."

"I shall answer it," Celeste said quickly as she rushed from the living room. Erin seemed likely to enthusiastically fling her arms around the next person to enter the house.

Dallas was at the door, and Celeste's relief was

immeasurable. She barely knew any of the other students currently occupying the living room, and Dallas's presence felt grounding. "You have changed the color of your hair again. Lavender is quite nice on you."

"Thanks, babe." Dallas shook her head. "Something different for me. Look, I brought Swedish fish." She held up a bag. "And other fun treats."

"Thank you. Please make yourself at home," Celeste said nervously.

Dallas followed her into the living room. Celeste scanned the sea of faces and locked eyes with Zeke. He widened his eyes and tipped his head slightly to his left side where there was a free spot.

She stepped delicately around students and led Dallas to a place by an end table. "There is adequate seating right here next to Zeke. He is the drummer for Flinch Noggins whom you met earlier today. Zeke, you remember Dallas, I am sure."

Dallas and Zeke were transfixed on each other, neither evidently capable of speaking.

Celeste cleared her throat. "Perhaps you would care to offer Zeke something to eat."

"Okay," Dallas said without moving.

"Zeke would you care for something called Swedish fish?" Celeste took the bag from Dallas' hand and frowned. "Or... pickled green beans? Or canned blueberries?"

"Any of those sound awesome," he said breathlessly.

Dallas looked as though she might faint.

Celeste put a hand on Dallas' back and gave her a small push forward. "Okay, then, wonderful. Such a colorful assortment of snack options. Why don't you have a seat, and we can begin."

She worked her way to the outskirts of the living room and surveyed the scene in front of her. The chatter died down as the students became aware that the college application discussion was going to begin. She could choose to be terrified and collapse right then and there, or she could choose to rise to the occasion. This gathering was her doing, and these people were now counting on her. Collapsing was not a smart option. And Celeste was smart.

So she faced them head on and forced a smile. "Welcome, everyone. I did not realize there would be so many of you here tonight, but I will do my best to lend any wisdom I have about how to tackle college applications." She took a deep breath. Everyone looked more worried than she felt. It was her job to inspire and empower, so do that she would. "This can be a most intimidating process. High school guidance counselors have the best of intentions, but their advice can often be rote and uninspired. Our futures are undecided. We do not know where we will be living next year, where we will be creating new lives. We are all on the brink of magnanimous change." She could hear her voice rising, her confidence growing. "Options are important, so together we will work to increase the margin for acceptance at multiple schools by delivering the most spellbinding applications these colleges and universities have ever seen. We will help ourselves and help our comrades! We will not be pushed aside any longer! We must fight the system and chase the dream!"

"Sing it, coach!" a boy she barely recognized yelled. "Let's do it!"

He clapped his hands together loudly a few times, and soon the room was applauding. For her. Although she knew she had likely turned redder than Dallas's canned cherries and she waved her hand dismissively, she did understand that something very nice was happening here. There would be time to question it later. Right now, she had a revolution to lead.

Celeste raised a fist into the air. "A change is gonna come!"

## CHAPTER 13
# CLARITY

ICY RAIN PATTERED against Celeste's bedroom window. She dropped her head back against her cozy chair and shivered. It seemed impossible to get and stay warm today. Even her fluffy fleece socks weren't helping. The weather was only going to get worse with the miserable months of January and February coming up. Winter sports were not in Celeste's repertoire, but it might behoove her to take up snowboarding or ice fishing or something so that she could get all sorts of thrilled by awful weather.

Warmth. She would kill for warm air and sunshine now. Celeste half laughed. She *had* filled out that Barton College application. Not that it'd been a real application in the sense that she hadn't submitted it, but it had served as a great modeling tool last week when her friends had been over. Maybe not friends, exactly. Fellow students. Whatever they were to her, they had been at her house every night, Monday through Friday, and all had solid applications completed. No one had said anything mean or taunting. No one had been sarcastic or critical. In fact, there had been joking and laughter and hard work. She had people to sit with at lunch and in class now, too. It was entirely possible that they felt an obligation to include her on some level because she'd been up late every night editing their essays. So maybe that was it. Or maybe they were friends? Either way, she found that, much to her surprise, she was grateful for the companionship. She was finding that it was less effort to *allow* social opportunities than to avoid them.

Another thing occurred to Celeste: she had not been a red-haired rocker chick, or a yogini, or anything else but herself. And no disaster struck. It was quite interesting.

A gush of wind slammed ice crystals against the windowpane. San Diego didn't sound half bad right now. Out of curiosity, she visited an online weather site and checked to see what miserable weather Californians were dealing with today. "Oh, pity the poor souls!" she called out. "Unseasonably warm at seventy-seven degrees today? How unfortunate!" Resenting San Diego residents was not, she knew, fair. It was not their fault that they had the good sense not to live in an arctic tundra, which was how Boston felt right then.

Her email icon lit up with a white number one in a red circle. The way her stomach went crazy every time a new message came in was really inexcusable. One should not come undone over a highlighted numeral. Really. It was unbecoming. And it was probably spam.

But it wasn't. It was what she had come to view in the past month as the most beautiful kind of email.

*Celeste!*

*Hi! Whatcha doing? You're in school right now, so you shouldn't be reading this because you should be paying attention to your teachers. Unless you're in a reeeeeeally boring lecture about chlorophyll or something. Nobody cares about chlorophyll. I mean some people do. And plants do. They love chlorophyll and tend to drone on for hours about how fabulous they are in the most obnoxious manner. "Check us out, being all full of sexy green pigment and stuff! We've got the super keenest biomolecule around! And, pfft, don't even get us started on our ability to photosynthesize. Who else makes energy from light? Who? That's. No one. At least no one that we know of. Fine, we don't know everybody, but we for sure make energy in a more fascinating way than anyone else could. In fact, to annually commemorate our being so superfly, we have a holiday. Did you know that? Yes. It's called Chlorophistmas, and it falls in August because there are no other holidays then. Obviously there's a Chlorophistmas tree, because, hello! GREEN! And a bunch of other important traditions that will be revealed over time because we don't want to overwhelm you with all of our spectacularness right away, but you're gonna love everything about us and this holiday or we will shoot out green pigment and wreck your beautiful outfit. So there!"*

*See? Told you. Plants are insufferable.*

*But speaking of holidays, I'm coming home on the 22nd. Or maybe it's the 23rd. I'll find out. Do you celebrate Christmas? I love Christmas. Not in any kind of a religious sense, really. I'm just a big fan of decorations. I get that from my dad, who clearly has some kind of Christmas disorder that compels him to go to extremes. Fortunately, he's not about mini-Santa collections or anything. It's all very tasteful. Lots of white snow-like stuff. And lights. And lights. Also, lights. Did I say lights? Our condo gets lit up like a glow stick. But it's fun. Although there are a lot of requirements for present wrapping. You know, no paper with cartoon reindeer or anything. It's white paper, mostly. White ribbons. OH GOD, GIVE ME COLOR! Hey... maybe the plants will lend me some chlorophyll?*

*So a white Christmas is our tradition. What about you? What does the Watkins family do every year that can compare?*

*Can I take you out again when I'm home? I say we hit up a sushi bar this time. Or you can come to my house to see the white lights. Don't wear white, though, or I might not see you. And that would be a tragedy from which I might never recover.*

*-Justin*

Only Justin could create a holiday for chlorophyll. But more notable was the fact that he wanted to *take her out*. And he wanted to take her out *again*.

It was only now, in this very moment, that Celeste really examined their night out together. It was looking more and more as though they had gone out together. On a date. Her first date.

For someone so intellectually gifted, she was an absolute dummy.

"I may have gone on a date with Justin," she whispered. "I may have had a date." Even saying the words aloud did not make this feel any more real. She wanted to jump up and down. To scream. To holler to the world that she had gone on an actual, real, very first date. With a cute boy. And the boy spilled things, and babbled, and bowed. Most of all, he delighted her on every level. However, she wasn't the sort of young woman who went bananas over this type of thing, was she? She wasn't sure. It seemed unbecoming.

For now, she would simply remember to breathe. She would not panic or have a boy-related anxiety attack. She would just take this one email at a time.

*Justin-*

*I am at home this afternoon because we had a shorter day due to teacher workshops, but had I been suffering through yet another lecture on chlorophyll, I would have been greatly relieved to have received your email during such a dull occasion. It does seem as though teachers have an unnatural fixation on chlorophyll, and photosynthesis, and such, does it not? Every science teacher spends an inordinate amount of time discussing the details of these as though there is nothing more important or interesting in the world than photosynthesis. Goodness, there are imaginary plant holidays that certainly warrant greater attention! I very much look forward to August this year now that I am aware that there is a celebration to be had. Are there gifts involved? I do enjoy gift giving.*

*As well as being someone who now celebrates Chlorophistmas with full gusto, I also celebrate the lesser known Christmas, as you do. Our family has not been much for passing down traditions, although I feel as though I should start one. My brother Matt's ex-girlfriend Julie is glued to her tradition of laying under the Christmas tree and looking up through the branches, taking in the candlelight (Yes, candlelight! From real candles!). Julie takes the opportunity to focus on the past year, the upcoming year, and essentially take stock of her life. Make a wish, have a dream. Things along those lines. She has a propensity for the romantic, and I believe this routine ties into that side of her. I myself do not wish to lose an eye, particularly as emergency rooms are quite harried during the holiday season, and thus do not cram my body under prickly branches in order to daydream. It sounds unsafe and uncomfortable, but I do quite like the idea of adopting some type of tradition as my own. Perhaps this year will be a first for me? I shall keep you updated, if you like.*

*The Boston area is full of culinary exploration opportunities, and I feel sure that we could keep quite busy restaurant hopping if you would like to get together again. Sushi would be another first for me. Or I am certainly amenable to visiting at your parents' place if you prefer that location. My room is done entirely in white, so I feel that your father and I might get along splendidly. Please do let me know when you will be home, and we can find a time that works for us.*

*I imagine that you are in the midst of your final exams right now, so I hope that those are going well for you. You do have an ample supply of coffee, yes?*

She stopped typing for a moment to think about what to say next. How to sign off. How risky to be.

*It will be lovely to see you again. I have missed you, and I don't have occasion to miss many people.*

*-Celeste*

Before she could rethink her wording, she hit the send button.

Today was about bravery.

She thought briefly of Finn and of his never-ending bravery. She opened the photos on her tablet and scrolled through until she found her favorite picture of him. Her grief would be forever; she knew that. Some days it was still excruciating and complex, but more and more, her grief was simple, clean. It was tolerable sadness. Sadness for the brother whom she lost, but also for the brother whom she could have had with her now. He would have gone on to… Well, to do *anything* really. He was wild that way. Unpredictable, curious, daring, extreme. She would love to know what sort of a man he would have grown into.

Today may have been made of small steps, but they were steps nonetheless. They mattered. Finn would, she knew, be very proud, even though her type of daring was different from his.

Her phone rang, Celeste assumed it would be one of her parents or Matt, but Justin's name appeared on the screen. The phone seemed to fly out of her hand, shoot across the room, and land on her bed. She couldn't talk to him on the phone! They hadn't done that! Oh God, why was he calling? But what if he hung up? It would be a missed opportunity. And she had just decided that today was a day of bravery.

Celeste scrambled out of the chair and dove onto the bed in a most ungainly manner, catching the call on what was surely its final ring. Controlling her voice and breath took some effort, but it would not do to answer her first call from Justin sounding all sorts of bananas. "Hello?"

"Why haven't we talked on the phone before?" he immediately asked.

Because there was no one to see her, she let herself smile broadly. "Hello, Justin. I do not know why we have not communicated by phone."

"Maybe we got so used to just emailing and texting that it didn't occur to us to use the phone?"

"Perhaps."

"Okay, that was a total lie. I've thought about calling you a million times."

"You have?"

"I'll refrain from being emotionally scarred by the implication that you've never once thought about talking to me on the phone, but, yes, I've totally wanted to call you. But I was nervous. In fact, I'm a little freaked out right now. But since you said that you were at home and all, I thought that I'd take the opportunity to be all brazen and assertive."

"Oh. Yes."

"How am I doing?"

"How are you doing with what?"

"Being brazen and assertive?"

"You are doing very well."

"I'm nervous. Is that weird? But you make me nervous. I mean, in an awesome way. But you make me nervous," he said.

Celeste rolled onto her back and stared at the smooth white ceiling. Justin's voice was wonderful. "I have also wondered about talking to you on the phone. And I, too, am quite nervous right now."

"You are? Really?"

"Yes. I am."

"How can you be nervous with me? I mean, it's *me*. I'm not exactly suave and polished." He laughed.

"That may be why. You are exceptionally comfortable with yourself." Celeste took a deep breath. She thought for a moment. Justin was decidedly direct. He was open and not afraid of showing his vulnerability. She should—and could—return his honesty. That was important. "And I am anything but. I admire that about you."

"Seriously? I'm totally not comfortable with myself. Are you kidding me? I love that you think that, but..."

"You are very self-aware, I find."

"Okay, I'll give you that. I'm pretty introspective, but you are, too, aren't you? You seem to know yourself well."

"In many ways, yes. I do know myself." Another big breath. "And it is because I know myself so well that I am uncomfortable. In many situations."

"What do you mean? Why?"

"Justin... I know that we do not care for clichés, but this is a rather large can of worms that you are attempting to pry open using a rusty can opener."

"Like one of those old creaky ones you'd find in a summer rental home? With the super skinny handles that hurt?"

Celeste laughed. "Yes. Like that."

"I like worms. You can let the worms out. But only if you

want. I won't make you talk about anything you don't want to."

She sighed and rubbed a hand over her eyes. How to explain so much to this boy? "It's just that... quite obviously, I am not the average high school girl."

"I love that."

"I do not have friends. Well, maybe I do now." She thought about Dallas and Zeke. She was friendly with them. And maybe getting to be friends. "But I do not fit well into any social mold whatsoever. That is not appealing to others."

"It's appealing to me."

Celeste didn't know what to say to this. "I do not use contractions. That is odd, I know that."

"Sometimes you do."

"I do?"

"You just did a minute ago. You said, '*It's* just that...' And you used a few the night we went out. Besides, who cares about whether or not you use contractions? They're overrated."

"If you say so."

"I do say so," Justin said emphatically. "Does using contractions or not using contractions have anything to do with the kind of person you are?"

"Well... no."

"So there. See? Who cares?"

"I have social difficulties. I do not always read situations properly. Or, more correctly, I do not always read people properly."

"Maybe people don't read *you* properly."

"That is a generous way to see me."

"It's the only way to see you."

Celeste could feel both tremendous tension and over-whelming gratitude course through her. Her mind was racing, and she had no idea what to say.

"Hey, Celeste?"

Her heart soared. "Hey, Justin?"

"Are you all right?"

"Yes. I'm very much all right."

"Then I'm very all right, too."

"Hey, Justin?"

"Hey, Celeste?"

"I would like to ask you a question, although I have worries about doing so."

"What kind of worries?" His voice was so gentle that she could cry.

"I am afraid that you will think me silly. Or find my question to be inappropriate. Or that I will embarrass myself due to my naiveté in this area."

"That won't happen. You can ask me anything. C'mon, lay it on me."

She would take the risk. "When you were last home, we went into Harvard Square together. We ate at a number of locations."

"We did," he prompted. "Keep going."

"When we made arrangements to connect that night, I had been under the impression that our evening was af-filiated with Barton. That you were a dining companion to a prospective student. You did not, however, discuss college at all that night. So it has only recently occurred to me that there is the slightest chance that we were not out together for admissions reasons, but... Obviously, nothing untoward occurred between us. I don't have experience in this area, so I am unclear... I believe us to be friends, but then there have been many so many emails between us, although all highly appropriate..." She was floundering. "And many, many texts of coffee froth and Rorschach tests. And you have asked to take me out again which leads me to think that... that you might... I am trying to define the nature of... of our status... as one person relating to another...." This was not going well. At all. "There is the undeniable fact that you are a sophomore in college and I am a senior in high school, so it is likely that you were just—"

"Celeste?"

"Yes?"

"I like you. Yes, as a friend, if that's what you want, but that's not all. I want to take you on a date. A real date. A not-just-friends date."

"Oh."

"And the last time that we went out, I wanted it to be a date, I really did, but I didn't know if you'd say yes, so I guess I didn't clarify on purpose. Then you could think of it as a date or not a date."

"Not having experience in this arena, it did not occur to me that you might have been exhibiting interest other than friendship."

"How could I not? You're you. And why you didn't run screaming after I doused you in ice water, I have no idea, but you didn't run."

"No, I didn't run."

"I had a great time that night."

"I did, as well."

"You tolerated all of my craziness. You made me happy."

"You did the same for me. *Do* the same. You create contractions."

"Because I make you all relaxed and full of warm fuzzies?" Justin may have been teasing, but he spoke the truth.

"Yes."

"Victory! But now we have a problem."

Celeste's stomach dropped. What had she fouled up? "I am listening."

"I messed up, not only our first date, but apparently *your* first date. That's not okay. In fact, it sucks. I want to fix that."

"You have not messed up anything."

"I did, and I feel like a schmuck. But you already agreed to a second date. Or rather, a real first date. And know something, Celeste?"

"What, Justin?"

"It's going to be good. It's going to be a really good first date. You deserve that."

She rolled onto her side and tucked a hand under her head. Justin was saying things that no one had ever said to her before. Trying to comprehend that his words were truly meant for her was going to make her brain explode. But he didn't strike her as one to lie. She would believe him because he was worth this risk. "I am very flattered that you would like to take me on a date."

First she'd had a group of peers at her house every night last week and now this. Her world was changing.

"And I'm honored that I get to take you on a date, so this works out well, what with all the flattering feelings flying far and fast. Did you like my use of alliteration?"

"Given how much I enjoy words, I really did."

Celeste heard some banging and grunting noises on the other end of the call. Justin groaned. "Oh geez, I can't find my poli sci book anywhere. Imagine that. I tried to move my desk, thinking that maybe it fell behind it, and I knocked over my lamp and broke the bulb. Anyway, I have to walk over to the campus store and then the architecture building. You wanna come or should we hang up? I should probably let you go. That'd be boring for you. You don't want to do errands with me. Oh, shoot, I have to check my mailbox. I haven't done that in, like, a week. Wait, where's my wallet? Got it. Okay. Sorry, do you want to go? I mean, go as in go with me or go as in go away from this progressively weird phone call. Are you still there?"

"I am still here. I would like to continue talking to you while you do your errands."

"Yeah?"

"Yes." She didn't want to let him go. Not yet.

"All right. But if you get bored, just tell me."

"I won't." Celeste sat up and moved back to her cozy chair. The ice outside didn't bother her anymore. "Do you have your keys?"

"What? My keys. Damn, thank you! Okay, now I'm ready. Remind me that I have to get milk at the store. Forget I said that. It's not your job to remind me to get milk. I don't know why I asked you that. My study group is at three today, so I've enough time. Wait, what time is it? It's not even nine; what am I worried about?"

She heard a door shut and listened happily as Justin talked aloud to himself while he worked his way out of his building.

"You still there? Wow, it's gorgeous out. Sorry, is it freezing there?"

"It is sleeting ice chips here, and the weather is perfectly miserable, so tell me more about your sunshine. And do not worry because I will remind you to get milk."

"You're a lifesaver, Celeste."

"No, you are my lifesaver, Justin."

## CHAPTER 14
# AFTERSHOCKS

THERE WAS NOTHING in her closet. There was too much in her closet. Celeste put her hands on her hips and scowled at the hangers. Justin had not told her what they were doing tonight, so she was unclear about what would be considered appropriate attire. Jeans? A hideous Christmas sweater with a pom-pom reindeer? A ball gown? She hoped not a ball gown, since she didn't own one; and it was snowing right now, so heels would be horrific footwear. It was a good thing that she had the entire day to figure this out. A first date was not to be taken lightly.

And she was taking this anything but lightly. She was in a near panic. Figuring out what to wear was the least of her worries. Date etiquette was entirely out of her repertoire, so this evening was weighing heavily on her. It appeared that one could want and not want something at the same time. Matt would make some Schrödinger's cat joke were he here, but Celeste was not in the mood for amusing analogies.

Julie would surely be able to help, but Celeste felt somewhat ashamed of relying on a twenty-something with a full life and friends her own age. Plus, calling her would cement this date as a monumental deal worthy of a complete freak-out.

There was Dallas. Celeste thought about her. She was a good choice.

> **Celeste:** Hi, Dallas. I hope that your winter break has started off nicely. I was hoping that you could help me with something.
>
> **Dallas:** Hey! I'm coloring my hair green today! What's up?
>
> **Celeste:** I wanted to consult with you because I have a date tonight, and I do not know what to wear. He has not told me where we are going.
>
> **Dallas:** Oooooh, a date, huh? Nice! Unless it's somewhere really formal, which I'm guessing it's not, what about that pretty pink sweater you have. It's soft and fuzzy looking. Then just do nice jeans and simple jewelry. Be you! You're always dressed so well, anyway, so nothing to worry about.
>
> **Celeste:** Thank you. Yes, I think that pink top might be a good choice.
>
> **Dallas:** Call me tomorrow and let me know how your date goes!
>
> **Celeste:** I will do that. Text me a photograph of your green hair if you like. I feel positive that you will look very much in the holiday spirit. Many thanks for your assistance. I am fortunate to have a friend who is knowledgeable in such matters!

> **Dallas:** And remind me to tell you about Zeke! God, he's so super-hot. Thank you for sitting me next to him at your house! We've been chatting on Facebook and stuff, and I think he might like me. Maybe you can ask him? No, that's dumb. But we'll catch up on that tomorrow, okay?

There. She had reached out to a friend and received a good response. This was a positive sign. Despite the overt differences between herself and Dallas, Celeste liked her quite a bit. And it seemed that Celeste's matchmaking maneuver had potential, so discovering that was a surprising bonus.

She retrieved the pink sweater from the closet and held it up against her chest, assessing her appearance in the mirror. Dallas was right; this was a good choice. As she was looking for a good pair of jeans, her phone dinged.

> **Justin:** Who invented time zones, huh? It's past noon and I'm just waking up. I'm going to UNINVENT them. Whatcha think about that?
>
> **Justin:** And good morning. I made you a coffee with a picture of me jet lagged and groggy.

Celeste laughed out loud at the chocolate face that rested on milk froth in the picture Justin attached to his text.

> **Celeste:** I think that you look dashing, but I am sorry that you are struggling to adjust to Eastern Time.

**Justin:** But have no fear, I will be caffeinated and alert tonight, okay? 7 still good for me to pick you up?

**Celeste:** Yes, that is fine. I am uncertain about proper attire, as I do not know what we are doing; but I have made a decision nonetheless.

**Justin:** I suggest a pirate costume. I'll bring extra peg legs in case you lose yours.

**Celeste:** As you wish.

**Justin:** Also, a pair of wings. And a squash racquet.

**Celeste:** My anxiety level is rising.

**Justin:** Then no squash racquet. Better?

**Celeste:** Slightly.

**Justin:** Are you actually nervous?

**Celeste:** Yes.

**Justin:** Why? It's just me. You know me. Nothing bad is going to happen. I mean, I might fall down or something, but YOU will be just fine. You need to trust me.

**Celeste:** I will do my best.

**Justin:** I have to go shopping, so as long as I'm not stampeded at the mall on this final Saturday before Christmas, I'll see you tonight. Wish me luck!

**Celeste:** I have minimal concerns about your outing, but I wish you luck nevertheless.

**Justin:** #amwearingprotectivegear #picturewithmallsantaforsure

She felt a bit better. He was right. It was *Justin*. Justin with whom she had been emailing whom she had been talking to and texting on the phone, and whom she had seen in person a total of three times.

She sighed. Three was not many. Still, it wasn't about the amount of face time one had with another, it was about the quality of the overall relationship, and she did believe that she and Justin had some level of connection. Or she was trying to believe that.

Life was getting better for her. Very slowly, bit by bit, she was allowing the walls she'd so carefully constructed to come down. Every move felt to be a most dangerous risk, but she was taking those risks, and they were paying off. The world might not be such a hateful place after all, and there was the faint hope that she might just be able to find a place in it.

Celeste abandoned her fretting and headed downstairs to tackle some gift wrapping. The dining room table was set up with wrapping paper, various bows and ribbons, tape, scissors, decorative bags, and tissue paper. Really, more materials than anyone would reasonably need, but Erin had become a big fan of elaborate gift presentation. Matt was coming over later to make use of the supplies. It was Celeste's understanding that twenty-six-year-old males were unable to purchase their own wrapping paper *and* that they often had hidden hopes that showing up at their families' houses would result in younger sisters taking over the wrapping of said gifts.

She finished affixing a piece of tape to the *Come to the nerd side. We have Pi.* T-shirt that she was wrapping for Matt. She had wanted to get him the shirt that read, *Dear Algebra, Stop asking us to find your X. She's not coming back,* because under normal circumstances he would find it funny. However, now it felt inappropriate, given that Matt's romantic life appeared to have stalled significantly since he and Julie ended their relationship. She still wasn't sure exactly what besides distance, if anything, had come between them, but perhaps that was enough to keep them apart. Although it had been two years since they'd broken up, it still bothered her. Matt and Julie not being together felt all wrong.

When her text alert sounded repeatedly, Celeste couldn't help but grin over her increased social network. Her stomach rarely dropped anymore when alerts came through.

> **Justin:** Michelle! Hope you got home with no layovers. I heard the Denver airport cancelled most flights yesterday. Miss you already. Winter break will fly by, and Kevin and I will throw a party the night everyone is back.
>
> **Justin:** And why didn't you let me take you to the airport? I'd even remembered to gas up my car the night before. I heard you leave, but by the time I was fully awake you were long gone. I would have gotten up with you (even at that ungodly hour of FIVE IN THE MORNING!).
>
> **Justin:** You left a shirt here, by the way, in case you're looking for it.

Celeste read the messages over and over. Obviously Justin had texted her in error, but that did not ease the nauseated feeling that threatened to choke her. The phone shook in her hand.

Celeste focused on Matt's present, and she finished wrapping it, carefully and methodically. Then she set his T-shirt under the tree and walked slowly up the stairs to her room. She took the pink sweater and placed it neatly back on the shelf in her closet and shut the door. The full-length mirror was in front of her now, and she turned away quickly. She couldn't stand the sight of her reflection.

Celeste pulled off her sweatshirt and pulled the blinds shut. She crawled into bed, wearing her jeans and tank top. The silent tears came easily, wetting her face in seconds. *Of course* Justin had a life outside of her, a real life with girls at his school who were fun and functional. Who were normal. How she had deceived herself into dreaming that anything meaningful could happen between Justin and herself was nearly incomprehensible. This date tonight could not happen because there was no point. And based on those text messages, Justin likely already had a girl, one who was in his room early in the mornings, one whom he was missing already.

She rolled onto her side and pulled the covers over her head. It was fortunate that her parents were gone for the day at the outlet stores, so that she could be alone. Explaining her devastation would be impossible. All she could feel right now was the depth of her total inadequacy when compared to every other girl her age. She would never, ever be a girl who could hold Justin's attention, and why he had even paid her any mind in the first place was a mystery.

Hours ticked by as Celeste lay still in her bed, her mind spinning. Justin had teased her. Maybe not intentionally, but he'd taunted her with the idea that maybe, just maybe, he could see beyond all of her strangeness. The things that she couldn't control, but the ones that made up who she was. Even if he had, for a split second, liked her to some degree, he clearly had a college full of women with whom he could engage on normal social levels. Romantic levels. Probably sexual levels, if she was being realistic.

The bedroom darkened as the afternoon wore on. If she could just hold on, time would take her through the night, through the next day, the next week. This day and this awful misery would ease. Celeste knew how pain lessened with time. So she would just hold on. She would cease to exist until tomorrow, after the time for her date had come and gone. Then it would be easier.

Her room was virtually pitch black when she heard Matt's voice. "Celeste? Are you in here?"

She didn't bother to move. She couldn't move anyway.

"Celeste?"

Through closed eyes, she saw the darkness lift a bit. He must have turned on the nightstand light. She felt him sit on the bed next to her. "Are you okay? What, do you have the flu or something else disgustingly gross and contagious? Do I need to begin a bloodletting routine or what?"

She wanted nothing more than for him to go away. As much as she loved her brother, he would not understand, and she was too embarrassed to tell him what was happening. Or to tell him who she really was: an utterly pathetic, despondent mess.

Matt put a hand on her shoulder and rolled her onto her back. She pulled away, and again he rolled her over. Celeste shoved him away, hard, and resumed her place on her side. She moved an arm over her eyes. "Leave me alone, Matthew."

"Hey, what the hell's going on?" He was angry now. Or maybe scared. Either way, she didn't care.

"I forgot that you would be coming to the house today. Just. Go. Away."

"Don't yell at me because you slept through your date."

"Get out of my room. Now."

"No," he said firmly. "No. You're going to tell me what this all about. All I know is that I was downstairs happily gift wrapping and listening to One Direction sing a fanciful medley of uplifting Christmas carols when that Justin character shows up at the house, saying that he's supposed to pick you up at seven."

"You were not listening to One Direction."

"Fine. It was Hillary Duff, but whatever. The point is that there is a dude in our front hall telling me that he's been texting and calling you for hours, and you're not answering. Are you supposed to go out with him?"

"Tell him to leave. I am not here."

"Well, you *are* here."

She didn't respond. She could wait him out. He would give up and leave soon enough. Except that he didn't. Ten minutes must have gone by when he said her name again. "Celeste. Please explain this to me." She felt him shift on the bed. "I wish that you would let me do something. Do you want me to kick him out of the house? Did he do something to you?"

Another voice echoed in her room. Justin's. "Maybe she'll talk to me?"

Oh God, why had Matt even let him in the house?

"Do you want him to stay?" Matt asked.

Silence.

"Celeste." Matt's frustration was evident, but she simply had nothing to say. "I don't know what to do here, so I'm going to have to give Justin a shot. Yell if you need anything." His weight lifted from the bed. Knowing Matt, he was likely staring Justin down as he left the room. He might not be a typical alpha male, but Celeste knew that Matt was fiercely protective when it came to her.

Willing herself to become invisible was not working, it seemed, because she heard Justin cross the room and then felt him next to her. The sound of his footsteps even tugged at her heart. She felt him kneeling next to the bed. "I've been trying to get a hold of you all day," he said softly.

This was an impossible situation. If she was lucky, he would give up on her, get back in his car, and vanish from her life altogether. It was the only way to recover from this.

"It took me six hours, but I finally realized that I texted you by mistake."

Despite herself, she nodded.

"And you're upset about that."

She nodded again.

"I think you're misunderstanding what you read. Will you let me explain?"

It was best to get this over with. She rubbed her eyes and turned to face him. It didn't matter that he looked distraught because that meant nothing to her right now. "I understand, Justin. I understand very clearly."

He moved a hand to her face and brushed the hair from her cheek. The sorrowful expression in his eyes made her feel worse. He felt sorry for her. "I don't think you do."

"I understand that having a girl in your room during early morning hours—"

"No," he said cutting her off. "No. It's not what you think it is. Michelle is my roommate Kevin's girlfriend. We live in a tiny dorm suite, and we each have our own miniature bedroom and a small common room. She slept in Kevin's room that night. I was just going to give her a ride to the airport. Yes, she's a friend of mine, but that's it. I met her on the first day of college last year, and we've been friends ever since I stopped her from taking one too many vodka shots and saved us all from having to listen to 'Don't Rain On My Parade' for the ninety-seventh time."

Celeste sniffed. "I dislike that song."

He smiled and touched a finger to her wet cheek. "Don't cry. Please. You don't have to hear it ever again."

Celeste couldn't smile back.

"Do you want to know a secret?" he whispered.

"Okay."

"Your brother really *was* listening to One Direction."

"He was not." But now she did smile just a bit.

"Oh, but he was. And I think I saw him dancing a little. It was subtle, but there was some foot tapping and a few shoulder shakes." Now he took both hands and rubbed his thumbs under her eyes. "Please don't cry."

"I do not think this is going to work out, Justin. I appreciate how kind you are being, but you should not have come here."

He shook his head. "Why would you say that? You understand now, right? That the texts were nothing."

"I do. But that does not change the inherent problem present. Even if Michelle is solely a platonic friend—"

"She *is*," he insisted.

"Even then, I was reminded today that you are immersed in a crowd of young women, all of whom likely possesses much more typically alluring traits than I."

"Celeste," he said, "you are beautiful."

"Perhaps physically, by cultural norms. But that only serves to make the non-physical parts of me even more unsuitable."

"What are you talking about?"

"I am not like other girls. I recognize that, and I understand that my traits are incompatible with what is traditionally desirable in a romantic partner. I cannot compete. That is all. I will never be regular."

Justin looked around the room as if searching for how to handle her. Then he rose from his kneeling crouch and stretched out on the bed, resting on his side next to her so that they were eye to eye. He took her hands in his. "You listen to me, okay? Listen. Yes, are you are a beautiful girl. Stunning, really. Anyone can see that. But that doesn't really mean anything to me. I see past your beauty, and I find more beauty. The important kind. Don't you know that? I'm doing something wrong if you don't, so let me be really clear here." Justin lifted her hands a bit and delicately kissed her fingers.

She could hardly breathe.

He looked at her again. "I am staggered by you. I am intoxicated by you. I think about you way more than I should. I want to get to know you as much as possible, but you have to let me. I mean, if that's what you want. Maybe you think I'm a huge jerk, and maybe you're done with me. So tell me that if you need to." He kissed her hands again and peeked up at her, his eyes sparkling. "But please don't, because I desperately want to take you out tonight."

Celeste was sure that he could hear her heartbeat. "Okay."

"Yeah?"

"Yes. But I'm afraid that I do not look very nice."

"You could wear a garbage bag, and I wouldn't mind a bit."

"I was not going to wear a garbage bag. Or this plain white shirt. I was going to wear a pink sweater."

Justin eased himself to sitting. "Then let's get your pink sweater." He looked behind him. "Closet or dresser?"

"Closet."

He squeezed her hands and let them go, getting up and going to her closet. He returned in a moment with her sweater. "This one?"

"Yes. Thank you."

Justin slid a hand under her back and gently pulled her to a sitting position. She watched him, mesmerized, as he lifted up the sweater, lowered it over her head, and then smoothed out the fabric as she eased her arms into the sleeves. He took one of her hands back into his. "You look very sad today."

"I am sorry. I am not an easy person."

He pointed back and forth between them. "Pot, kettle." He winked. "Are you sad just because of me, or is there something else?"

Celeste thought for a moment. "I am sad because of me. I am embarrassed."

"Tell me why."

Celeste dropped her head while she spoke. "I am embarrassed because things that are easy for other people are challenging for me. Going on a date with you should not be as monumentally terrifying as it is."

"What can I do to make you feel better?"

Celeste had no idea. She looked at him, helpless.

"Would it help if I told you that there is no pressure here? We're just going to go out and have a good time. Neither of us gets to have performance anxiety, okay? We don't. If at any point tonight you decide that you want to go home, I'll take you home. That's it. I won't be angry, or think less of you, or anything. Deal? I'm humbled that you would let me take you out when, as you said, this feels hard for you."

"It is not your fault. I have issues centered around loss. Perceived abandonment. Solitude, which I both crave and detest. It's too much to explain."

Justin looked down and thought for a moment. "I saw a picture downstairs while I was waiting for you. In the front hall. It's a picture of you and Matt…"

She finished the sentence for him. "And Finn."

"A second brother."

"Yes," she said. "Older than Matthew. He died when I was much younger. I did not handle his death well. Nobody did. It is my assessment that my personality type, coupled with a high level of family dysfunction and a mother with unmanaged depression at the time, was not adequate to cope with losing Finn." She couldn't tell him about Flat Finn. Not now, not ever. It would be the ultimate deal breaker, revealing that she had relied on a cardboard copy of her brother to get her through even the most basic basics of daily life for almost two years. She could only expect a certain degree of understanding and tolerance, and Justin had already gone above and beyond. "Finn was my savior, and then he was dead. Some days the aftershocks can still be felt."

"We all have aftershocks." Justin stood up, pulling Celeste with him, and bringing her into his chest. She tucked her arms up between them, letting him hold her.

"It feels as though I must work very hard for everything. It's not easy."

"You're in a war."

It was a painfully accurate way to describe her state. "I am."

"I understand that. There are battles, some greater than others. But they are worth getting through." He held her tighter. "This is the fight, Celeste. You're in the middle of it. I feel that."

"Because you have endured your own?"

"Yes. I got through mine, and you will get through yours."

## CHAPTER 15
# QUITE BEGUILED

CELESTE COULD STAY wrapped in Justin's arms forever, but eventually he pulled back a bit and lifted her face to his. "You ready to go?"

"You still want to take me out?"

"I want to take you out more now."

"Because you feel sorry for me that I have a dead brother and formerly crazy parents?"

He laughed. "No. Because I like that you shared something with me. I feel closer to you. Don't you feel closer to me?"

Celeste studied his face. "You often surprise me with your candor."

Justin shrugged. "I spent a few years in therapy. I learned that I like being truthful."

"I, too, have been in therapy. It was helpful in many ways, but it did not change who I am at the core."

"That's a relief." Justin jostled her shoulders and then slid one arm behind her neck. "Let's go to dinner, and you can tell me about it."

She stopped them at the top of the stairs. "Justin? Thank you for being so kind to me, tonight and all of the times we have communicated. Quite often my experiences with being myself have resulted in rejection by others. I have tried to change who I am so that the average person will accept me, but that has not met with much success."

"Did that red hair and bodysuit thing have anything to do with that?"

"Perhaps. And perhaps, I will also tell you about that over dinner." She led the way downstairs, and even though the stairs creaked like crazy, she did not miss the sound of Matt scrambling off the lower risers into the dining room.

"IT'S BEGINNING TO LOOK A LOT LIKE CHRISTMAS!" he half-sang, half-shouted. "If Christmas looks like mangled paper and shredded ribbons."

"Matty?" Celeste stepped through the archway to where Matt was poised over a mound of crumpled snowman paper.

"Oh, hey, didn't see you there."

"You are not a good actor, Matthew, but I appreciate your effort to act as though I did not treat you atrociously earlier tonight."

"What? Nah, don't worry about. What you should worry about is whether or not I go insane and hurl all of this gift-wrapping nonsense into the fireplace."

Celeste walked to her brother. "Matthew."

"Fine, fine, I won't burn it all. I'll save the roll that has the naked Mrs. Clauses."

"That is Dad's favorite." She touched Matt's arm. "I should not have yelled at you the way I did. You were trying to help."

Matt refused to look at her and continued to fuss with trying to curl a ribbon. "I didn't do a good job, did I?"

"That was not your fault," she said.

"He made you feel better, though? That's all that matters."

"This is not a competition."

"I didn't say it was."

"No, you did not. But you sound flippant. Please stop making unsuccessful ribbon curls and listen to me, Matty."

He dropped the scissors loudly. "What?"

"I'm sorry."

He softened his voice. "It's okay. I'm just in a bad mood. It's not you. I really am glad that you feel better." Matt stepped back from the table and looked at Justin. "You two going out for dinner?"

Justin nodded. "Sushi. I hear your sister has never tried it."

Matt crossed his arms and smiled. "I'm liking you more and more. Which restaurant?"

"FuGaKyu on Beacon Street in Brookline. Have you been there?"

"I have. That's a great place. Make her get the clam. Or octopus. Don't go easy on her."

Justin raised his eyebrows. "I don't know; I may have already pushed her enough for one day."

Celeste was trying to interpret how Matt was looking at

Justin. Whatever that look meant, he still stepped forward, put a hand on Celeste's shoulder, and turned to Justin. "Okay, then. Well, go have fun. Mom and Dad know you'll be out?"

"Yes," Celeste said. "And I have my phone. Would you turn off my computer for me? I believe that I left it on."

"Yes, your highness." Then, in what Celeste felt to be a very sweet move, Matt reached out to shake Justin's hand. "Good to see you, Justin."

Justin nodded. "You too. I'll have her home by midnight."

"Or eleven-thirty." Matt said.

Celeste put her arm through Justin's and steered them to the front hall for her coat. "Or midnight. Good night, Matty. I love you."

"Girls... They're impossible. Always pushing limits." Matt's voice followed them as they went out the front door. "Be nice, or I'll return the Hello Kitty purse that I bought you for Christmas."

When she was buckled into the front seat, Justin pulled the car out of the driveway. She could see Matt through the living room window. He raised his hand in a small wave, and she felt a striking pang of emotion. Celeste waved back at her brother.

He looked so terribly alone tonight. But maybe that was just her interpretation because she had been brusque with him. She would have to apologize again for that. It did seem to Celeste, however, that Matthew was not as happy as he had been when he was with Julie. Celeste missed them as a couple probably as much as Matt did.

"You lost in thought there?"

"Huh? Oh. Yes, I believe I was. I was just thinking about Matt." She turned to Justin. "I do believe he likes you."

"You surprised?"

"A bit. Not because of who you are, but because I don't think Matt develops fondness for people easily."

"Then I'm especially glad that I passed his filters." He turned on the wipers to brush away the light snow. "Maybe you'll come over and meet my parents? They'll worship you; I already know that."

"How could you know that?"

"Because some things you just know."

"Yes. I think you are right about that. Some things you do just know. I would be pleased to meet them."

"New Year's Eve, maybe? They always do a fun cocktail party at their house. You could bring your family, too, if you want."

"You have not arranged to spend that holiday with friends from home? I was under the impression that college students who returned home for vacations were interested in reconnecting with high school friends."

"Well, to be honest, I didn't have that many friends in high school. There's not really anyone who I want to see."

"But you have good friends at Barton?"

"Yeah. My roommate, Kevin, is awesome. Despite the poor introduction from my texts, you'd love him and Michelle."

Celeste was not sure they would love *her*, but Justin had good intentions.

"You ready for your first sushi?"

She nodded. "Given that this is a night of firsts, I feel it fitting. I will be brave."

"You've already been brave."

She leaned back in her seat and gazed at the boy next to her. "I have a question for you."

"Sure."

"You have spoken very forthrightly about your struggles with distractibility. How you are easily scattered."

"Yes."

"But tonight, upstairs with me, you were very focused," She paused. "On me."

He smiled. "Important things can ground me. People who matter can ground me. It's, like, I get jarred into clarity. Some of the endless static in my head quiets. It's not as though I can never pay attention."

"No, no," she said quickly. "I did not mean to imply that."

"Oh, I know you didn't. You get me more than most people do. Your patience with me? It means a lot."

"You have many different sides."

"Some of them more grating than others?" he asked with a laugh.

"Absolutely not. I like all sides of you very much."

"You're the first person to say that."

"Then our night of firsts is going very well."

Justin ran a hand through his hair. "You're calming for me. You can settle me somehow in a way that nobody else has. I can't explain it."

"That is exceptionally nice to hear." The way he looked

under the evening streetlights was too much. Celeste lifted a hand and brushed the back of her fingers against his cheek.

Justin was quiet for a minute. "I didn't like seeing you upset tonight." He tipped his head into her hand.

"You made it better," she said. "You fixed me."

"We can only fix ourselves." He braked at a red light and turned to her. "I was just there to support you while you did that."

He let her stroke her hand over his skin, lightly touching his hair. She was so unused to physical contact of this sort—much less wanting it—that she was undeniably entranced. It was one thing to snuggle with Julie on the couch when she was younger, or loop her arms though Matt's when they walked. But this? This was an entirely different category of touch. Celeste let her hand trail down to the back of his neck before she felt obligated to pull away.

"Don't… don't stop. I mean, unless you want to. It's just… That felt good."

Without speaking, she moved her hand to the top of his arm, to his shoulder, settling again to the soft skin that peeked out from his sweatshirt.

Justin parked the car on a side street off of Beacon in Coolidge Corner. She let him open the door for her because he seemed to like doing that. As they walked the short block through the soft snow, her hand falling naturally into his, she realized something.

"Hey, Justin?"

"Hey, Celeste?"

"I do not feel scared anymore."

"Neither do I."

So they ate sushi.

Justin slid into the seat next to her, saying, "I get to be closer to you this way. Is that all right?"

She touched the menu that sat on her plate. "Yes."

"And," he continued as he draped an arm over her shoulder. "This all right, too?"

Nodding was all that she could manage.

He moved the menu between them and opened it up. "We're going to order one of everything—and extra clam just to please your brother—but we can look at what they have anyway."

"You have quite the appetite."

"Fine, we won't really order one of everything, but it's the thought that counts."

"I think that you may need to choose our selections," she said as she scanned the menu. "I have no idea where to begin. I will rely on you for recommendations."

Justin walked her through the menu, moving his fingers over the pages, describing different fish for her and asking what sounded good. She was fairly sure that she missed half of what he said because having his arm over her shoulder now caused her to be the one with significant attention issues, but she nodded and otherwise responded when she could. He never took his arm away from holding her.

Later, a colorful selection arrived, and plate after plate of dumplings, tempura, sushi, sashimi, maki, none of which Celeste could have identified on her own. There were vinegar sauces, spicy add-ons, and sweet soy. And while her taste buds danced in reaction to so many explosive new flavors, she listened to Justin. As much as she had enjoyed their many emails over the past few months, she was quickly learning that the sound of his voice had a powerfully wonderful effect on her. It might do well for her to become more comfortable talking on the phone.

"The way you speak, Justin, I find it quite beguiling."

"What do you mean?"

"I feel as though I might well be able to listen to you all night. There is a pleasing quality about your phrasing, your word choices, the intonation and animation in your speech. It captures me."

"Really? That's particularly complimentary considering that I had a horrible stutter when I was a kid."

"You did? I would not have guessed."

"Oh God, it was awful. I could hear what I wanted to say in my head, but delivering it was an entirely different matter. Some words were worse than others. It only added to everyone's impatience with me. Nobody wanted to wait for me to ask yet another question. I was that kid, you know? The one who followed every question with another question. It drove people nuts, but I wanted answers and explanations. *Why is it raining? But why do the clouds do that? But why some clouds and not others?* And my poor parents. *Why do I have to go to sleep now? But why do you say so? What happens if I'm tired tomorrow? Why can't I read another book? Why is this book square and others are rectangular? Why is the caterpillar so very hungry and where did he find all of those random foods just scattered in the middle of nowhere?* There was no end to my questions."

"You were curious. That is a fine quality and indicative of intelligence."

"Positive rephrasing. I like it."

"I feel confident that I would have liked your many questions *and* your stutter because I am sure that you pulled off both with very sharp style."

Justin raised his eyebrows and shook his head. "I have no idea what to make of you, Celeste Watkins."

"Oh." She could feel her body tense.

He rubbed her shoulder. "Hey, easy. I mean that in the most complimentary way."

"Oh," she said again. But this time she had to restrain herself from jumping out of her seat with happiness. "Thank you."

When the bill came, Celeste tried very hard to convince Justin to let her pay for dinner. When he vehemently refused, she tried to get him to agree to split it. "My father was insistent that he treat us to dinner. He dramatically shoved money at me and said that the Watkins family would like to thank you for—"

"Absolutely not. You tell your father that there is no way that I am letting anyone else but me pay for your first date. But say that with lots of respect and stuff." He winked. "Now, that's enough of that. We have somewhere to be." He checked the time on his phone. "Yeah, we need to scoot."

"Where are we going?"

"It's a surprise."

"You are not going to tell me?"

He led them through the busy restaurant to the door. "Can you trust me?"

"I believe that I can."

"Okay. I'm the one who should be nervous, not you. What if you hate it? What if you call me a stupid moron and roll your eyes and faint because you can't fathom how you agreed to blindly follow such a strange fellow on an unnamed adventure?"

Celeste laughed and dusted snowflakes from her sleeves. "I am highly doubtful that will happen."

"You're not cold, are you?"

"Not at all. Even with the snow, it is quite agreeable out tonight, don't you think?"

"Okay, good."

"You have on only a sweatshirt. Are you not chilly?"

"I have a hood. And I have you." He pulled her closer. "Damn, I think I forgot my wallet. Oh, no, I didn't. It's fine. Anyway, you up for a little bit of a drive?"

"I am." She would drive across the country if that's what he wanted.

# CHAPTER 16
# JOY

**T**HEY WOVE THROUGH busy Saturday night traffic, eventually making their way onto Route 9, heading west. Since he'd seemed pleased with having her hand on him during the earlier drive, she returned to the place on the back of his neck that he seemed to like. His hairline was damp from melted snow, something that Celeste found endearing. It did, however, seem that she found everything about him endearing, so it was quite likely that he could belch out the alphabet and she would be delighted. Not that she would suggest that to him.

Justin took them past a town sign for Dedham and soon slowed, pulling into a parking area. Celeste looked out the window and smiled. "We have arrived at a Christmas tree lot?" She clapped her hands together. "Are we buying a tree?"

Justin parked the car in a row by the entrance. "Better. Or I hope better. But if buying a Christmas tree is the true ultimate in your list of awesome things, then I will absolutely buy you a tree. Although you already have one at your house, so your parents might think that I found something ginormously offensive about their tree and was so horrified that I felt forced to replace it. I'd prefer they like me and not see me as some kind of jerk who goes around passing judgment on Christmas tree adequacy."

She slipped her arm through his as they strolled through the lot, the snow still swirling softly in the night breeze. "I feel confident that they like you very much."

An older man in a khaki parka with grey hair peeking out from under a Santa hat waved with one hand as he pulled a tree behind him with the other. "Justin! There you are!" He righted the tree against a chain link fence and walked to close the gap between them. "This must be Celeste. Pleasure to meet you, miss." He held out a hand and flashed a mustached smile. "I'm Steve. Welcome to Steve's Trees, and excuse the cheesy name."

"It is very nice to meet you. You own this cheerful establishment?" Celeste had no idea what they were doing here, but she liked it.

"Your girl looks mighty confused," Steve said. "You didn't tell her?"

Justin grinned. "Nope. I'll take her over now. Thanks, Steve." Justin patted the man's arm as they walked by.

"What are we doing?" she asked. Justin was leading her through the stacks of snow-dusted trees, winding among shoppers who were examining shapes and sizes, and eventually taking them to a back gate.

"You ready?" His eyes were full of mischief. "I hope you like this. But it's not a big deal if you don't."

He opened the gate and Celeste stepped forward to find

herself at the start of a path. A tunnel, really, of evergreen trees that grew rounded over the path in such a way as to nearly obscure the sky. She was surrounded by what must be thousands of mini white lights.

She walked into the glow, a shimmery hue now cast over her. "Justin."

He dropped her hand and stepped back, watching as she began to move through the tunnel. His hands slipped into his pockets, and he bounced on his feet as she slowly moved ahead.

She touched both hands to her cheeks. "It's magical. A place for fairies or other enchanted beings."

Justin hopped to her side. "Or snow goddesses. Like you. Is it okay?"

"It's beautiful."

"I used to work here every Christmas season since I was a kid, so Steve let me set this up for you," he said excitedly.

Dazed, Celeste stopped in one spot and pivoted in a circle, taking in what Justin had done for her. When she circled back to face forward, Justin was ten yards ahead of her.

"Look at you," he called laughing. "You're just gorgeous."

"And you," she said. "You look like... like Mr. Darcy. The most romantic of leading men."

He tossed up his hands in a cheer. "I'll take that compliment. Usually I get told that I look like a boy band member, so this is huge."

She giggled and shook her head as he made a little hip-thrust-spin dance move in the snow. "I didn't know Mr. Darcy could dance."

"Well, he can. And very sexily, I might point out. Come

on." Justin beckoned her to join him, so she ran under the arched trees to catch up. He grabbed her hand and tugged. "I want you to see something else."

The path was longer than she would have thought, the wooded trail curving in a few spots. She could stay in this cozy fortress forever, only Justin and her. The perfection of this moment was all she would ever need.

The lighted walk eventually ended, and they emerged into a circular clearing. She gasped again. One massive fir tree sat before them, magnificent and alone. Justin walked her through the snow around the edge of the clearing, stopping by a wide driveway. "So this tree? This is sort of my tree. My parents' tree, I guess. They've known Steve for years, and when Steve cleared out this area to use for smaller outdoor weddings and other events, my parents convinced him to leave this tree because it's so amazing. The fall that they adopted me, they kind of adopted this tree, too."

Celeste turned to him. "I was not aware that you were adopted."

"I didn't tell you that? But I am. Well, when you have two dads, it's pretty common."

"You have two dads?"

Justin smacked a hand against his forehead. "I didn't tell you that either? Oh God... Yup, me and my gay dads."

"You've always just said *parents*."

"I guess you're right. Are you weirded out?"

"I don't understand what you mean."

"Um..." Justin looked so nervous. "Does this... change anything for you?"

"Change what?"

Justin kicked the snow. "Us."

"You think I might find you less… less everything wonderful that you are because you have two fathers?"

"Some people think it's totally creepy that I grew up with gay parents."

"Are they creepy parents?"

"They're awesome actually."

"Unless there is good reason for me to deem them neglectful or otherwise nasty parents, I find nothing even vaguely hair-raising about this. Plus, they adopted a tree in your honor, an act that is quite moving. Your fathers are thoughtful, and they appreciate symbolism."

"I'm glad you like the tree."

"I like more than the tree," she said, glad to see Justin happy again.

"Okay, so, we're going to light this baby up. Me and you, okay?" He knelt down and brushed around snow on the ground and then moved to stand behind Celeste and wrap his arms around her as he rested his chin on her shoulder. In each hand he held an end of an extension cord. "Take them. This is your tree tonight, and you're in charge of turning it on."

She leaned back into him. "We should do this together."

"If that's what you want." He put his hands over hers. "Ready? On three. One… two… three!"

Together, they joined the plugs, and the tree instantly brightened with red and green lights. She couldn't speak for a minute, so she just nestled her head into the crook of his neck and looked at the picturesque vision in front of her.

"Spectacular," he murmured.

"Yes, you are."

"*We* are." He rocked them back and forth as he hugged her.

"You did this just for me?"

"I've been here all day. My dads helped, too."

"I don't know what to say," she whispered. "I am touched. Indescribably so."

"I think there's missing something, though, don't you?"

"I can't imagine what."

He squeezed her shoulders. "A star, silly. Every tree should have a star on top."

"Unless we both turn into spider monkeys, I do not think that possible."

"Anything's possible, even for us non-monkey types."

He pulled away and bounded in front of her until he faced the tree-lined rugged road next to them. He waved his arms over his head. Within seconds, a truck was shining bright headlights their way, driving out across the snow into the clearing, and parking close to the tree.

"What in the world..." Celeste wondered. "Why is there a truck from the phone company here?"

"I'll show you."

They walked over to the driver's side, and the window rolled down. "Justin! What's up, bro?"

Justin clamped his hand into the driver's and leaned in for a quick hug. "Right on time. This is Celeste. Celeste, meet my friend Trent."

She looked up into the cab and waved shyly. Even in this

cold, he had on a navy shirt, the sleeves cut off and revealing large muscled biceps. She wasn't sure that the knitted striped watch cap he wore was enough compensation, but Trent's warm smile conveyed no indication that he was near hypothermia. "Hello."

"And hello to you, sweet thing. We've all been dying to meet you." He fist bumped Justin. "You said she's even smarter and cooler than she is pretty, so this girl must be the most badass genius in the world, huh?"

"Don't make me look pathetic, man. But, yeah, pretty much."

Celeste felt a flutter run through her. "May I ask why you have driven this bucket truck onto this field?"

"Because my friend here has the most bitchin' crush—"

"Hey, hey, that's enough." Justin smacked Trent's arm and then explained. "Trent works for the phone company. He's going to give us a lift." He looked to the top of the tree. "Follow me."

"Take your time, lovers," Trent said. He left the window down and cranked up the radio.

At the back of the truck was a ladder. Justin helped Celeste climb up, then joined her and escorted her into the standing bucket attached to a long, jointed steel arm. "You ready?"

"It is hard to say whether one could ever be ready for something like this, but I believe so."

"Let 'er rip!" Justin called to Trent.

The bucket gave a jolt and Celeste let out a sound of excitement as she clutched onto Justin's waist.

He laughed. "You okay?"

"Yes, very much so!" She was giddy as the bucket lifted them from the truck toward the winter sky until they were poised far above the ground. Her grip on him grew tighter as they veered sideways and swung nearer to the branches of the great tree. Trent skillfully brought them so close to the top of the tree that Celeste could reach out and touch the tips. They stopped moving, and she surveyed the view around her. Dedham looked rather spectacular tonight. City lights twinkled in a sky that was fading from navy to jet black, cars flowed evenly over the nearby bridge, and plenty of evergreen trees nestled in between snow mounds, breaking up the small downtown.

Her hold on Justin was still fierce, and he tipped her face to his. "You're not afraid of heights, are you?"

"Apparently not. At least not when I am with you."

"Good." He reached down and picked up a bag. "I brought a pen and paper for you to write something. Anything you like." He winked. "We'll save it in a waterproof container and tuck it under the star. It will stay safe there for you."

"I think that is a wonderful idea. Now you lean over and look at the tree, and I shall make use of your back as a sort of writing desk."

"I'm just an object to you, aren't I?" he said with a laugh. But he did as she asked. "And don't tell me what you're writing. This is just for you."

So Celeste took the small notepad and pen and thought. She had everything to say and also nothing. Justin was making her feel as though anything might be possible, and that was overwhelming. But then she knew what to put down to paper. Celeste wrote in perfect cursive writing, taking her time because she enjoyed the intimate quiet.

She tore off the lower half of the paper with her words and folded it up. "Now it is your turn."

"But this is just for you," he protested.

"This is for *us*." She turned, offering her back for him to write on.

"If that's what my snow goddess wants, that's what my snow goddess gets." Justin took his time, but she finally heard the tear of paper as he took his words from the notepad and folded them up.

Together, they set their papers into the small box, and Justin sealed it up. "Now hold me so I don't fall out of this rickety old truck bucket. You know my terrible balance. I don't want to fly out of this thing, because I didn't bring my parachute."

She rolled her eyes in fun, but put her hands on him as he leaned to tuck the box among the top branches.

"I'm falling! Catastrophe is imminent!"

She laughed. "You are not falling!"

He pulled himself up hard, with no small amount of drama. "Whew. You saved me. Did you see how I almost went careening off the side? So close."

"You are very silly."

He reached into the bag again. "And now, my beautiful snow goddess, this is the star for the top of the tree." Justin produced a star that was at least a foot wide and handed it to her.

"For me?"

"Of course. Just reach out. Don't worry, I'll hold on to you."

She took a deep breath and stretched her arms over the edge, while Justin kept his hands on her waist. The star went easily onto the uppermost evergreen branch, the one that stood nearly perfectly straight up as if waiting for its finishing touch.

"Do you see the plug there? Hook them together."

Celeste lit up the star, showering them both in the bright golden light.

"Now look down," Justin said softly.

Celeste set her hands on the small ledge and did as he asked. The red and green lights hung on the ends of branches, so many of them. It must have taken hours of work. She took in the patterns, the networks, the way the branches held their own but also intertwined so seamlessly with each other. Minutes went by as she got lost in the view. A feeling of joy—of pure unencumbered joy—coursed through her body and soul. In this moment, she felt the possibility of a wonderful future. This might be the most extraordinary moment of her life.

And then she saw. She knew what Justin had done. Her eyes grew damp, and she did not fight the force of her emotion.

"Oh, Justin." It was staggering, this beautiful act. "Thank you." Those two words were inadequate, but they were all she had in this face of beauty. She could not tear herself from what she was looking at, even though the lights began to blur together as her eyes welled. "You knew that I did not care for *under* a tree, so you have given me the opposite." Celeste shook her head in disbelief. "You have given me *over* a tree."

"Yes." His mouth was by her ear as he leaned in with her.

Justin held her while she continued to lean over the side,

rejoicing in the magic of this gift. When the urge—the necessity— to be in Justin's arms grew too strong, she stood up and turned to him. His hands slid around her waist and hers lifted around his neck. He was so beautiful, this boy, in all senses of the word. He made her feel raw and exposed and vulnerable, but in doing so, he was healing her and empowering her. She knew that.

He looked at her for a long time before he took her hand and moved it to his chest. "My heart is pounding. Do you feel that? You make me so nervous, but I'm so comfortable at the same time. I don't know how to make sense of those two things happening at the same time."

"Why are you nervous?"

He squeezed her hand. "Because I'm going to kiss you." A touch of a smile crossed his lips. "And I better do a good job because I want you to like it."

Celeste's voice was shaky. "I feel sure that I will."

"How could you know that?"

"Because it is you." There was no fear, no worry.

She loved the sweetness he evoked as he inched closer. When his mouth first touched hers, she closed her eyes and drifted. His kiss was tentative initially, one soft kiss before he pulled back a hint. He kissed her like that again, just a brief connection before backing up. The cold on his lips was a stark contrast to the heat Celeste was starting to feel. This was a new kind of heat, different from any that she had ever experienced. It did not arrive on the surface of her skin as from the sun, but came from within. These light kisses had ignited her. She was the one who should be nervous and unsure, but she could sense Justin was the one filled with caution.

She could taste it on him.

Celeste eased her hands from around his neck, moving over his skin until his face was in her hands. Justin kissed her fully now, pressing his mouth against hers, moving so smoothly and so perfectly. He was guiding her, making it impossibly easy to respond. For a split second he pulled away. "You give me such clarity," he said. She felt the breath of his words on her mouth. And that felt like everything she could possibly hope for.

Celeste couldn't stand not to be kissing him. So she did. Justin had awoken a monster, one starved for a taste of romance and of touch. She kissed him harder, wanting more. More of the kiss and more of him. And then, at the height of their intensity, just for a moment, his tongue brushed against hers.

Her knees almost gave out. Real life blacked out. Intrinsic emotion and need took over. And Celeste allowed it. For once—God, for once—she let go of outside forces.

When their kissing finally slowed, Celeste had to put her hands to his chest and gently push him from her. It was becoming difficult to kiss when smiling could not be held off.

Justin smiled back at her, the twinkle in his eye undeniable. "I did good?"

"Yes, Justin." She didn't know whether to laugh or cry. "Yes, you did good."

Celeste realized that Trent's music was still blaring from the truck. It was funny, she noted, how when one is so deeply engaged in joy, all else ceases to exist.

Joy, she decided, wins out over everything.

## CHAPTER 17
# MIDNIGHT

"JULIE!" CELESTE BELLOWED into the phone. "Julie!"

"Good morning," Julie grumbled. "What time is it?"

"It is already eight. Why are you still sleeping?"

"Because I am exhausted from work, and I'm trying to get some sleep before I have to fly home to Ohio and deal with crazy relatives."

"You are cranky this morning. You are not looking forward to going home?"

"I'm all right," she said without sounding all right. "What's going on with you?"

"I am calling with very important news," Celeste said seriously. She lay on her back on the floor of her bedroom and kicked her feet in the air. "I do believe that I have a suitor."

"A suitor?"

"Indeed."

"Justin?"

"Yes."

"You guys have been talking for a few months, and now… what? Something changed?"

"He took me out last night. Oh, Julie, I have had a sexual awakening!" Celeste exclaimed.

Julie was alert now. "You've had a what?"

"There is no cause for alarm."

"What exactly did you do last night?"

"Justin escorted me to dinner, and I had sushi for the first time. It turns out that sushi is a very sensual food, what with all the silken raw fish and such. My taste buds were ravenous due to the myriad of new flavors."

"It's not your taste buds that I'm worried about being ravenous."

"Just listen. And then he took me—" Celeste stopped herself. Perhaps she shouldn't tell Julie about the Christmas tree. It would remind her of Matt and what she'd had. And what she'd lost. "Well, anyway, he kissed me. I kissed him. There was a mutual kissing that occurred!"

"And there were clothes on and stuff?" Julie asked.

"Good God, yes, there were clothes on! It was my first kiss! I didn't exactly fling myself at him and strip down after one kiss. Granted, it was totally spectacular kiss, and, as I mentioned, I experienced some sort of primal sexual awakening, but that didn't mean that I was ready for intercourse."

"Oh, man, it's too early for this."

"Too early? I'm eighteen. It's not too early. It's late. Most girls my age have much more physical experience than I. Now, what others do is honestly of no importance to me because I am not going to be one to up and make love to someone I've known for a matter of a few months, but... Oh, Julie, the point here is that Justin was a gentleman. And in that kiss, a part of me came to life."

Celeste detailed the drive from the house and dinner, how Justin stayed close to her the entire night. How she felt safe and inspired and totally in awe of this boy.

"I like hearing this, Celeste. He sounds so cool. And I'm glad this 'coming to life' bit is innocent. Justin sounds very romantic."

Celeste sighed happily. "He really is. Is this what it was like with you and Matt when you first got together?" She froze. "I should not have mentioned him. I'm sorry. It's just that, as far as I know, he is the sole great romance you have had, so naturally, I apologize."

"It's okay. It's not like you can't say his name. He's your brother."

"But I'm right, am I not? Matthew has been the one great love of your life."

"Just because I haven't been involved with anyone else really doesn't mean... I don't know. It doesn't mean anything."

"I'm sorry. I wanted it to work out between you two. I believe it should have. And that it still can. He loves you."

"No. Not anymore."

"And you love him," Celeste insisted.

"No. I don't. I don't love Matt anymore." But Julie's voice broke.

Celeste waited a moment. "Fine, then. You don't love Matt; Matt doesn't love you. There, all settled."

"Look, I'm glad you're having a good time with Justin and enjoying being all googley-eyed, but that doesn't make you an expert on everyone else's life. You have no idea what Matt and I have been through. How complicated relationships can get. It's not fair to act like I just gave up on us for no reason. It was a two-way street. It's been two years. It's over." Julie had raised her voice, and Celeste heard a sniff. "Sometimes love is not enough, and it doesn't matter how much you want it. Want *him*. And even if nobody else compares to that person, it doesn't mean that you're supposed to be with him."

Celeste sat up suddenly and smiled. Whether she knew it or not, Julie was giving her wonderful news. "You're right," she said matter-of-factly. "There is no hope. It's over. I'm very sure that Matthew has no feelings for you either. He has likely forgotten your name. I won't mention your hopeless relationship again."

Julie blew her nose in a most noisy manner. "Now, why don't you tell me about colleges? Any idea where you might end up?"

"I'm still not sure."

"Still no interest in flying? Stanford's not too shabby. And near me."

"I would not mind an acceptance letter from such a prestigious school, but traveling across country by train so many times is impractical."

"Understood."

"College is boring. Let us continue talking about Justin."

Julie laughed. "Okay. Let's talk."

■ ■ ■

Celeste helped herself to another pizelle and leaned back into the couch. Justin's father, Filippo Milano, had been coerced into telling her what Justin was like as a child, and she was soaking in every word. Filippo leaned in from his spot on a chair next to her. "Bundle. Of. Energy. Which I'm sure doesn't surprise you. That kid was non-stop. But he was adorable. You think that boy is cute now? He was just as cute as a baby. We totally let Justin's charms work for us. We used to jump lines, get discounts at the bakery, that sort of thing. Anything for free cannoli, am I right? Have you ever tried to make those from scratch?" He rolled his eyes. "Who has time for that?"

Erin playfully swatted his arm. "Oh, Filippo, you are a riot."

"Truly, Luka and I were so thrilled when Justin arrived. Now, truth be told, he never slept, so there were moments when both of us wondered if we might die from fatigue. I know the toddler years are rough for all parents, but dear God, he was exhausting. Moved nonstop, talked nonstop. Even in grade school, he barely slept. Up all night chatting to himself. But what an *interesting* child. Some children are dull, right? Let's be honest. But Justin was anything but. Rather draining," Filippo said with a laugh, "but he was and remains our darling baby."

Erin nodded and stared a little too intently. "Don't they always stay our babies? I cannot believe Celeste is off to college next year."

"Happens in the blink of an eye." Filippo rose from his seat. "May I get you ladies something to drink? Sparkling cherry water with an orange slice? And I know that the roasted pepper dip will be coming out of the oven in just a few minutes. Shall I stop here first with it?"

"Absolutely," Erin said. "I'm sure I'll want to get that recipe from you, too."

"Then I will be back in a few, my dears. Erin, I want to hear more about your gardening."

Erin practically blushed.

Celeste nibbled on a delicious waffle cookie and glared at her mother. "You do realize that man is *gay*, don't you?"

Erin ran a hand through her hair. "Yes, of course, he's gay. It doesn't mean that anyone should pretend that he's not absolutely gorgeous."

"Mom!" Celeste laughed.

"Well, he is! Don't you agree? That sleek black hair, the dark Italian complexion…"

"I may regurgitate all of the culinary treats I've consumed this evening. That man is Justin's father. I am not going to comment on his appearance." She touched a napkin to her mouth. "But he is gorgeous."

"See?" she practically squeaked.

The New Year's Eve party at Justin's house was lovely. Although their condo in Needham was small, that had not stopped them from inviting what Celeste assumed to be every person the family had ever met. The condo was certainly modest compared to the Watkins' house, but it had a genuinely warm feel with bright colors on the furniture and framed pictures that dotted the walls. And Justin had not been exaggerating when he'd spoken about white lights; the house was positively covered with candles and strings of lights. She loved it, probably because it was so reminiscent of the path that led to the Christmas tree.

Erin brushed a few crumbs from her red dress. "I think I'll go help Filippo in the kitchen."

"Oh, God."

"What? Can't a girl have a little harmless fun? It's New Year's Eve!"

"Perhaps I can take your place?"

Celeste looked up to see Justin's other father, Luka. She'd spent the first part of the evening with him glued to her side, and she liked him immensely. He had the same deep kindness that Justin did. Luka offered his hand to Erin and helped her to stand.

"Such gracious manners around here," she said. "Where is Roger? He could use a few lessons from these two."

"I do believe he's in the kitchen already, helping with the meatballs."

"He is? How sexy."

"Mother!" Celeste was horrified. Yet underneath her sheer embarrassment, she was pleased to see her mother in such good spirits. And so relaxed. There were days when it was hard to even remember Erin's depression, her consistently serious tone, and her exclusive focus on work and her children's school performance. This new Erin? She was happier.

Still, Celeste was relieved when Erin took off after the men and Luka sat down with her.

"I very much like your tuxedo," she said.

"There are so few excuses in life to wear a tuxedo, so I take New Year's to do so." Luka had lovely grey hair on the side of his head that blended smoothly into the darker pieces. He had a very neatly trimmed beard and mustache, just a hint more than stubble, she thought, and all in all, there was something quite distinguished about him. "And you, in that silver dress? All sorts of sparkles? Did you wear that to impress your boyfriend's gay parents?"

"Oh. I had not thought of that." She looked at Luka, loving the dimples that appeared on his cheeks. "Are you impressed or does it appear that I am attempting to suck up?" This was, without question, the first time that Celeste had every said the words *suck up*, but it seemed appropriate.

"Impressed. With the dress, yes, but more with you. I don't think that I've seen Justin this happy, maybe ever. He's talked about you incessantly."

"I hope not to the point that you now find me uninteresting."

"Never." Luka lifted his glass. "I toast you, my dear. And I'm glad that your family came here tonight. Is it making you nervous to have the families colliding? Parents and siblings meeting and trading who knows what?"

"Aside from my mother's inappropriate flirtation with your husband, the evening is going nicely, don't you think?"

"I do," he agreed. "And your mother is a spitfire. Now where is your brother. Matthew? I haven't had a chance to speak to him."

Celeste lifted her head to catch sight of Matt, who was standing with Justin by a very tall bookcase. "He's there," she pointed. "Do you know whom they are speaking with?"

"Ah, yes. That's my niece. Twenty-five, grad student at Tufts. Very cute. Think your brother would be interested?"

"I think it is worth a try. Matthew is reticent to become involved with anyone due to his stubborn nature."

"An ex-girlfriend?" Luka guessed.

"Yes."

"Maybe she shouldn't be an ex."

"Precisely."

"I'll give it a try anyway."

Justin had made his way through the crowd to them. "Dad, are you raking Celeste over the coals?"

"I was not. I was talking about the possibility of Matthew and your cousin Amanda."

"Yeah, good luck. I gave it a shot. She might as well be talking about rocks, he looks so bored."

"Actually," Celeste said, "Matthew is fascinated by rocks. You might suggest that to her. I did not realize that you were a family of matchmakers, but your attempts to bring a romance into Matthew's life are very much appreciated. At least by me."

Justin stretched an arm over her shoulder and gave her a noisy kiss on the cheek. She couldn't get enough of him. They'd seen each other nearly every day of winter break so far, and kissing him, getting to hold him, being held... How was she going to give this up when he went back to school? She couldn't think about that now.

"Love is love is love," Justin said decidedly. "And we all need it. But I think Trent is about to pounce on Amanda if Matt doesn't pick up speed. It's too bad. She looks interested in Matt."

"You never know," Luka said. "When the clock strikes

midnight, your brother may get bitten by the New Year's bug and make an unexpected move."

"That would be unlikely behavior from Matthew. He is not known for impulsive gestures."

"Impulsive is good," Justin said. "It means you're speaking from your gut. Or your heart. Or something like that. Some kind of important body part. Not, like, your elbow or something. Of course, we all enjoy our elbows because they're good for jabbing people who misbehave, but speaking from one's elbow doesn't carry the same weight, right, because we don't have a lot of feeling there? Fine, we have physical feeling, particularly the funny bone, so I suppose you could speak from your elbow if you're a stand-up comedian. In any case... um..."

"Impulsivity," Celeste prompted.

"Right! Being impulsive means you've let down your guard and are going after what you want."

Celeste looked at Matt. Her brother could stand to unleash a little impulsivity. Really, if Celeste could brave this new world of dating and socializing, Matthew could take a few risks of his own.

She would have to work on encouraging this. Later.

For now, she had someone to kiss at midnight.

And when the clock sounded and the room cheered and music blared throughout the house—and she and Justin were in a more secluded hallway out of sight of their parents—she got her kiss. And it was somehow even more delicious than all of the others. In fact, every time they kissed, it was better. Not that they'd had anything but a phenomenal base to start from, but now he tasted more like him. Or more like them. Because she knew him on a deeper level, and she felt him in everything he did. Every move of his hand, every touch of his lips to hers, every breath he took as he whispered in her ear.

When they reluctantly eased apart from each other, Justin lifted her hand in his and started slow dancing in the hall, slowing turning them in a circle.

"Why are we dancing?" she asked.

"Why not? It's an excuse to hold you, how's that?"

"I like that excuse very much." She rested her head on his shoulder. She had never danced with anyone before. "Hey, Justin?"

"Hey, Celeste?"

"You are going back to school soon."

He paused. "I know. Don't remind me. But we still have a few weeks."

"What will happen then? I am unfamiliar with how a situation such as ours should be handled."

"I think it's up to us."

"What is your preference?" She felt nearly sick asking this question.

"My preference is to pack you in my suitcase, but those TSA people are so picky, and there's some kind of stupid regulation about human trafficking and—"

"Justin. This is serious."

"I know." He entwined his fingers in her hair. "Blondie, I don't like that we're going to be apart, but we don't have to feel apart. It's just physical distance."

She thought immediately of Matt and Julie and how

heinously distance had worked out for them, but she pushed that thought away.

"Am I to understand that I am your girlfriend?" She jerked away from him and put a hand over her eyes. "I apologize. Was that a strange question to ask? I am sure there are unspoken rules about things such as this of which I am unaware, and I should not have... Oh God, this is awful..." She peeked out at him from behind her fingers. "Do not look at me like that. Do not be all understanding and patient. It's extraordinarily weird that I do not know what to do here."

"No, no," he said. "It's good that you asked me that. You don't play games, Celeste. I love how honest you are, how you say what you think. And you're not missing anything here. There's no set rule that we have to follow. We do what we want. This is between us and only us."

"I am still embarrassed."

"I can't have my girlfriend feeling embarrassed. That won't do at all."

Celeste dropped her hand and looked at him fully now. *Girlfriend.* "Really?"

"I mean, if you'd like that."

"I would." She said. "I think that I would like that quite a bit."

"Then, my lady, we shall be boyfriend and girlfriend, and we will figure out the long-distance thing as we go."

And with that, he encircled her waist and dipped her most formally.

## CHAPTER 18
# TO THE FUTURE

**Justin:** I'm going surfing today! I've never been, but I feel sure that I am on the edge of a professional boarding career.

**Celeste:** The water will allow you to surf without developing hypothermia now? It's almost March, lest you have forgotten.

**Justin:** What? I thought it was August. August of 1975. Wait, what year is it? Where am I?

**Celeste:** Very funny. I was simply concerned for your well-being.

**Justin:** And I am super touched and all heartmelty.

**Celeste:** "Heartmelty" is not a word, I do not believe.

**Justin:** I'm a wordsmith, an inventor of words that should be. And "melty" is a word, didya know that, smartie girl? Ergo, "heartmelty" needed to be invented.

**Celeste:** If I recall, Webster's fell to pressure and

only very reluctantly added "melty" to their lexicon. "Didya" and "smartie," however, are not... Well, never mind.

**Justin:** Celeste!

**Celeste:** Okay, fine.

**Celeste:** Didya think it is smartie to go surfing in the cold weather?

**Justin:** Look at you all sexy with the goofy words. And it's still warm here, so don't worry about me. This winter has been unusually gorgeous. It's almost 80 today. Plus, I'll be wearing some sort of protective bodysuit thing. Whatever it is that surfers wear. I best get the terminology down for my impending high-profile career. #Sharksbetternotbitemybutt

**Celeste:** Please report back with your surf tales. I will be eager to hear. And to know that you are in one piece, without half of you making its way through a shark's digestive tract. I have lunch now, so I must run.

**Justin:** I'll call you tonight! Surf's up, dude!

**Justin:** Did that sound lame? Probably. Let's pretend I didn't write that. I will investigate socially awesome surf talk today.

**Celeste:** I would not be opposed should you want to text a photograph of yourself.

**Justin:** In my sexy bodysuit?

**Celeste:** Perhaps. Then we would be even, you know, since you have seen me in a bodysuit.

**Justin:** Don't think I've forgotten that. I'll see what I can do.

Celeste was becoming quite expert at walking and texting, although evidently her ability to attend to the rest of the world fell to the wayside when Justin was involved. Especially when a wet-suited boyfriend picture might be coming her way.

Boyfriend.

What a colossally glorious word. Not because having a boyfriend met some standard of teen life that she had finally attained. Celeste didn't much care about that. What she did care about—what moved her heart so dramatically—was that she had Justin in her life. He was the first person with whom she could relax fully. And therefore, life was more vibrant.

In her distraction, Celeste bumped into another student. She quickly apologized, embarrassed at being so lost in boyfriend thoughts that she noticed too late the scene ahead of her.

Finding herself in the hallway of her high school with a swarm of screaming students swarming directly toward her triggered a sharp feeling of dread. Now what? Things had been going so well.

She counted her attackers. Perhaps it wasn't really a swarm. There were five people. Yet it felt like an out-of-control mob. Something had gone terribly wrong. Her few months of happiness were over. And now, on this Friday afternoon during late February, she was about to be flogged or otherwise assaulted by this group, all waving their arms and hollering at her. "Celeste!" She heard Dallas's voice rise above the others'. "Celeste, come with us!"

Before she could react, Dallas had grabbed her by the arm and was pulling her along with the whooping crowd toward

Mr. Gil's classroom. Classmates were patting her arms and back, chanting her name.... It was all incredibly disconcerting. Panic inducing, really.

"Dallas, I do not have philosophy class now. I have lunch." Celeste could hear the tremor in her voice. She was going to run out of air any second, she knew it. "I need to go. I must go now."

"I know, silly!" Dallas swung open the door, and Celeste was moved forward. "We have lunch for you here."

Celeste looked into the room. Every person whom she had tutored through college applications was here. Jennifer held a cake, and a stack of pizza boxes sat on Mr. Gil's desk. She inched forward and looked at the cake. Blue lettering spelled out *Thank you!* Confused, she looked at Dallas. "I do not understand."

Leighann stepped out from behind her. "We've been waiting until we all heard, but it's official. All of us got into college."

"Even me!" Zeke piped up. "And into Kenyon at that."

Celeste gasped. "That was your top choice!"

"I know, right? Top choice *and* a reach." He threw his arms around her. "And financial aid. You made that happen."

"What?"

"My application was really strong. They complimented me on my essay. The one you made me redo forty-seven times. I couldn't have done it without you."

Then she was getting hugs and handshakes and listening to college acceptance stories from everyone there. It was overwhelming.

"Speech!" Mr. Gil broke through the crowd. "Speech, Miss Watkins!"

Soda was poured into red cups, and Celeste did what she could to gather her thoughts. Someone handed her a drink and the room grew silent. She looked to Mr. Gil. He smiled kindly and gave her a supportive nod.

Celeste touched a hand to her heart, trying to compose herself.

"I… I do not know what to say…" She cleared her throat. "This is an honor. I am so very happy for all of you. Tremendously proud. All I did was to help you channel skills that you already had within you." She paused, suddenly quite emotional. "I do believe that you did the same for me. Thank you for giving me that chance." It was all that she could bring herself to say. It hit her that all of these new friends, her new level of social comfort, was going to come to an abrupt end upon graduation, less than four months away. She turned to Dallas, who knew—as a friend does—to rescue her.

Dallas raised her cup high. "To Celeste."

"To Celeste!" the room cheered.

When pizza had been eaten, more thanks offered, and the celebration had started to wind down, Celeste found herself alone with Dallas and Mr. Gil, a few chair-desks pushed together. Her philosophy teacher nibbled on crust. "So, Dallas, where are you going to end up?"

"Yes, where will you study next year? I did not get to hear during the earlier chaos," Celeste said.

Dallas tried to suppress a smile, but gave up and flashed a full-on beam. "USC. Film school."

"Oh, Dallas, you did it." Celeste practically jumped out of

her seat. "I am unequivocally thrilled for you. I do think that you will take Los Angeles by the proverbial storm."

Dallas blushed. "I'm really happy. Really. And you helped me pull together exactly what I needed for the application. I can't believe it. What about you? Have you decided?"

She fidgeted with a napkin. "I am unsure which to accept."

Mr. Gil reached for another slice. "Where have you gotten in?"

"Harvard, Wesleyan, Yale, Columbia, Princeton. Um... I can't recall where else at the moment."

"Don't be modest. You got in everywhere you applied, right?" Dallas raised her eyebrows. "Right? C'mon, brag a little."

The napkin was now shredded. "I did." She forced a happy tone in her voice. "I don't know how to pick. This is a hard choice."

"You'll figure it out. All good options," Dallas said.

"Did any California schools make it onto your list?" Mr. Gil asked way too casually.

"What? Cambridge's own Harvard isn't good enough for her?" Dallas said, laughing.

He waved his hand. "No, no, it's not that. I was just curious."

"I am not one for flying," Celeste confessed. She did not want him to think her ungrateful, as she knew he was the one who had spoken to Barton about her. "But I appreciate the interest that I've had from west coast schools."

"Ah, well, not wanting to fly could be a problem. In any case, I'm very happy for you both, and I'll miss you next year."

He stood. "I'm going to get a head start on grading some essays, but the room is yours as long as you like it. And these are for you." He slapped two small papers onto the desk. "A couple of passes to keep you free for another period. Benefits of being my favorite students. It's a half day today anyhow. Enjoy it."

"Yes!" Dallas clapped her hands in the air. "Best. Day. Ever."

Even Celeste, who was not one to be in favor of skipping classes, felt that she would not mind missing a class today. Just for once.

"You girls have fun. And congratulations to both of you." Mr. Gil grabbed yet another slice of pizza and made his way out.

Dallas leaned in. "Okay, now that the teacher is gone, tell me what's up with you and Justin?"

"Our relationship is…" Celeste didn't know how to explain how perfect it felt without sounding trite. How she missed him every second of the day, but how they stayed in touch so much that she felt as if he were here. She sighed, more dreamily than she would have liked. "He's just stupendous. He is not only a suitable first boyfriend, but a rather ideal one at that. Our phone conversations are quite wonderful, his emails detailed and engaging, and every morning he sends me a coffee picture."

"He sends you a picture of his coffee?"

"Yes, it's charming. See he takes a photograph of… Well, never mind. The point is that I am in the throes of my first romance, and I'm deliriously happy."

"So what are you going to do? There's that flying issue you

have, which I really think you need to get over. And next year? I mean, you're not going to school out there, are you? Not like you didn't get into enough good schools on this coast, ."

"Yeah."

"And you sound *so* happy about it." Dallas glared at her. "What is your problem?"

Celeste got up and paced the floor. "Oh, I don't know, Dallas. This entire college process has not been what I expected."

"How so?"

"Despite having worked my entire life to be in this position, I am unsatisfied. Unenthused. Academics are all that I have ever had. But I am just now stepping into new waters and exploring other sides of myself."

"You can't do that in college?"

"I can. It just seems a monstrous task to manage the level of work and stress associated with an Ivy League school with other parts of life that I already find so intimidating."

Dallas thought for a moment. "Are you freaked out about you and Justin?"

"I am unclear on what you are asking."

"I mean, you're going to be out here somewhere, and he's still going to be in San Diego."

"Yes?"

"That's going to become a problem, don't you think? You can't manage to sustain a relationship like that, can you? It's not like you two were a solid couple for a long time, and then he left. Then you'd have a better base. But even then…"

Celeste finished the sentence. "Even then it would be near impossible at our ages."

"Kind of."

"What about you and Zeke? You two will be separated. That is unfair." Celeste was getting riled up now. "Having just found each other, your relationship will be ripped apart at the seams come September. That is tragic, is it not? What are we to do? The heartache of the high school senior must be like none other." She flopped back into her chair and chugged down some soda. "Of course, even my brother and his long-term girlfriend, Julie, who had, as you called it, a solid base, could not survive great physical distance."

"You're right. We are in big trouble here." Dallas dropped her head onto the desk, smushing her cheek and almost making Celeste laugh despite herself. "You could apply to Stanford late. I bet they'd take you. That's not far from San Diego, and you'd be near me. Oh wait, but the plane thing. Damn it. So I guess Barton is out, too."

"Dallas, that is outrageous. One does not make crucial, life-impacting choices, such as which college to attend, based on a boy. One chooses an educational institution after careful consideration of what the school offers one intellectually and academically. End of story."

"There's more to college than just classwork, you know."

"I know that. That's the part that I'm not good at!" she said with near panic.

"Easy girl, easy." Dallas half smiled. "You're doing just fine."

Celeste sighed. "Thanks. And sorry. I am a bit emotional."

The girls indulged in their crankiness over what they saw

as the impending demise of their relationships, both emitting the occasional whimper of dramatic misery. Celeste drummed her fingers on the table over and over until Dallas finally slapped her hand over them.

Celeste didn't like this. All of her recent happiness was going to come undone.

"Dallas?" she whispered.

"What?"

"Do you happen to have a fake ID?"

"Are you kidding me?"

"I do not mean to stereotype. That was terrifically unfair of me. But if I were to go by cultural stereotypes, you would strike me as the sort who might, just perhaps, have a form of false identification for the occasional—but I'm sure responsible—purchase of alcohol."

Dallas sat up. She looked Celeste in the eyes. "I'm shocked and horrified."

"Oh. I apologize. I'm really terribly sorry to have offended you. Please forgive me. That was very rude."

Dallas started laughing and cracked her knuckles. "I totally have a fake ID. Whatcha need?"

She shrugged. "This will sound silly, but Justin once mentioned drinking something called an Old Fashioned, and I feel as though sipping a drink might somehow... Oh, this is nutty."

"I think it's sort of adorable. You drinking your boyfriend's favorite drink, thinking about him, letting the warm glow of alcohol make you even more googley–eyed."

"I don't know. I miss Justin. And all this talk about college makes me refocus on how difficult I will find the social transition. As you can imagine. I think it is reasonable to want to have my first drink before I am already at a new school, and my parents are away, so it seems an opportune time."

"Look at you, being all quintessential teenagery and stuff. Well, I've got plans with Zeke tonight that don't involve drinking, so you're just going to drink alone?"

"It's just a cocktail. I'll call my sweet boyfriend and chat with him." Celeste pulled out her phone and opened a browser. "Do you know anything about muddling bitters?"

CHAPTER 19

# HAVE A DRINK ON ME

I T WAS FRIDAY afternoon, and her parents were gone until Wednesday at a conference in Philadelphia. Despite her assurances that she would be fine on her own, Matt insisted on coming over, and he'd be here any minute. The truth was that she liked having him around, and the thought of being alone in that big house for four nights was intimidating. She probably could have asked Dallas to stay over. Girlfriends did things like that, didn't they? Were they too old for that? Or was that just something fictionalized in the movies? Dallas would certainly laugh and lovingly correct any misperceptions she had, but investigating the validity of sleepovers would have to wait.

Celeste rearranged the glasses and bottles on the kitchen counter for the fifth time. Presentation and mood felt important here if she was going to prevent Matt from completely flipping out. She turned on a country radio station because most country songs were about pining over love or about drinking, and both seemed fitting. She heard the front door rattle and then struck a casual pose by her display.

"Hello, my open-minded, sweet brother. I am most looking forward to our weekend together." She flashed Matt a smile. "Have you eaten lunch yet?"

Matt tossed his overnight bag on the floor. "I did. Pasta from an Italian place near my apartment."

"Carbs! Perfect. You may need them."

"Why would I need—" Matt looked around. "What's going on? Why do I feel as though I walked into an old fashioned saloon?"

"It's funny that you should say *old fashioned* because—"

"What's up with all the booze?"

Matt looked exhausted, more pale than usual. His dirty blond hair had again grown longer than she knew he liked, and he appeared generally washed out. In need of some sunshine, she thought. And happiness.

"I am eighteen, heading off to college in a matter of months, and I thought it appropriate to try my first drink. It seemed best to do that under brotherly supervision. And there is the added bonus in that it will be a bonding experience. Afternoon-cocktail-hour-in-the-library type situation. Fun, yes?"

"Illegal is more like it," he scowled. "I think this is a terrible idea. We don't even have a library in this house. What exactly are you planning on doing with bourbon and gin? I feel sick already."

"You do not feel sick," she protested. "You feel festive and ready to partake in relationship building with your sister."

Celeste rounded the kitchen island and tossed one arm around Matt. "Matthew, do not be so uptight."

"Uptight? *I'm* uptight?"

Celeste frowned. "Fine. Perhaps we both could use a little loosening up. Let's have a cocktail together, shall we? I find it rather civilized, the idea of sitting back with a fancy drink on this dark afternoon."

Matt laughed lightly. "You know what? Sure. Let's have a drink. One drink, okay? That's it. One." He pulled out a barstool and sat down. "What are we having, bar wench?"

"Assuming you do not again refer to me as *bar wench*, we will be starting with an Old Fashioned."

Matt wrinkled his nose. "An Old Fashioned? That's rather an odd choice. Although perhaps not for you. But maybe you should start with something fruity with parasols and fizz?"

"Absolutely not! How undignified. Although I will confess that while I do not have parasols, I do have mini swords for piercing the orange peel and cherry."

"Mini swords?"

"I hear they are a fine finishing touch for cocktail presentation. One is simply not going to haphazardly slosh liquor into a cup and chug it."

"Well, no, we couldn't have that."

"Besides, Justin mentioned Old Fashioneds one time, and my curiosity has been piqued. I spent a decent amount of time investigating various methods to mix this drink, though all involve muddling, a term I find undeniably charming. Then we can move on to the classic gin and tonic, always a solid choice from what my research tells me."

"Nice to hear you've been so thorough." He crossed his arms. "Hey, didn't I say *one* drink?"

"Yes, we'll see. Anyhow, first I am going to douse this sugar cube in bitters and then smash it up in the bottom of the glass until it takes on the look of a syrup." Celeste narrated as she concocted the first drink, not unaware of the bemused look on Matt's face. "Because I did not have access to a true muddling device or whatever it is termed, I have opted to use the handle of this oversized wooden spoon. Now I shall squeeze the oils from this slice of orange peel and incorporate that essence into my muddled… my muddled stuff. Ahem. Then, a few ounces of this lovely bourbon, poured slowly and mixed in nicely to dissolve the sugar. Now some ice cubes, another quick splash of bourbon and garnished with another spritz of orange peel that I will then affix to this garish mini sword along with a disgusting maraschino cherry." Celeste carefully carried the nearly overflowing glass over to Matt and set it down gently onto a coaster. "For the gentleman."

"You've lost your mind."

"I have not. Now try it," she ordered.

Matt lifted the glass to his lips, took a tiny sip, and then winced exaggeratedly. "Oh dear Lord! Horror of horrors."

Celeste stomped her foot and tried not to giggle. "Matthew, that is not funny. How is it really?"

He took another taste. "Actually, it's pretty damned good, I must admit."

"Fabulous. Now I will make one for myself."

"For the record, I'm not encouraging you to have a drink, but since I think you'd go ahead and do it anyway, I am here to supervise."

"Yes. You be the responsible adult, and I shall be the out-of-control teenager who is experimenting with alcohol consumption."

"Great. Role playing in its most pathological form. Fine." He swirled the glass, clinking ice cubes before having another longer drink.

Two hours later, when Matt had finished his third Old Fashioned and was halfway through a gin and tonic, he and Celeste found themselves sprawled on the living room floor. Her own gin and tonic was going down rather easily, and the country music was sounding better and better. She rolled over onto her back and reached for the volume on the stereo.

"This is fun, Matty, isn't it? Cocktail hour is intoxicating."

"It is."

"I made a little joke there."

"It was a riot." Matt was on his stomach with his chin in his hands. "It is kinda fun. I think I might be a little drunk."

"Good for you, Matty! If I don't go to college next year, I could be a bartender, huh?"

"Yeah, totally."

"I know this country tune," she said loudly. "This is a very famous song called 'The Gambler' by Mr. Kenneth Rogers."

Matt started laughing uncontrollably. "I think he just goes by Kenny."

"Whatever. The point is that I know it." She started singing from her spot on the floor, and much to her surprise, Matt was soon belting out lyrics with her. "I had no idea that you had such a country–boy side to you."

He paused in his now near-screaming singing. "I do not

have a country side to me, but everyone knows this song." When the song ended, he tapped her shoulder repeatedly. "Celeste."

"What?"

"I have to know what song you sang for that rock band audition."

"They were skate punk, not rock," she corrected him. "That is important."

"Fine. What song?"

"A very meaningful song by Joan Baez called 'The Night They—'"

Matt finished the title with her. "'Drove Old Dixie Down'!"

She rolled over so that they were practically nose to nose. "How could you possibly know that song?"

Matt smiled drunkenly. "You don't remember, do you? You were probably too little."

"Remember what?"

He looked at her for a moment. "You know how much Mom hates any sort of hippie political folk music singer stuff? Like, Arlo Guthrie makes her gag?"

Celeste nodded vehemently. "And Pete Seeger. And Bob Dylan."

"Right. So Finn used to piggyback you around the backyard. And he'd sing that Dixie song at the top of his lungs while he ran around and around with you bouncing on his back, laughing the whole time. Mom used to hate it, and she'd yell at him to knock it off, but the more she yelled, the louder he'd sing."

Celeste's jaw dropped. "And he would say to me..." The memory was coming back. "'Here comes the chorus,' every time so that I would join in. I'd forgotten."

"That's right. He was very good with you."

Celeste put her hand on top of Matt's head. "You are very good with me."

"I never gave you piggybacks."

"That's okay, Matty. You give me other things. You always have."

"Like the T-shirt that I gave you for Christmas?"

"No, not like that, dummy! And that shirt is inappropriate."

"Is not. You like science. That's not inappropriate."

"The shirt says, *All This Science Gives Me a Hadron.* I understand the play on words, and it's inappropriate. I can't even get a *Hadron*, Matthew! I don't have the right parts."

"But it's funny," Matt snickered.

"Okay, it kind of is," she agreed.

Celeste grabbed for the coffee table to lift herself to a seated position. Her hand landed on a stack of mail that she pulled onto her face, causing her to fall into a fit of giggles. "That did not work out as I planned." She managed to sit up and started to gather the envelopes. Matt was looking rather glazed over, but he made a sudden swipe for one envelope.

"What's that?" she asked.

"Nothing. I'm just helping." He picked up a flyer. "Oh, look, how fascinating. Do you need a new roof?"

She squinted her eyes and held out a hand. "Gimme."

"I had no idea you cared so much about shingles, but

you're in luck because they have a wide assortment for your roofing pleasure."

"Give me the envelope that you are hiding!"

"It's just a personal letter from the roofer threatening to sneak on over and poke holes in"—Matt jabbed his finger in the general direction of the ceiling—"this here roof if he is not hired. Desperate times and all. So sad."

Celeste lunged for the letter and snatched it from Matt. "You have delayed reflexes, brother. I win."

"Celeste..." Matt mumbled as he crawled to a stand, slammed back the rest of his drink, and headed for the kitchen. "Don't get all crazy mad, okay?"

The letter was addressed to her, and she tore it open. She read it three times. "MATTHEW!"

"I said don't get all crazy mad," he called back.

She stood unsteadily and marched after him, waving the paper around. "Either I am more inebriated than I think I am, or this is a letter from Barton College."

Matt pushed his glass under the ice dispenser and did a terrible job disguising his amusement. "Is it? How interesting."

"What?" she shrieked. "It is not interesting. The words on this page indicate that I have been accepted into Barton College for next fall, something which I find confusing because I did not apply to Barton College."

"Well, that's weird." Matt refused to look at her as he poured another gin and tonic. "Are you gonna go there?"

"No, I'm not *gonna go* there, Matthew Watkins!" she said snidely.

"Why did you apply then?"

"I don't know. I guess I thought that Justin said so many good things— Wait, stop that. I did not apply to Barton!"

"See? You *do* want to go there!"

"Maybe *you* want to go there, Matty. *You* filled out the application."

"Technically *you* filled out the application."

In the back of her head, Celeste could hear her own words from last December. *Oh, would you turn off my computer for me? I believe that I left it on.* She gasped. "The online application on my computer. You sent that? You went snooping through my computer? That was... that was not a real application," she protested. "It was just for demonstration purposes."

Matt raised one of his eyebrows and held out his drink in the most pompous of manners. "Or was it? One might conclude that you had secret hopes and dreams of attending the school in question."

She balked at his drunken accusation. "Oh, please." She took the glass from his hand and gulped down a mouthful. "I got into... into... other places."

Matt laughed. "You don't even know where you got in 'cause you don't even care, do you?"

"I care! Bunches! And bushels! And... other amounts that start with the letter B."

"Barrels?"

"Yes."

"Bounds?"

"Yes."

"Banshees?"

"One cannot," she said waving a finger at him, "care banshees about something."

"That is not true. I care banshees about you, my dear sister."

"You do?" Celeste clapped her hands to her heart. "Matty, that's so sweet of you. I care banjos about you, too."

"Banshees! Not banjos!" Matt added a second lime slice to his drink.

"Whatever. Anything with a B is cool beans with me."

Matt laughed. "Beans starts with B, too."

"It really does, doesn't it? We are so smart."

"Know what else starts with that letter?"

"Burlesque?"

"No. Fine, it does, but," he said as he leaned over the counter, "I was thinking of Barton."

She nodded. "You are correct."

"I think you might like it there."

"Matthew, you are clearly drunk beyond sanity." Celeste rolled her eyes and started pouring herself another gin and tonic.

"I think you might. Really."

"Why would you say that?" she asked with a slight slur. "You wanted me to go to Yale."

"I want you to be happy."

"I am happy."

"Okay. I just want you to stay that way." Matt was then silent.

Celeste peered at him. "Do you like Justin?"

"I do." He nodded. "Very much."

Celeste circled around the kitchen island and leaned over the counter, shoulder to shoulder with Matt. "I know another word that starts with B," she whispered. "Beach."

He nodded.

"Matty, I wanna go to the beach."

"It's winter. Too cold," he said. "Too dark."

"We could go."

He thought for a moment. "Know where they have nice beaches?"

"Brazil? Bali?"

"California."

Celeste continued to whisper. "That does not start with the correct letter."

"Still…"

"Then we should go to California and look at some beaches."

"That sounds fun. I think we have to," he agreed. "We could look at Barton."

"Okay, let's go."

"You could see that boyfriend of yours."

"Okay, let's go."

"It would be sunny."

"Okay, let's go."

"We could catch a plane right now, I bet. We should go to California."

Celeste nodded. "We should do that. Book us a flight. I shall go pack for our travels."

Matt was already tapping at the screen on his phone. "Do we like first class?"

Celeste stood up tall and clamped her hands on her hips. "I believe that sounds very elitist and obnoxious."

Matt looked up briefly to stick out his lower lip. "Fine. You can fly for the first time in the cramped section of the plane, and I'm gonna stretch out in first class."

"Oh. Well, okay then. I do not want to be separated from you."

"Then it's first class, baby!" Matt whooped.

"Okay, let's go," Celeste said and started to make her way rather clumsily to the front door before stopping in her tracks. "Oh wait. I must pack. Didn't I already say that? And we must call a taxi cab because I do not want to walk to Logan Airport. It is cold. And far away."

Matt continued booking their flight online. "Wait. Do *I* need to pack?"

"Yes, that's a good idea. You need to wear clothes in California." Celeste spun around to go for the stairs, but tripped over his weekend bag that he'd thrown on the floor. "Oh look! You already packed!"

"God, I'm so smart," he muttered.

"You really are, Matt." Celeste was floundering up the stairs to her room.

"You should tell Justin we're coming." Matt's voice carried up the stairwell.

"You have had yet another smart idea, Matthew Watkins. I shall do that. I shall tell him that we are listening to our guts and behaving impulsively. He will like that!"

"Hurry up. The cab will be here in fifteen minutes, and our flight leaves in two hours."

"Yes, sir, boss man. I shall do as instructed." She barreled into her room and delved into her closet to locate a suitable bag. As she rooted through her dresser and tossed clothes into the bag, she called Justin. "Ouch!" She tripped over a shoe and dropped her phone, but thankfully caught herself before she careened into her desk. It would not due to show up to see Justin with a giant lumpy bruise on her head.

She heard the beep of voice mail from where her phone had landed across the room. "I AM COMING TO SAN DIEGO IN AN ACT OF IMPUSLIVITY! WE SHOULD HAVE LUNCH OR SOMETHING ALONG THOSE LINES! I WILL BE ARRIVING LATE TONIGHT, SO I SHALL SEE YOU ANON, MY BELOVED ONE!" she shouted. Well, hopefully he caught all of that. She knelt in front of her dresser and grabbed a handful of… well, she didn't know what, but they were items. Items for a spontaneous trip. Another few handfuls from more drawers, a quick trip to the bathroom for supplies, and she was back downstairs.

"You ready, oh world traveler?" Matt asked. He was leaning against the wall in the front hall and halfway through a drink.

"I am, oh distinguished escort." She took the glass from him and downed a sizable gulp.

"Cool beans," he said with a wink. "Our chariot awaits."

They stumbled through the doorway, and Matt locked the house. "Hop on," he said as he patted his back.

"Woo hoo, Matty! You are piggybacking me, yes?"

"Yes, ma'am."

The two miraculously made it down the front steps and up the icy path to the concerned cab driver. "You two goin' to Logan?"

"That is indeed our destination," Celeste said. "We are taking a spontaneous journey together for the purpose of... spontaneous journeying." She scooted in beside Matt. "It's a really good idea; I'm sure you'll agree."

"Yeah. Great." The driver started the meter.

Celeste immediately started a search on her phone for airport protocol, as this would be her first experience with security and such. One must appear to know the part. She read for a few minutes. "Psst, Matty, did you know that we have to take off our shoes to go through the line thingie?"

"I know."

"I," she said drawing out her words, "find that to be an entirely civilized custom."

"It's not really a custom so much as a requirement."

"I shall enjoy this part so much."

She continued reading. "Oh no, Matty." She leaned in to whisper in his ear. Or at least what she thought was whispering.

"What is it?"

"It says here that we are not to be inebriated when flying or they might deny us access to the airplane."

"Then don't act drunk."

"We are inebriated."

"Don't act inebriated."

"Sir?" Celeste tapped on the heavy plastic panel that separated them from the front of the cab. "Sir?"

"Yeah?"

"Sir? Do we look inebriated to you?"

"Pretty much."

"That's not okay. We cannot look inebriated. We would like to fly via airplane, and inebriated is not allowed. Do you have a suggestion for how not to be inebriated?"

"Don't drink?"

She waved her hands. "Too late. Now what?"

"A breath mint wouldn't kill you. And don't talk when you go through security. Or board the plane. Or at all."

"Aha!" She slapped Matt's knee. "Our chauffeur has a set of brilliant ideas which we will incorporate into our sneaky scheme. Matt, are you paying attention here?"

"What? I was just booking us a hotel room."

"Ohmigod. How are we paying for this trip?"

He leaned, or perhaps tipped slightly, into her and said, "I got a buncha money."

"You have what?"

"I dunno. I mean, I make money and don't spend a lot. I saved up. Then I never spent it."

"What did you save up for?"

He started to say something and then stopped. "Nothing really. I'm just stingy."

"You're not so stingy. You are taking us on this trip."

"Then I'm a big spender."

"Hey, big spender…." Celeste started to sing.

"Don't sing. It makes you look inebriated."

"Oh. We can't be inebriated, or they won't let us on the plane."

"I know."

"Inebriated is not appropriate travel behavior."

"Calm down. Don't be scared. It's just a dumb airplane."

"I'm not scared. I'm going to think about seeing Justin. And you'll be with me. I will be fine. That is what I have decided."

"Check out the new Celeste, all ballsy and stuff."

"Matty! Do not say *ballsy*! That is disgusting." She sunk into the seat and looked out the window. "But I am gettin' ballsy, aren't I? It's fun."

## CHAPTER 20
# HEY, CELESTE?

"WE'RE ABOUT TO hit a little turbulence, folks, so I'm going to keep the seatbelt sign on. We should be through this pocket in about ten minutes."

Celeste winced with every word from the captain. "Flying is not fun, flying is not fun, flying is not fun," she whispered.

Despite the luxurious first-class seats, she was anything but comfortable. She leaned against Matt, grabbing his arm and resting her head against him. True, she couldn't fault him for being asleep considering how much he'd had to drink. However, he was not being particularly helpful right now, but it was slightly comforting to clutch onto him each time the airplane bounced. She couldn't decide if closing her eyes or keeping them open was worse, but when shut, every noise and movement did seem intensified, so she settled on bug-eyed awake. Old Fashioneds and gin and tonics had certainly eased the take-off, but now that she was sobering up... Well, just one more hour and they would land. Presumably with all of their limbs still intact. The good news was that there was a reward at the end of this misery: Justin.

> **Celeste:** Our plane should begin its descent in approximately 40 minutes.
>
> **Justin:** Your what should what?
>
> **Celeste:** The airplane that I am on will be landing soon.
>
> **Justin:** You're on an airplane?
>
> **Celeste:** Have you not checked your voice mail? I left you a message. I'm almost in San Diego.
>
> **Justin:** Hold on...
>
> **Justin:** I don't have a message from you, but, OH MY GOD, you are? You seriously got on an airplane? I'm freaking out. And totally damn happy.

Oh dear. She knew for sure that she had called him, but... Of course, she had been a bit under the influence of alcohol and perhaps her memory was failing her. There was, she realized, a very distinct possibility that she had not actually phoned him. Or worse, that she had phoned someone else.

> **Celeste:** Matthew and I were experimenting with cocktail hour, and it seems that things got a bit out of hand.
>
> **Justin:** So you two got drunk and flew to California?
>
> **Celeste:** "Drunk" may not be accurate, as I feel

painfully sober and my senses are astronomically heightened by this hideous air travel venture.

**Celeste:** Was this a bad idea? Are you unnerved?

**Justin:** No! It's only the BEST IDEA EVER! I didn't think I'd see you until the summer. This is more than I could have asked for. How long are you here for? Do you want me to pick you up at the airport? Where are you staying? SO MANY QUESTIONS THAT NEED ANSWERS!

**Celeste:** We have not arranged a return flight yet. That was evidently not part of the Old Fashioned planning process. We have a hotel, and I think a car, as well. Given how many drinks Matthew had, it might be best to get him to the hotel as soon as possible, and I do not want to put you out. I am able to drive him with no concerns.

**Justin:** Understood. But I can't wait to see you! Tomorrow morning, then? Text me when you wake up, okay? I'll take you all over campus, and I know a great place for dinner. Maybe hit the beach?

**Celeste:** I, too, am excited to see you.

The plane dipped. Hard. She clenched her teeth and fought for nerves of steel. Of course, *nerves of steel* was a nauseating cliché, but she didn't have the damn nerves of steel to come up with an alternative.

**Celeste:** I do not like flying. It will be a relief to land. This is stressful.

**Justin:** I'm very impressed with you for getting on that plane, even if it took some liquid courage.

*Liquid courage.* Celeste liked that phrase. It must mean bravery through alcohol consumption. Not that Celeste was going to take to drink on a regular basis—or frankly ever again based on how her stomach was feeling—but the term was quite amusing. Besides, courage should come through the strength of one's character, not the strength of one's bourbon. She was still working on that.

**Celeste:** There is turbulence. I am vehemently displeased with it.
**Justin:** Would it help to tell you that I'm waiting for you?
**Celeste:** Yes.
**Justin:** That when I see you, I will take my most fabulous girlfriend in my arms and pull her in close?

Celeste checked to make sure that Matthew was still asleep.

**Celeste:** Yes. That helps.
**Celeste:** Justin, I would very much prefer to be with you at this time. I have had a phobia of air travel that was based solely on fantasy, and now that fantasy is becoming reality.
**Justin:** There are much better fantasies, right? So listen to me. Celeste, listen to me, because I can't

stand that you're scared. Push that fear aside. Focus on a fantasy of... whatever suspends from you from this.

**Justin:** Let's talk fantasies. For me, there has been a fantasy about getting to kiss you again. Before, I was so rushed with you. Over the holidays. It was perfect and moving... but I want time. I want time to settle with you. Relax. I miss you. I miss the way you feel. And the way you make me feel. You sort of settle me, Celeste. If that makes any kind of sense. So my fantasy is to feel wholly me again. But me again with you.

**Celeste:** I miss you, Justin. So very much.

**Justin:** When I see you tomorrow, I am going to kiss you so deeply that you will forget about this horrible flight. I'll make the memory go away.

The plane thumped sharply, and Celeste caught her breath and gripped the armrest. Her eyes rimmed with tears. She truly wanted off this plane.

**Celeste:** It will have to be the best kiss that has ever taken place, because I am most decidedly unhappy at the moment.

**Celeste:** I wish you were here in the seat next to me. Justin, I do not like this. I am quite scared.

There was a devastating quiet from him now. She should not spaz out. Dallas loved the word "spaz," and it was mildly helpful to think of her friend. It was possible to manage this plane terror herself if she had to, so if Justin had been distracted by… well, any of the myriad of things that might distract him… she would get through this. She would not spaz out. But then her phone buzzed, and a wave of relief hit her. It was everything.

> **Justin:** I'm leaving my dorm now.
>
> **Celeste:** Justin, please… I do not want to be a bother. It is quite late.
>
> **Justin:** I don't care. It's college. There is no "late." I need to see you. To know you're okay. And I swear to you that you are going to be okay. Turbulence is just air pockets. Bumps.
>
> **Celeste:** Okay. Just air pockets.
>
> **Justin:** Exactly. That's all. I'm going to be there the minute that you land.
>
> **Celeste:** I would very much like that. Thank you.
>
> **Justin:** Hey, Celeste?

She smiled.

> **Celeste:** Hey, Justin?
>
> **Justin:** I want to tell you something.
>
> **Celeste:** Yes?
>
> **Justin:** I shouldn't say this over text, but I don't know that I can say it in person.
>
> **Justin:** You're scared now. I feel that. But I am more scared, and I want to tell you why anyway.

As the plane jostled sideways, the captain came over the speakers with another jarring warning about remaining seated. Celeste could feel her chest tighten with anxiety. Not just about the plane.

> **Celeste:** If it is something that could be helpful for one under duress, I would advise you to speak up. Immediately, for instance.

Justin did not reply for a few minutes. She stared at her phone's screen, silently begging him to say something. Anything. Anything at all would do. Even a diatribe on shrimp. Finally she saw the blinking dots that told her he was typing.

> **Justin:** I am falling so in love with you.

Her body electrified. Celeste wiped her eyes and read his text again. The drone of the plane disappeared; the turbulence was no more. There was only Justin and his words.

> **Justin:** I lose myself and find myself at the same time with you.
> **Justin:** I need you, Celeste. I need you as part of my world, because for the first time, I am connected to someone in a way that has meaning. And truth. Maybe our distance has strengthened what I feel

between us since we're not grounded in habit or daily convenience. We have to fight for what we have.

Celeste didn't bother to dry her eyes again because there was no point. It was so rare that one cried with happiness that she allowed it without shame.

**Justin:** I don't know if I can equate what I feel for you with anything else. Except maybe one thing, if this makes any sense.

**Justin:** I go to this spot at Sunset Cliffs sometimes. It's usually a place crowded with tourists, but certain times of year are quieter. I like it then. And there's a high spot on the sandstone cliff, surrounded by this gorgeous ice plant, and it overlooks the most beautiful water view you've ever seen. I'm on top of the world there, it seems.

**Justin:** And everything fits, you know? Life feels right. As though I could take on anything, do anything. And sometimes, when I'm feeling overcome with gratitude for the view and for what I have, I jump so that I remember to continue to be courageous because not every piece of life will feel so in place.

**Justin:** It's a twenty-foot drop, the water is only in the high fifties, and it's a damn scary experience. But it's a wonderful fear. One that I know I can get through and one that I want.

**Justin:** That's what it's like with you. I am scared because you are so beyond anything I could have imagined. I become so much more with you beside me. That's terrifying, by the way. But I will be brave because my fear only comes from finally having something deeply powerful to lose. That's my connection with you. It would be a massive loss.

**Justin:** And now I am in the car and about to see you, so don't reply. I'm too flipping terrified to hear what you think of my rant. It's hard not to pour my heart out once I start. If you think I'm out of mind, just wave your hands in horror when you spot the lovesick guy at the airport.

Ten minutes went by. He had said not to reply, so she hadn't.

**Justin:** Let's hope I don't get pulled over for speeding... but I'm at a stoplight now.

**Justin:** God, I hope you aren't... aren't... something bad.

**Celeste:** Hey, Justin?

**Justin:** I TOLD YOU NOT TO REPLY!

**Justin:** I know, I know. But I'm happy you did because I lost it there for a minute.

**Celeste:** HEY, JUSTIN?

**Justin:** Sorry... Hey, Celeste?

**Celeste:** I am, unequivocally and wholly falling in love with you, too.

**Justin:** Now I'm definitely speeding. I will see you soon.

Celeste turned off her phone. Now she was able to shut her eyes without fear. The landing gear thudded as it lowered for their final descent, the vibrations ran through her, and she barely noticed. What she did notice was her intense desire to be held by Justin, to feel his mouth against hers and his hands in her hair as they kissed. He made her feel... feminine. Cherished. His touch and his tenderness created the first desire she'd had for more. A curiosity. Maybe one day, they would even—

"Oh my God, what the hell is going on?" Matt groaned from his seat next to her. "Why am I on an airplane?"

"Oh dear. Do you not remember?"

He touched a hand to his forehead and didn't answer.

"We shared some cocktails during a very lovely brother-sister bonding afternoon, and then we decided to do some cross-country traveling."

"I bought us first-class tickets?"

"You did. It was very generous of you."

"You don't fly," he said weakly. "Are you okay?"

"I am quite well. Quite well indeed."

"You sound perky. Why are you perky?"

"Look out the window! San Diego is stunning at night. The city lights push through the dark sky, creating a most spectacular scene before us. You should look, Matty."

"I don't think I feel well enough to look out of a window."

"I see. Do you have a hangover? Why do they call it a hangover? What is one hanging over?"

"I feel a little sick," he mumbled to himself.

"Oh, I see! One might possibly hang one's upper body

over a toilet! Ergo, a hangover. Quite clever. Are you going to vomit? Earlier, I located a vomit bag as I was exploring what was offered to us in this seat pocket."

"Please don't say vomit."

"Should I say barf? That starts with the letter B and continues our earlier joke."

"I do not want a bag of any sort."

"'Bag' also starts with... Never mind. Could I then offer you an in-flight magazine?"

"No."

"The airline offers a catalog that sells extremely unusual items." She retrieved it. "Here, for instance, is a biker gnome statue. Or a bigfoot yeti carving that attaches to a tree trunk. Magic shower heads? These look interesting. They light up the water with various colors so you could bathe in green or purple. A multitude of colors are offered."

"I don't want a green shower."

"Something else for the bathroom, perhaps? An Egyptian goddess toilet paper holder?"

"Please stop talking about toilets and bathrooms."

"Sorry. Here's something you might like. Star Trek pajamas for adults."

"I'm going to kill you."

"For the traveler, they sell a convenient clothesline. You could wash your underwear and hang them up in the hotel bathroom—Oops, I mentioned a bathroom again. Well, it's not my fault that this catalog features many bathroom items. Aha, how about a gargoyle bottle opener?"

"Celeste..."

"No, sorry, that's no good. It probably makes you think of beer or wine, and you are experiencing nausea and a headache, I suspect."

"Why are you so chipper?"

"Because we are on an exciting adventure!"

Matt rubbed his eye and stretched. "That's true. This was certainly unexpected. Where are we staying?"

"You made a hotel reservation."

"I did?"

"Yes. You likely have a confirmation on your phone. Justin is meeting us at the airport in his car."

"He is? That's nice of him…"

"How long are we staying here, Matty?"

He laughed lightly. "I have no idea. I suppose we better be home before Mom and Dad get back. They wouldn't like this. So whatever you do, don't tell them we're here. Just pretend we're at home, okay?"

"Oooooh, we are being very mischievous and naughty! How unlike both of us!"

"Shhhh. My head is pounding. Let's just focus on getting to the hotel so that I can pass out again."

"Okay, that's a wise plan. Good thinking, Matthew." She leaned into him more and gave him a hug. "I am sorry that you don't feel well, but this trip is terrifically exciting for me."

He put an arm over her shoulder and pulled her in, kissing the top of her head. "I'm glad you're happy. I feel like hell, but I'm glad you're happy."

The landing was smooth, and in fact, Celeste found that she liked the rush she felt from being pushed back against her seat as the plane braked to a stop. It was a build, the force picking up gradually until reaching a peak, then gently easing up. She almost wanted more. What she had feared so much was now what she craved.

Or, she thought with no small degree of embarrassment, braking in an airplane was not what she craved. Justin's texts may have ignited something else.

When the lights came on and the seatbelt sign pinged off, she and Matt retrieved their bags from the overhead bins and stood to exit. The flight attendant nodded as they walked by. "Thank you for a most pleasant flying experience," Celeste said. "My first flight was significantly less traumatizing than I imagined. A job well done! Please extend my thanks to the pilot." Celeste beamed and stepped off of the plane.

"You really liked flying that much?" Matt asked, sounding more than a little surprised.

"Well, I confess that I was unnerved for most of the flight. But then, Matt?" She stopped them in a crowd. "Justin texted me."

"Okay. And?"

"Matty, he said wonderfully kind things to me. He said… he said…" Celeste was now uncertain how, or if, she should tell him. "Well… that he… had feelings of a certain nature…."

Matt frowned. "What the hell do you mean *of a certain nature*? I don't like the sound of that."

"Matthew! Not that nature! The sweet sort."

"Oh." He relaxed his expression. "Oh. Then, I guess that's okay. I mean, that's good."

"He is quite romantic."

Matt nodded and started walking again. "Then let's go see him."

Celeste followed Matt, suddenly a bit nervous with anticipation. But then they passed by security and took the escalator downstairs. And he was there.

Justin stood looking up at them as they descended, his hands in the pockets of his leather jacket, a baseball hat pulling the hair from his face so that she could see every handsome feature of his face. When they reached the bottom, Matt had to nudge Celeste forward. She couldn't stop staring, could barely remember how to walk. Justin didn't move either, seemingly as transfixed on her as she was on him.

"Oh God, go. Go get him," Matt said with a laugh. He shoved her forward until she walked slowly toward Justin.

Nearly crippled by the sight of him, she couldn't get herself to move faster. But then she involuntarily let out a sound, a near cry of emotion, when his arms clutched her to his chest and held her body against his. She squeezed back, not able to get enough of him. The only reason she eventually pulled away was for one reason. His mouth. The urgency to kiss him.

So she eased her head back, letting her lips find his. How she had missed this. Missed him. Just as Celeste's tongue started to touch his, he pulled back. "Boy, do you taste like bourbon."

Celeste blushed. "Oh no…"

"And also gin. And you're delicious, and I'm going to give you that proper kiss I promised, but right now your brother is glaring at me."

"Oh! Indeed." She got her breathing under control, and turned to Matt, slipping her hand into Justin's. "Sorry."

He rolled his eyes. "It's okay. Hi, Justin."

"Matt, good to see you!"

Celeste smiled when they shook hands. Matt genuinely did seem to approve of her boyfriend. That was important to her.

"Look, we need to rent a car, but the fact is I'm likely still hammered out of my mind, so you'll need to drive. Justin, would you mind leading us to our hotel? I don't think either of us should be responsible for locating anything right now."

"Of course. Where are you staying?"

Matt shrugged and laughed at himself. "I have no idea." He checked his phone. "Apparently someplace called The Grand Del Mar?"

"Really?"

"Yeah, why? Is it a dump?"

"Um… no. Quite the opposite. You'll like it."

Matt continued staring at his phone and shaking his head with a bemused look. "It also seems that I reserved a car already. It's being delivered here."

"Well, all right, man!" Justin patted him on the back. "Nice going?"

"What?" Celeste was confused. "What does this mean?"

"It means," Justin said, "that your brother rented a luxury car that's not available for rental from any old regular agency. I like how you think, Matt," Justin said tapping his head with a finger. "I really do."

Thirty minutes later, Celeste was behind the wheel and following Justin's old two-door Ford. "I am flabbergasted at your choice of vehicles, Matty. This is quite unlike you." She shifted the car into fourth gear and sped up. "If you ask me, a black Corvette convertible is a bit much for our needs. And perhaps on the cliché end, although not that I am complaining. The weather is magnificent. I gather this is unusually warm for this time of year, but the wind feels lovely. It turns out that I may very well have been a race car driver in another lifetime. If I believed in other lifetimes, that is. But this convertible? Not what I would have expected from you. I don't even remember you ordering this. I mean, Matt, you had to make special arrangements to have this car waiting for us."

"Just let me have my mid-life crisis." Matt had his eyes shut and his head tipped into the headrest while the wind blew his hair around.

Celeste had tossed hers into a bun on the top of her head so that she could see enough to drive. "You are too young for a mid-life crisis. But I will enjoy whatever episode you are having." She took a corner hard, reveling in the control. "I quite like this vehicle."

"Please don't kill us before we get to the hotel."

"I shall not kill us because based on the first-class airplane seats and now this car, I cannot wait to see the hotel. Oh, here it is!" She pulled up to the hotel behind Justin's car, driving past a lit-up fountain and under illuminated palm trees, and let the valet help her from the car. "Matthew, the Grand Del Mar is indeed grand! I had no idea that you had such good taste. Given your wardrobe and general chintzy nature, I am entirely shocked, albeit delighted."

Justin left his car for the valet and strode over to the Corvette.

Matt looked at the outside of the hotel and just shook his head in disbelief. "Justin?"

"Yeah, Matt?"

"Oh God. What have I done?"

"Look, you treated yourself to a nice hotel. So what?"

"Okay, yeah. You're right. So what?"

So when they all stood at the desk and the clerk confirmed their two-bedroom suite, Matt simply nodded as though this was exactly how they traveled all the time. Celeste was awed by the massive arches, the wide wrought iron staircase, and the marble pillars and floors. But Matt didn't so much as flinch when they walked into the living room of the luxurious suite, or when he looked out the window to see the stunning view and the glowing moon. He simply flung himself onto the striped couch and smiled sleepily. "This was an awesome idea. Do you know they have a pool? I'm never leaving this place."

Celeste put her hands on her hips. "You are having some sort of severe psychiatric break, are you not? You could have changed our room to a more reasonable one, you know."

"I don't care. I like this room. It's very distinguished and formal. Perfect for you. I want to keep it forever. Let's move in here. Let's never leave. Let's have more of those crazy Old Fashioneds."

It was all she could do not to stomp her foot. "We are never drinking Old Fashioneds again. Look at us!"

"I know, right?" Matt giggled. "We're awesome."

Celeste sighed as Justin rubbed her back. "Fine. We are rather awesome. And one of us is most definitely still intoxicated and should not have continued drinking on the airplane.

But if it were not for the multitude of cocktails, I would not be here with Justin, so I can thank alcohol for that. But from now on, we are staying away from it."

"I think I should get to bed," Matt said. "I feel heinously awful."

"Well, for heaven's sake go sleep in one of the expensive beds that you paid for."

"I should probably get going…" Justin started.

"What?" Celeste said with alarm. "No, you mustn't go. You can't."

"Well…" He tipped his head toward Matt.

"Matthew, may Justin stay for a bit?"

"Sure." Matt pulled himself up. "On two conditions. One, if you ever tell Mom and Dad, I'll disown you as my sister. Two, if anyone takes off even a single item of clothing, I—"

"Matt!" Celeste said loudly. "Honestly!"

"Yes, honestly."

"I can go, really," Justin said.

Matt yawned and got up, now squinting and shuffling to the far bedroom. "It's totally fine. I'm just giving you a hard time. I was young and in love once, so I have a vague memory of it. I get it." He leaned on the door jamb. "'Night."

Celeste couldn't help herself. She rushed across the room and flung her arms around him. The sad, even bitter, edge in his voice pained her. "Thank you, Matt. Thank you for this trip. And for being with me."

"Yeah, yeah. Calm down. Don't be up too late. It's four in the morning or something."

"It is only one o'clock. Time change, silly."

"Whatever. Stay up all night." He shut the door. "But all clothing stays on; or someone loses an eye, and it won't be Celeste!" he shouted from his room.

Justin dropped his head onto Celeste's shoulder. "Really. I should probably go. I don't want to upset Matt. And you must be exhausted."

"I am tired. Very tired. But I cannot bear to have you leave. Please stay." She hesitated, but then said what she felt. "I want to fall asleep with you. Would that be all right?"

"I'm so glad you said that." He nuzzled his face into her and kissed her neck softly. "I would like nothing more."

She smiled. "I believe that I must take a shower and brush my teeth. I cannot possibly smell anything less than questionable."

"I'll take you in any condition, but you may feel better after a shower."

She led him into the second bedroom and then stopped short, causing him to crash into her.

"Ugh, sorry. I knew I couldn't get through the night without doing something klutzy."

"No, no. That was my doing. Justin?" She couldn't look at him. "I am suddenly aware that I am taking you into a bedroom. And that may indicate... something... um, something..."

"I know. And I understand. I told you that I'm not like that, okay? And I can still leave now. I just want to be close with you. That's all."

"I want that, too."

He zipped in front of her and jumped onto the bed. "But

that doesn't mean that I don't appreciate a fancy hotel bed. It's good for bouncing, see?"

Celeste left Justin to bounce and took a steaming shower in the luxurious bathroom before slipping into one of the hotel robes. "Justin, would you hand me my bag that I left out there?"

"Of course, doll."

She cracked the door and took her bag. She looked through it for a moment and nearly screamed. "Oh perfect!"

"What's the trouble?"

"It appears one should not pack for a trip after drinking. I have an unusual assortment of items, but we are in luck should either of us require knee socks with rainbows and unicorns. My mother thought they were a funny Christmas gift. Well, I'll just have to make do."

"But, but, but *I* might have interest in the unicorn socks!" Justin teased. "Unicorns represent purity, and truth, and strength, and stuff like that. I like to wear my value system on my feet."

"You will do no such thing." Celeste emerged in soft shorts and the *All This Science Gives Me a Hadron* shirt that Matt had given her. "Please do not acknowledge this shirt."

Justin raised his eyebrows. "You want me to pretend it's not there? That you're not wearing a top? If that's what you want…"

"Justin!" Celeste laughed.

He softened his look. "Come here, you. You've got to get some sleep." He pulled back the bed covers for her.

"I do." She turned off the lights so the room was barely lit by the lamp in the living room.

Celeste slipped under the sheet and Justin lay on his side, his head propped on his hand. He kissed her cheek, then her lips, very gently. "Sleep, baby."

She was exhausted now. Drained and overwhelmed, and desperately needing to fall into a deep slumber. Justin started to move from the bed. "You're leaving?"

"Call me when you get up, okay?" he whispered.

"Stay," she said. "Stay."

"Sleep here?"

"Yes. I want to wake up with you."

He dropped his head down onto the pillow. "And I want to wake up with you."

"I like that I can say that to you."

"I like that you can, too."

Celeste rolled into his chest, and Justin's arm moved over her waist. And enveloped in each other, they slept, and they dreamed.

## CHAPTER 21
# WATCHING PERFECTION

WAKING UP IN San Diego was less disorienting than Celeste would have imagined. That may have been because she was in Justin's arms, he on his back and she with her body in the crook of his arm and her head on his chest. She felt whole and at home. It was odd, however, that she felt so physically comfortable with someone she wasn't able to see on a regular basis. But she did. And she wouldn't question it now because who knew how many times she would have this opportunity.

She glanced at the clock to see that it was just after eight. He had not moved from her all night, but was now under the covers, still close to her, with his legs entwined with hers. Celeste eased down the covers and slipped into the bathroom to brush her teeth. This may be the first time that she was waking up next to a boy, but she had common sense. When she had freshened up and run her fingers through her hair, she returned to her spot in bed and in Justin's hold.

She placed her hand on his chest. In the early morning light, she watched the way her hand moved with his breathing. It was watching perfection. Her hand slowly moved over his shirt, up to his shoulder, down his arm as she explored the shape of his body while he slept. Celeste slid her hand down to his waist, accidentally catching the hem of his shirt. Then her hand was on his stomach, his skin hot and wet.

Never had she felt this way. She had to laugh at herself; this was by far the most intimate moment of her life, and the other person wasn't even conscious. She hoped this wasn't creepy, but touching him, feeling his body under her hand… Well, she didn't know exactly what she wanted, but she wanted something. And she was scared out of her mind about what she might want. But nonetheless, she let her fingers inch up under his shirt a bit more. Justin sighed in his sleep and rolled to lie facing her, and she eased her palm over his waist to his lower back. His workouts must be more frequent than he let on, she decided, because she could feel how toned he was, the dip of his spine surrounded by muscle. She'd known he wasn't so muscular that he was bulky, but it was only now that she felt how defined his body was.

Oh God, what was she doing?

Justin stirred, smiling even before his eyes were open. "Well, hello. This person reaching up my shirt better be who I think it is, or I'm gonna freak out."

Celeste pulled her hand away quickly. "Sorry."

"Oh good, it is you," he murmured. "Why is there stopping? Why is there no more hand being all cute and awesome?"

"Because you woke up."

He considered this for a moment. "You can't touch me when I'm awake?"

"I'm nervous."

"About what?"

"What I'll do. What you might do."

"You don't have to be nervous. Nothing's going to get out of control."

"It isn't?"

"No. I'm not going to let anything happen."

"Oh."

He opened his sleepy eyes. "Not because I don't want anything to happen, because believe me I am a perfectly horny college boy. But I'm assuming that since I was your first kiss, every step will be a first. And firsts are important. Or they should be. So we go step by step when each feels right. We don't just jump down a staircase. Or jump up it. Whatever. My metaphor sucks. I'm not awake yet. The point is that I'm not about to rush ahead, and neither are you."

"In that case, good morning." She returned her hand to his back and moved her fingers over his skin.

"I can't *not* taste you any longer." Without saying anything else, he lifted his shoulders from the bed and leaned over her. His mouth grazed over her neck, the tip of his tongue running over her as he kissed slowly down to the top hem of her shirt. Her totally unsexy, geeky Hadron shirt, of all things! Celeste was going to kill Matt. He'd better improve his gift-giving skills by next Christmas.

Matt. She'd forgotten about him. The bedroom door was open. He had to be sleeping still, right?

She lifted her chin as Justin moved his kisses up one side of her throat and over to the other side. There was this one particular spot, she discovered, just below and behind her ear where she really, really quite liked having his mouth. That spot, the way he lightly sucked her skin, made her body tremble. She would have been disappointed when he stopped, except that his lips were then on hers, his chest barely touching hers as he held himself over her.

When he'd kissed her as deeply as he had assured her he would during last night's texting, and when the outside world had all but disappeared, he stopped and rubbed his nose against hers. "We need coffee. We have a big day."

Celeste liked coffee as much as the next person, but it was significantly less enticing than what they were already doing.

"Yes. Coffee is important," she said halfheartedly.

"Don't sound so sad." He kissed her cheek and rested his mouth by her ear. "Believe me, I'd like to do this all day, but your protective brother is next door, and I want to keep both of my eyeballs. Besides, I want to show you the city."

She nodded, trying to regain control of herself. Justin was right. They needed to get out of here.

"Hey, Celeste?"

"Hey, Justin?"

He continued to whisper in her ear, hiding his face from her. His breath and the sound of his voice were driving her wonderfully crazy. "Are you okay with what I said last night? When you were on the plane?"

She smiled. "Were you okay with what *I* said?"

"I asked you first, silly, but I was damn thrilled with what you said."

"I was very much okay with what you said."

"It's all right if you want to change your mind. You might have felt pressured. I mean, not the cabin pressure, although that could have messed with your ears and made you dizzy and unable to think clearly. Have your ears popped yet? Did you know about popping ears? But, you know, if you felt emotionally pressured because I said something that—"

"Justin?"

"Yeah?"

"I did not feel pressure, cabin related or otherwise."

"Good."

It was another fifteen minutes before Justin insisted that they really had to get out of that room because he could feel one of his eyes developing a stabbing pain at the thought of Matt waking up.

"I want to take you to Barton, so you can see where I go to school. We can have lunch there and hang out. You cool with that? Is that all right? Do you want to wake up Matt?"

"Yes, I shall check on Matthew."

"I'll jump in the shower real quick. We can stop by my room so I can change, too."

Celeste remembered her unsuitable packing job. "I may need to borrow a sweatshirt or something. I'm not sure what I have."

"I would be more than happy to see you in one of my shirts." Justin crawled out of bed, looking so dashingly sexy with his messy hair and rumpled clothing that Celeste actually checked to see if she was drooling. She didn't know if that was just an expression or true physiological reaction that one could have when enamored, so she had to be sure. So far, so good.

Celeste had to stop herself from following her boyfriend into the shower. That was a crazy idea, of course. She wasn't near ready for anything close to that, and yet there was a distinct pull for more contact with him. She took a deep breath and opened the curtains, trying to distract herself from the utter hotness that was now probably totally naked and lathering himself up with expensive hotel body soap—

She really had to stop this. Being flooded with outrageous sex-crazed thoughts was completely out of character. Of course, she'd never had a boyfriend before, or really even much of a crush, so reasonably, this was not abnormal. Just abnormal for her.

She stared out of the window. Okay, the view was extraordinary. Totally blue skies and full sunshine. As much as the whole idea of making out with Justin all day had sounded pretty fantastic, she simply had to get out to see this lush city. She found another pair of shorts, and tossed those on with a non-geeky layered, flowy cream tank top. It seemed that her drunken packing had not been entirely terrible. Her hair was unmanageable after having slept on it wet, so she yanked it into a high ponytail.

Matt's door was shut, so she opened it just a crack to peek in. He was definitely still asleep. She checked the mini fridge and then left him a note pointing out that there was cold bottled water for him. When she opened the living room curtains, her need to get out into the city skyrocketed. She banged on the bathroom door. "Justin! I want to see the ocean! Can we see the ocean?" she said with excitement. "It's sunny and wonderful outside. We must go!"

She heard him laugh. "Anything you want, love." The shower turned off.

Celeste turned her back to the door and slumped to the floor. He called her *love*. What was happening? This was so much good, so much romantic, and so much categorically outside of how her life had been thus far. There was also the nakedness happening close by. That was out of the ordinary for sure. *He was entirely unclothed behind that door!* She had to stop herself from squealing. That would be undignified. One should be composed even in proximity of such a gorgeous showering boyfriend.

Her mind drifted. What he'd said about going step by step, she liked. He was right. That was important to think about, and it wasn't a decision to make in the heat of the moment. The fact was that she was an eighteen-year-old young woman, and she knew it was perfectly normal to have such physical attractions. It was allowed; it was healthy. And she was responsible. It was good, though, that Justin was responsible too. He was so caring, so respectful, and so stunningly thoughtful. It only made her feelings more intense. Celeste closed her eyes, imagining what might be the next step, what she wanted, what would keep her comfortable…

Suddenly she fell back onto the tile as Justin opened the door, clothed, but dripping water from his hair. She looked up at him. "Hello."

"Hello," he said grinning as he knelt down over her, his head upside down to hers. "Whatcha doing?"

She reached up and took his face in her hands and pulled

him in, sinking her tongue into his mouth with more assertiveness than she knew she had. When she was done, she continued holding him and said, "I want to see Barton. And I want to see the beach. And I want coffee. And more palm trees and sunshine. And most of all, more you. More kissing."

"I can give you all of those. Promise. You ready?"

"I have a fear, though."

"What's that?"

She hesitated, but being truthful with Justin always made her feel better. "Will we be speaking with other students? With your friends?"

"I don't know. Maybe. I'm not sure who's around today." He paused. "Why?"

"You know that I have difficulty in social situations." Her voice nearly disappeared. "I do not want to embarrass you."

He kissed her again. "Stop that."

"It is a legitimate concern."

"The only legitimate concern I have is that you will be appalled by the unhygienic state of my dorm room. Now, come on up." He grabbed her hands and pulled her up to a stand. "No Matt?" he asked.

She shook her head. "No Matt. I have hope he might contact us later and join in our adventures. Er, well, not all of them."

"Yeah. Agreed."

When they were finally in the car, Justin handed her one of the to-go cappuccinos he'd bought. She took off the top to sip the foam, but stopped. It was the most beautiful cappuccino any girl had ever received, because a perfectly symmetric heart was floating in the foam.

"Of all the foam coffees you have presented me with, I do believe it is fair to say that this is my favorite."

"Usually I cheat because I draw with syrup, so I hired a pro for the important one. I have no idea how they make pictures out of foam like that, but as an architecture student I'm annoyed with myself that I can't do it. I should be able to build foam sculptures for you. Anyway… You like?"

"I like." She placed a hand on his cheek, running a finger over his lips for a bit. "I like very much." She leaned over from her seat and kissed him. It was all too easy to get used to being able to touch him. To watch him. To simply be in his presence and the power that was Justin.

He revved the engine and took them toward the Barton campus.

As they drove down a road that ran beside the ocean, Celeste's phone rang.

"Hello, Julie! Guess where I am? You will not believe it."

"You're in San Diego. I got your message."

Celeste's heart nearly stopped. Immediately, she knew what had happened. What she'd done. The message intended for Justin had instead gone to Julie. Their names were right by each other on her favorites speed-dial list. "Yes. My message."

"I'm dying to see you! I can drive down and get there for lunch and stuff tomorrow afternoon. Is that good?"

No, this was not good at all. This was a nightmare.

Or was it?

"Yes, that would be delightful. Justin and I shall pick you

up, so simply let me know of your arrival time, and we will have lunch. The three of us. Justin, you, and me. A trio. Just a small group."

"Is everything okay?"

"Everything is violently perfect! Why would you ask?"

"*Violently perfect*? That's an odd word choice…"

"I am in the car and about to experience a full day in a new city, so I feel that I deserve to use whatever words strike my fancy at a moment's notice. I am feeling whimsical and robust."

"*Whimsical*? *Robust*? Celeste, what is going on?"

"Sexual tension levels are at an all-time high, and there are linguistic repercussions!" she shouted.

"Oh my God."

"Text me later. Can't wait to see you!" Celeste hung up. That hadn't exactly gone smoothly. And she couldn't even *look* at Justin.

"So," he said and made a big production of clearing his throat. "What was that you said about sexual tension?"

She put a hand over her face. "Perhaps we could skip over some of what you heard?"

He playfully pulled her hand from her face. "I like the sexual tension discussion! More of that! This deserves details!"

Celeste busied herself with retying her ponytail. "I got nervous and didn't know what to say. I have some thinking to do in that area."

"Really? Then you think and report back in later. Although not in essay fashion. I hate reports in general, but essays are so sterile and boring. How about with a pie chart? Or a diorama? Dioramas are fun. You could include little action figures.

Although that might be creepy. I think my parents were very disappointed that I didn't like action figures, I have to tell you. They have a collection of vintage superhero ones still in the boxes, but I was more about trains and building blocks. They hated Legos, probably because I left them all over the house, and one time Luka stepped on one and when he was screaming and hopping on one leg, he fell and landed on more and had Lego indents on his face for a few days. Oh, I missed my exit. Hold on."

Celeste put a hand on his and then rubbed his forearm. She loved his meandering talk.

"Sorry, what were we saying? Julie called, that's right. What's up with her?"

"It seems that I called her instead of you last night and invited her to come down from Los Angeles to see me."

"Oops. Isn't that going to be weird with Matt here?"

"Extremely." She was working over a plan in her head. "Although I am choosing to see this as a sign. It is my belief that Matthew and Julie still love each other very much. If we get them together over lunch, then I feel sure they can recapture their former romance. Or, rather, see that it is still there. Wouldn't that be exciting?"

"Oh God, Celeste, this sounds very sketchy to me."

"What do you mean by sketchy?"

"Like, that it's not well thought out. Many areas for highly problematic angles and such. Unlikely to end well."

"That is not very romantic of you. You should adopt a more positive attitude. We should show them they must fight for their love. Fight for all loves destroyed by the hazards of distance. They have something that is worth saving, and I know their connection remains after all this time. This could be very exciting!"

"You think they'll see each other and the stars will align?"

"I do. Yes." Celeste was pleased about the mix-up. It *clearly* did indicate *some* sort of aligning of the stars. She must have accidentally left a message for Julie for a good reason, and here it was. Matthew had seemed so down for so long, and she was about to fix that by reuniting him with his true love. It was all very romantic! "Can you suggest a waterside restaurant for lunch? I think that would be picturesque."

"You bet. Tell her to meet us at Island Prime. You guys will love it." Justin turned the car to the right. "Up ahead. That's Barton."

Together, they spent hours covering the campus. She saw Justin's dorm room, which admittedly gave her pause as she was reminded of the impending roommate situation that she would face next year. Still, it was nice to see where Justin lived and where he was during many of their phone conversations. Now she would be able to picture him in his environment. His room wasn't nearly as unsanitary as he'd led her to believe, so that was a treat. She leafed through his architecture books and saw some sketches he was working on, thoroughly impressed with his attention to detail and his creative side. She briefly met his roommate (during which time nothing vile occurred) and was then given a very thorough tour of the campus. It was beautiful, more beautiful even than in the brochure or online photographs. Mesmerizing, really. Brick and stucco and archways. Palm trees and flowers abounded. Justin didn't complain once as she explored every inch of the library, nor did he mind taking her through each department building, even introducing her to a few professors who were working over the weekend. Justin bought them lunch at the student union and insisted on getting her a Barton College T-shirt, and she immediately pulled it over her tank top.

"You look good in my school colors." He tugged on the navy shirt that had the school name in a pale green. "But you'd look good in any colors."

It was late afternoon now, and they'd found a grassy spot on a hill that overlooked an area where students were gathered in groups, reading or studying or just talking. She saw laughter; she saw friends. She saw life.

Justin was leaning back on his arms, taking in the scene as she was.

"You are quieter than usual," she said. "Are you troubled?"

"The opposite." A warm wind blew over them, and he lifted his face into the breeze. "I feel better than I have in a while. I told you: you ground me. Being with you lets me pull myself together more."

Celeste lay down, resting her head on his legs, and Justin stroked her hair. They stayed like that for a long time, relishing every minute in the warmth of their togetherness. According to Matt's texts and pictures, he was busy at the hotel, soaking up sunshine by the pool and snacking on nearly every menu item, and he seemed happy. Or as happy as Matt got these days. He'd spoken to their parents and told some egregious lie about a trip to the Museum of Natural History followed by Indian food.

She would have stayed like this, in this glorious moment with Justin, for the rest of the afternoon if she could. However, they were interrupted by a group of students, all chatting at once and clamoring for Justin's attention.

Justin eased her to sitting. "Celeste, this is Michelle," he said excitedly.

Ah, Michelle from the Christmastime text mix-up.

"It's so nice to meet you!" Michelle's dark waves fell over her face as she reached out a hand. "Justin didn't tell us you were coming. How cool!" She introduced Celeste to the other students with her and then plopped down on the grass. "So this is perfect. Maybe you can help us out with something?"

"I should be happy to assist you if possible." Celeste was excruciatingly nervous all of a sudden.

"We're doing this play, and one of our girls is down with food poisoning. Don't worry, it wasn't from campus food. Anyway," she said as she pulled out a binder from her bag, "we're supposed to rehearse this huge scene, and we need a female actress. Any chance we could get you to run lines with us for a bit?"

"Run lines means that I read your friend's role?" Celeste asked.

"Yeah, exactly."

Celeste looked to Justin, and he gave her an encouraging look. "We've got time before we head to Sunset Cliffs. Go ahead."

"You really don't want me for this. I have never done any acting before. I may not be helpful in this situation." Celeste protested.

"Please! You'll be great. And you don't have to memorize anything. Just read the lines and we'll work around you, okay? I promise that there's nothing to be nervous about."

Celeste nodded and took the binder that Michelle offered

to her. She read the title and brightened. "Oh! The Importance of Being Earnest!" She looked at the people surrounding her now. "This is a delightful play. Gwendylon believes she can only fall in love with a man named Ernest, and quite the hilarity ensues when a man named Jack... Well, of course you know all of that. But I certainly admire this piece."

"Awesome! We need you to play Cecily."

"I am terribly sorry to hear that your Cecily has food poisoning, but I am most certainly a fan of this character. How wonderful." Celeste could still feel her hands shaking, but she knew this play. Adored it, really. She could likely take on Cecily's lines without even looking at the pages.

The cast initially stayed on their spots in the grass, reading from the script, but by the end of the hour, all were staged in front of Justin as they ran lines and moved as their characters would. Celeste got lost, fascinated by the way these acting students changed into character so quickly, how they dropped their roles when one made a goof, and how they moved their bodies and expressions for different scenes. Although she felt rather stiff and hesitant, she made an effort to add her own touch of flair to a few of Cecily's lines, even eliciting some good laughter from the others.

A boy named Ronnie patted her on the back as they wound down. "You're really good. I can't believe you haven't acted before."

"Me?"

"Yes. You're great. You should think about theatre. Where are you going to school next year?"

Justin was at her side then. "The poor girl has to choose

between Harvard, Yale, Princeton... Oh, the endless list of pathetic schools goes on and on..."

She swatted him with a hand. "I have not decided yet."

"Well, any of those will have a great acting program. You might like it." He lifted a knapsack over his shoulder. "Glad to finally meet the famous Celeste."

She shook hands or waved to everyone as the group disassembled. While Justin was talking to someone else, Michelle huddled in close. "Justin is damn crazy about you. I hope you know that. It's so good to see him this happy."

Celeste didn't know what to say.

"Really. It's not like he was a depressed mess before you, but... I don't know." She shrugged. "He's in a good place. He's got... light. If that makes any sense."

"It does." Celeste smiled at Michelle. "Justin gives me light, too."

"I'm glad. Listen, I've got to run, but I'm going to get your number from Justin. His birthday is coming up in May, and my boyfriend, Kevin, is trying to figure out what to do. Maybe you'll have some ideas."

"Kevin is Justin's roommate, correct?"

"You got it. And he's hooooooooot!" Michelle sang out.

Celeste laughed. "I would be happy to advise you on a birthday celebration, although you may know better what is appropriate for college festivities."

"Eh, you never know. Besides, the girlfriends of roommates should be in touch anyway, don't you think?"

"Oh. Yes. I like that idea," Celeste agreed. "I will make sure Justin gives you my contact information." She paused. "Thank you for including me in your acting work today. It was most unexpected."

"Cool. You rocked it, and I'm glad you had fun. Catch you later." Michelle surprised her with a quick hug before she took off.

Justin said, "Matt just texted me again. He's still by the pool reading a book called *God Created the Integers* and said we should go to dinner without him. He also sent a picture of a dirty martini, so I'm thinking there's a hair-of-the-dog situation going on. Frankly, I might need a drink if I tried to read that book, too, but the point is that he sounded content and relaxed. Ready to go watch a corny sunset with your boyfriend? We should hustle if we want to catch it. Sun sets at five forty-three. I checked. It's so awesome how you can find anything online, right? Like, we could find out about the world's most giant lobster right now. Or watch a video on how to change the water filter in a fridge. Or learn how they make those weird gel thingies in running shoes. Or—Hey, are you with me? Oh, I've done it. I finally lost you because I'm impossible to follow."

Celeste was transfixed on the campus before her. The buildings, the softening sunlight, the noise of students as they flowed over the lawn.

"Celeste?"

"Yes? Did you need to change a filter? Or find a lobster?" she asked with a glazed look.

"You okay?"

"Yes." She watched someone send a Frisbee sailing through the air. Perhaps Frisbee was not to be as lamented as she thought. She slipped her hand into his. "I am ready for our sunset."

## CHAPTER 22
# THE SHAPE OF US

"USUALLY IT'S MORE crowded here, but it's not really tourist season right now, so we get the view all to ourselves. Also, I paid everyone to stay away." Justin held her hand as they walked across sandstone and past the ice plant that covered the area. "Careful. It gets slippery here, so watch your step. There's a super-steep path that goes down to the water, but I don't want to take you down there without better shoes. Sometimes people sleep down there on the beach. Couples and stuff. But this is the spot I told you about right here. Where people jump off into the water. It's illegal, but people do it anyway. You just have to be careful that you don't jump on anyone."

Celeste peered over the edge of the cliff area. It was a good jump. Not insanely terrifying, but a very high jump indeed. "This is the place you wrote about in your texts?"

"Yes." He looked at her curiously. "Why? Do you want to do it?"

"No," she said quickly. "Never." Finn would have. Matt would. Even Julie. But she would not. "There is no reason to."

"It's not for no reason."

"What's the reason?"

"It's different for everyone."

"Tell me more about why you jump."

He looked down and kicked a pebble out into the ocean. When he lifted his head, the light caught his face in such a way that he managed to look all the more handsome to her. She loved the shape of his face, his full lips, his perpetually disheveled hair. Celeste was again achingly aware of how much he meant to her. It bordered on painful.

"I suppose," he said, "that I jumped for a lot of reasons. Is this good?" He surveyed the rocky cliff and seemed satisfied. "Yeah. Let's sit."

Celeste took a seat next to him and took in the unbelievable skyscape. The dark ocean rolling out before them, the jagged and richly-colored cliffs, and the sun brilliantly orange and just starting to finish its day with them.

"I came out here last year and hurled myself off the side. No, don't look worried. It wasn't like that. It was an empowering choice. I guess… I don't know. I'd been struggling a bit with who I was. Accepting that I've got pretty decent attentional issues. I have struggles. I'm probably diagnosable, but I don't really care to know. I've figured out how to work with my wiring for the most part. I hit a point when I finally got comfortable with that and with knowing that some people won't get me. That's okay. But I had years and years of baggage to deal with. Look, you spend your entire life with people telling you how annoying you are, or that you're dumb and will never manage more than a menial job… That's a lot to get over. I like proving them wrong. All the teachers who never bothered to see past certain pieces of me? All the kids who tortured me when I still stuttered? Screw them, you know? I'm proud of myself. I like myself now. So I jumped to maybe celebrate that. Because I was grateful that I dealt with what I had to, and I got myself to a place where I could enjoy a gorgeous view like this one. I was happy enough to do that."

Celeste was quiet. She eased into Justin's hold as he wrapped his arms around her to watch the sunset. She understood why couples did this sort of thing together. It was, she recognized, undeniably clichéd. Yet, God, it was breathtaking.

"Whatcha thinking about there, sweets?" he asked.

She focused on the pattern that the sun was making across the water. "Did you see me today? Did you see what happened with your friends?"

"What do you mean?"

"That they did not react unfavorably to me."

"Celeste…" He pulled her in more. "Not everybody is an asshole."

"Do not say *asshole*. Foul language is uncalled for here and should be saved for special occasions. But I am thinking that I, too, am diagnosable." She took a long, slow breath while he waited. "Sometimes I begin to type in words to do an internet search, but then I stop."

"And why do you stop?"

"Because I am scared."

"Would you find something helpful? Would you find

something that would make you change? I don't know about you, but I'd hate that."

She said nothing.

"Celeste, you are who you are. Don't be ashamed of yourself. At all. Surround yourself with people who cheer you on. That's all."

"I would hate to have a label. To be categorized."

"I agree. I feel the same way. For some, for many probably, it's helpful. But there are spectrums of personality types, and I don't believe everyone belongs on a chart."

"I have not had many friends. People find me weird; I know that. I have tried—really, really tried, Justin—to conform, but I do believe there must be something quite wrong with me that I fall outside the spectrum of what is perceived as normal."

"You just explained it," he said softly.

"What?"

"What is *perceived as normal*. That makes it other people's failings. Deficits. Not yours. Who the hell sets the standards, huh? Who gets to say how we are supposed to be? Or who we are supposed to be? And how dare anyone make you feel inadequate for being who you are? It's not okay. It pisses me off."

"You are angry," she commented.

"Well, yeah. Aren't you? I want to destroy anyone who has hurt you for a dumb reason like just being yourself. What? Do we want the entire universe made up of people who are all clones of each other? How damn boring would that be? You know the expression that love makes the world go 'round? That might be true, but love comes from the way differences interact. How personalities interact. How we bounce off of each other, challenge each other, and how we push and pull. It's through those tensions that we connect with others and with ourselves. And it's how we fall in love. Because there is magic in diversity. Without the Celestes, the world wouldn't go 'round. Do you see that?"

"I would offer that is the Justins that make the world go 'round."

"Justins, Celestes, whatever." He sighed. "You don't see it yet, do you? You don't see who you are and what you have to offer. You will, though. When you're ready, you will. One day, you won't be surprised when people are nice to you. Or," he said as the sun dropped below the water line, "when they love you."

She nodded, trying to trust his words.

"Something else to consider," he started, "is that you don't want to miss out on people. If you assume everyone is out to get you, then you're going to shut them down before they have a chance to prove you wrong. So…" He sighed. "I don't want that for you. I see you leaving that behind, so don't stop."

He was right.

For now, she listened to the water hitting the rocks and inhaled the sea air while she nestled into Justin's hold.

Later, when it was totally dark and a chill took over the evening, Justin took her to dinner. Rustic Kitchen, he told her, was his favorite restaurant in the entire city, and that said a lot because San Diego offered excellent dining. She had tuna sashimi with guacamole and grapefruit, a most unusual combination that she decided worked so well, it was almost sensual. And the burrata that Justin had mentioned in one of his first emails: it was bliss, the mozzarella cream unlike anything she had ever tasted. Maybe everything had a sensual quality tonight because of the company.

After, they walked across the street to Chocolat Bistro, where Justin fed her truffles, and then to a flower shop. Together, she and Justin selected lilies, hydrangea, gerbera daisies, and a few roses. She thought it silly for him to buy her flowers when she would be gone soon and not able to enjoy them fully, but he insisted. Celeste watched with interest as the shopkeeper held the flowers up in the air and intricately wove string through the stems to tie the bunch together. Then he wrapped the bouquet in plastic and then brown paper before he presented her with the mammoth bundle.

When they were in the car, she struggled to fasten her seatbelt until Justin lifted the bouquet and set it in the back seat. "I think we got carried away with the flowers," he said laughing.

"Perhaps a bit. But they are very elegant. Thank you. And thank you for dinner and dessert. I feel quite spoiled by this most romantic date."

"You are more than welcome."

Her text alert sounded, and she looked to see a message from Matt. "Oh dear. It seems Matthew's day of martinis and a second book called *The Road to Reality: A Complete Guide to the Laws of the Universe* has gotten the best of him, and he is going to bed."

"I hope he's in better shape tomorrow when you surprise him with his ex-girlfriend."

"Yes. I'd almost forgotten about that because you have

kept me very busy and distracted today. I am looking forward to what I feel sure will be a joyous reunion."

"I like your positive attitude, but don't be disappointed if it doesn't work out."

"I know them, Justin. I know that there is still love between them, and Matthew is not moving on with his life without her. He is stuck, part of him still hoping to reconnect with his one true love. They have not seen each other in two years, and it will take one look between them for whatever silly problems they've created to evaporate."

"If you say so," Justin said skeptically. "So, should I take you back to your hotel? You must be tired. Probably a bit jet lagged, huh?"

"Yes, the hotel, please."

The drive felt eternal, the Saturday night traffic slowing them down, and she was antsy to be alone with Justin.

Finally, they reached the hotel. "You will come in, right?" she asked. "You'll stay? You're staying, right? You can't leave."

Justin smiled. "Easy there. I'm not going anywhere."

"Okay. Good. I… just wanted to make sure."

He had the valet take the car, and they rode the elevator up to her floor in silence. She loved how he looked at her with such affection, the way he didn't take his eyes off of her as they passed floor after floor. They tiptoed into the room, and she was relieved that Matthew's door was closed.

"Not that I condone Matthew's weekend of drinking, but it is working in my favor. I prefer not to parade you past him and into my bedroom, but I would do so if necessary."

"Aren't you all brazen this weekend?" he said with a bit

of pride. "Flying on airplanes, marching your boyfriend around... I like it."

"Justin, I have done some thinking today," she said, leading him into her room and gently shutting the door.

"Okay...." Justin sounded nervous now.

"I haven't been carried away and made any giant decisions. Don't worry. But I do want to talk to you."

He nodded and followed her as she crawled onto the bed. He lay on his side and smiled. "Okay. Let's talk."

"I think it is important to have open communication. About our physical relationship."

"I agree." He put his hand to hers, intertwining their fingers.

"You talked this morning about steps. And firsts. And I assume that you've had many more firsts in this area than I have."

Justin took a deep breath and looked a bit embarrassed. "You want to know if I've had sex."

She nodded. "You are about to turn twenty years old. It would certainly not be unusual. I just think it's a good idea for me to know."

"I understand that. So... yes," he said, somewhat reluctantly. "I have. I had a girlfriend for a little while last year, and to be truthful, I think I felt pressured. Not really from her, but just... I don't know." He thought for a minute. "Looking back, I don't think it was the right choice for me. I mean, it's not like I didn't want to at all' I'm not going to lie," he said laughing. "But I think that I should have waited. I wasn't really in love. It didn't mean what it should have. But I did let myself feel the pressure to do what it seemed like everyone else was doing. I'm not particularly proud of saying that, but it's true."

"Justin, I am not judging you."

"No, I know you aren't. It's one of the things I love about you. That you don't judge people. Ever, really. Although, as I said, I do think you assume that people won't like you. But that's different. You're still kind to everyone. Always. You're a very good listener, and you're very understanding. Look, I felt pressured, and it's not the end of the world for me. Yeah, I'd probably make a different choice if I were in the same situation now, but I'm not going to drown in what I can't change. I just want to be sure that you don't ever, not for one split second, feel as though you need to do something with me that you don't want to. Fully."

"You don't need to worry about that." She reached a hand up and lowered his mouth to hers. They kissed gently.

"It's just, I would feel awful if—"

"Justin," she cut him off with a smile. "Do. Not. Worry. I told you that I have done some thinking. So you are clear, this is not about your wanting things and my simply agreeing or not agreeing. I want things too. I want intimacy and touch too." She paused. "I was going for your method of directness, and now I am a bit uncomfortable."

"I think these conversations are naturally awkward, but I think we still need to have them."

"Yes," she agreed.

"But maybe we can make it easier." He smiled and gave her a deeper kiss, his tongue moving into her mouth just enough to tease her. "So, kissing is obviously something you want. That stays on the approved list."

"It does."

"So what else makes up the list?"

"This morning... you kissed my neck... a spot that felt very good."

"Ahhh," he whispered. "This spot right here?" He lowered his mouth and—ever so slowly—brushed his lips down her neck, landing just below her ear.

"Yes, and back just a little," she said.

She felt his tongue touch her skin, moving where she wanted, and she instinctively moved her hands until she was stroking his arms. "Yes," she said a bit breathlessly. "Exactly there." She turned into him, enjoying the way he took his time with her, not rushing, not making her feel in any way as though this was not something he would willingly and happily do all night.

"And I might very well like it," she finally continued, "if your hands moved here..." With her hand over his, she moved to her waist, slipping under her shirt and across her stomach. "And higher."

"That's what you want?" he whispered.

"Yes," she whispered back. "And another thing."

"Tell me."

"I don't think you need your shirt on. Nor will I need anything on my top. I want... to feel you against me. That closeness. The shape of you and the shape of me."

"And the shape of us."

"Yes."

Justin moved so that he could ease her shirt up a hint and kiss her stomach. "So waist up?" he confirmed. "You're good with that?"

"I'm not just good with it. That sounds as though I've had to agree. It's what I choose."

"I'm kind of a fan of that choice." He lifted up on his arms so that his body was above her and they were eye to eye. "And you'll tell me if you change your mind."

Celeste glided her palms under the back of his shirt, touching his lower back as she had this morning. She nodded, rather distracted by the feel of his body under her hands. The curve of his spine, the muscles that were taut, the heat that radiated from his skin.

"Celeste?"

"Yes. I'll tell you." She was barely conscious of her own voice.

"Because I might take off my shirt and you might be horrified by the giant Winnie the Pooh tattoo that covers my chest. Honey pot and all."

She laughed. "I would have guessed Tigger, but I will not be horrified."

"And the *Hot Rod Mama* tattoo on my back."

"I certainly don't believe that."

Justin dipped down and pressed his mouth to hers, his lips soft but assured. "I think you should check."

"I think," she said happily as she began to lift his shirt, "that I should indeed check."

"This is getting significantly less awkward," he said with a grin. "See? I knew we could do it. Just a little honesty goes a long way, and now I feel closer to you. Don't you feel closer to me? And please do not be disappointed when you learn the truth about the tattoo thing, okay? You've been reading all those books with alpha males and their full-body tattoos, so I'm probably going to be a huge disappointment when you don't find anything. If you really want, I could get one, although I have a low threshold for pain, so there may be crying involv—"

"Justin?" She giggled and touched a finger to his lips. And as she looked into his eyes, she raised the shirt more until he lifted an arm to help get it over his head. Celeste lowered her gaze and took in his bare upper body. Involuntarily, she took a rather ragged breath. "Stop. Talking."

And so he did.

## CHAPTER 23
# SHIFTING GEARS

CELESTE GLARED AT Matt. "That is what you're wearing to lunch?"

"What?"

"*Don't Stop Me From Having a Helvetica Good Time*? Do you not have one single shirt uncluttered with a saying of some sort?"

"We're just going to a casual restaurant. Unless the dress code requires a three-piece suit—and in that case I'm probably not going—then I see no problem with what I'm wearing."

Celeste sighed. Well, Julie would probably find it endearing, but there was part of her that hoped he might wear something more stylish and handsome. She walked over to him and pulled at his wrinkled sleeve and smoothed down bunching fabric that hung over his jeans. "Have you completed your alcohol-consumption spree? I should hope so. You look puffy. You are probably dehydrated and need water. It is too bad you chose to continue sullying your body with cocktails because you got some color yesterday during your poolside respite, and you might look a bit more dashing were it not for the—"

"What's going on?" He frowned. "You're acting more than a little high-strung today."

"What? Nothing! Nothing is out of the norm! Right, Justin? Tell him. Everything is as it always is, only with the addition of sunshine and lovely breezes. No one is behaving in any manner that could conceivably be deemed high-strung!" She did, however, notice that she was talking too loudly. And too quickly. She would have to calm down.

Matt put his hands on his hips and looked to Justin.

"I'm starving. Let's go eat!" He shook his keys with more enthusiasm than necessary. "Should I drive or are we taking the 'vette?"

"Two cars! I prefer that we take two cars!" Celeste said immediately. "Er, perhaps you and I might like to go out on our own after lunch."

"Okay, okay, Miss Thing. Jeez." Matt held up his hands. "We'll take two cars."

Island Prime was known as the "restaurant on stilts" because it hung out over the water, so Justin had chosen well. Celeste liked the place from the minute she saw it. They parked the cars, and Celeste made a quick visual sweep of the lot. She didn't see Julie yet. The doors to the restaurant were nearly twice Celeste's height, and she had to use two hands to pull one open.

"This is a blatant case of form over function," she announced. "One does not need to enter an establishment via gargantuan doorways, although I do have an appreciation for the architectural style. Justin, do you have commentary to add about these big doors." She grunted and slid though the opening

"They are... very large... Um... grandiose?" Justin placed a hand on the door panel and swung it fully open for Matt.

When they were seated on the outdoor deck and looking at menus, Celeste could feel her nervousness growing. The words on the page in front of her were blurry and meaning-less. The only thing that had meaning now was Julie's arrival. She was torn between chattering on about the blissful location and alternately not saying anything at all.

"With an ocean front location such as this, I imagine this establishment must prioritize the quality of the seafood served, since one could not possibly expect anything less than out-standing when dining under the sunshine, inhaling the salt air, and marveling at the boats that pass by. Oh, look! One of the menu selections is entitled *A Study in Lobster*. How charming." There. She had made the words come into focus. "Although one must question the validity of whether a dish can truly be considered a *study*, unless of course it comes served with an es-say on lobster culture or something else equally ridiculous—"

Matt slammed down his menu. "Okay, that's enough. What the hell is going on?"

Celeste looked up at him. It did not feel nice to trick Matthew, as she was never deceitful. Well, until this weekend...

Justin calmly took a drink of water. "Celeste, I think you need to tell him."

"Tell me what?"

"Matt." Julie was there. Standing right at the end of the table. Her voice was already broken, pain already on her face. She was as beautiful as ever, though, Celeste thought. Her dark brown hair now had highlights and was much longer than Celeste had ever seen it, but she looked quintessentially Julie in a long, lightly patterned sundress.

The shock on Matt's face was all too evident, his emotion palpable.

Celeste jumped from her seat and rushed to Julie's side, throwing her arms around her old friend. "How I have missed you. Terrifically delighted that you were willing to make the drive to see us. This is Justin, whom you have heard much about."

"Hi, Justin. It's very nice to meet you," Julie managed to say from under Celeste's tight hug.

"You, too." Celeste could feel Justin and Julie shake hands. "Celeste, you might want to let your friend breathe."

"Oh. Of course. Terribly sorry." Celeste stepped back.

Julie kept her back to Matt and put her hands on Celeste's arms. "You look wonderful. I can't believe how long it's been."

"You, as well, look wonderful. And…" Celeste gestured grandly, "Matt is here. Whom you remember, I'm sure. I mean, of course you remember him."

Julie pursed her lips together and gave Celeste a look. "I assumed that you would be here with Roger or Erin."

"I do not know why you would have thought that," Celeste said with exaggerated confusion. "I did not mention them, did I?"

"No," Julie said pointedly. "No, you did not."

Celeste spun Julie around and shoved her toward the empty seat beside Matt. Julie slowly made her way over and sat down. Neither Matt nor Julie looked at the other. In fact, neither looked even slightly happy.

Matt's expression was bleak, and he kept his head down. "Celeste... what have you done?" She could barely hear him.

She looked to Justin, dumbfounded. He shook his head slightly, clearly at a loss for how to handle this.

"I can't... I can't do this..." Julie's emotions were raw as she held back tears. "I love you, Celeste, but you had no right."

"I just... I just thought it would be helpful for you two to see each other." Celeste's heart began to race as she looked back and forth between them. She would have to get them to break through whatever wall was here. "I know—I know with great conviction, that you still love each other. There. That is the simple truth. It is solely stubbornness or a similar characteristic that is standing in the way of what we all know to be right."

But then Julie had her hands over her face, unable to hold back. Matt continued to look down. He lifted a hand and just barely touched Julie's shoulder before she brushed him off quickly, finally looking directly at him. Her eyes held fury and hurt. "You broke my heart, Matt. You broke my heart. I don't want to see you. I can't."

Every word cut through Celeste. She could only imagine what it was doing to Matt. She was frozen in her chair. This was not supposed to happen. Justin was pulling on her hand, eventually putting an arm around her to lift up. He guided them to a table across the deck and out of Matt and Julie's view. "Let's give them a little space, okay?"

She sat down dumbly at the new table, Justin now across from her and holding her hand in his.

"Here have some water." He pushed a glass in her direction.

She shook her head and looked out over the bay. She would wait. Matt and Julie would take a few minutes to get over whatever hurdle had been keeping them apart, and then they would ease back into their love. They could do this. Neither had left the table, and therefore they must be talking things through. So she would hold Justin's hand and wait.

She counted boats that went by. She watched the single cloud as it traversed slowly through the bright blue sky. And she counted more boats.

There were many unfortunate things about this moment, not the least of which was that the deck was nearly empty of other customers. Julie and Matt's conversation could now be heard all too clearly. Justin squeezed her hand as Julie's voice drifted their way.

"You wouldn't leave. You wouldn't choose me. I asked you to come to California, and you said no."

"You know why," Matt said. "Julie, you know I couldn't leave."

Julie said nothing for a minute. "I know. I know that she needed you. But maybe you didn't trust her enough to do what she needed to do. She's strong."

Celeste turned her head slightly.

"You haven't seen her. You haven't seen how she's been." Matt was louder now. "It's only been since she met Justin that she's come alive and pulled things together. She'd been lying to us about having friends at school and who knows what else. That's only changed recently. She depended on me, maybe still does, and I'm not about to abandon her. If she accepts at

Barton, then Justin will be there for her. It'd be different. She would be safe. But it wasn't fair that you asked me to leave her two years ago. You know better than anyone what it means to feel protective of her."

"I do. I know. I just… I just wanted to be with you."

"You left me, Julie. *You* left *me*!"

Justin tried to get Celeste to look at him, but she refused. "You applied to Barton? And got in? Why… why didn't you tell me?"

How was she going to explain this? "Matt sent in the application. I just found out," she said numbly.

"You told me to go," Julie was now saying. "You told me to take the job!" The hurt in her voice was too much. "You said that we would be okay, Matt. You promised."

"I know. I thought we would." Matt's tone softened, apologetic and sad. "I don't know what happened. You couldn't forgive me for staying."

"It's not like Celeste was still carrying Flat Finn everywhere."

Celeste stopped breathing; her body went rigid.

Justin tugged her hand. "What is she talking about? Your brother Finn?"

It was all falling apart now, Celeste knew. There would be no recovery from this.

"She put your cardboard brother in the attic, remember?" Julie continued angrily. "Years ago. It was over. She didn't need him propped outside her bedroom door anymore; she didn't to talk to him to feel stable, and she didn't rely on Flat Finn to get her through the most basic parts of daily life. I think she would have been okay without you."

"You just said it. You *think*. I couldn't take that risk. What if I'd run off to Los Angeles to be with you, and she lost everything? Don't you dare blame her."

"I'm not blaming her, but what was I supposed to do? Not take the job?"

"I didn't say that," Matt said. "I understand. You had to take care of yourself, and I had to take care of Celeste."

"It's the same thing all over again, back where we were before we were even together. You keep sacrificing yourself for her, and then you have nothing left to give. "

"I'll do it for the rest of my life if I have to." Matt was angry now.

"That's not fair to her, and it's not fair to you. You *know* this, Matt. You're making her responsible for what happened to us, and maybe you were just too afraid to commit to me. I think that's the real reason. You used her as a crutch because you were scared. And so I left. And then you stopped loving me. We were too far apart. In every sense."

"That's not true. Don't say that."

"I could feel it. And now, I can't forgive you."

Celeste slammed her chair back and rushed to their table.

"I thought you were gone—" Matt started.

"Oh God, Celeste, I'm sorry," Julie begged. "I'm so sorry."

She grabbed the car keys from the table and ran from the deck. Tables, diners, and staff nearly invisible to her as she found her way to the parking lot.

*Fight or flight.*

There was no fight to win here. She couldn't. Flight was her only option. And so she flew.

"Celeste!" Justin was running toward her as she started up the Corvette and slammed it into reverse. There was panic and confusion and shock in his demeanor. It was awful.

She wanted to pretend he didn't exist, to just escape. And so she did. She soared out of the lot and drove. And drove and drove.

Shifting from third gear to fourth felt good, but every stoplight agitated her more. Then she pulled onto a highway. Fifth gear felt better, stronger. She stepped on the gas until she was doing ninety and passing cars that were going too slow for what she needed. The power felt good, the speed freeing. She found the ocean on her left and drove up the coast, changing lanes often, leaving everything behind her. It was a rush, intoxicating, distracting. Driving took her out of herself, and that was needed because she couldn't stand to be who she was now. Maybe not ever.

But she couldn't shake Flat Finn. Of all the things for Justin to know about, there would be no recovering from that one. Humiliation coursed through her entire being. It didn't matter that Flat Finn had been gone for years. The simple fact was that he had indeed been her constant companion for a long time. It was not normal, even though she'd been much younger, and it was not anything that she could explain away. Or even laugh about. Even today—*even today*—she couldn't laugh about him. Because she missed that cardboard representation of Finn; he'd given her strength and an ability to cope that she hadn't been able to muster on her own in the wake of her brother's death.

How truly weak it was, what she had needed then. And how pathetic it was what she needed now, now in this day of ruin.

It was forty minutes before Celeste pulled over onto a beach area. She could breathe again, her thoughts crystallizing.

The slam of the door followed her as she took off her shoes and walked across the hot sand. Her feet were probably burning, but she kept a slow pace, dragging them through the sand until she reached the shoreline. Celeste dropped to her knees, letting the last edge of a wave inch toward her before pulling back. Gone again. Then another one approached, testing what it was like to become part of her, and then leaving. As every one would. And as *everyone* would.

When the sand was bare, she noticed, there was nothing left. No imprint, no pattern, just nothing. As though the wave had never been there.

It was what she would do. It would be as though this year had never happened. It would simply disappear.

But then he was next to her. Justin. And now she would have to make him disappear, too.

He knelt down. "Celeste. You're hard to track down, did you know that? I mean, I like fast driving, but I lost you about ten miles back, so I just followed the coast line and hoped I'd find you. Guess the Corvette was a good choice, because it stands out."

Another wave, another exit as the water ripped away from her.

"I mean, if you'd been driving a Civic or something, it might have been impossible to ever find you. Too many of those around. Are you hungry? We didn't get to eat. You must be starving. I know another really good place to take you. Let's just go. Let's get out of here together. I can leave my car. Or whatever you want?"

She dug her toes into the wet sand, grinding the rough feel into her skin.

"Celeste, please. It's okay." He dropped down all the way now, sitting in front of her in the path of the water. "Why didn't you tell me that you got into Barton? I know you won't go, but you should have told me. Obviously, you'll go to Harvard or any of the other amazing schools you got into, but you still should have told me."

In order for this to end, she would have to speak. So she forced herself.

"There are a lot of things I should have told you, Justin, so that you would have known that I am not someone you are able to save."

# CHAPTER 24
# DREAMS AND TRUTH

"WHAT ARE YOU talking about?" Justin was gentle. More than he should be, given what she was about to say.

"I am not going to dream anymore. I am not going to pretend that I am anything that I am not. That I could never be, not really."

"I don't understand."

"Are you not able to see? Your understanding of me is clouded because you think you have feelings for me."

"I *do* have feelings for you."

"They are not real. They are not grounded in truth."

"I know who you are, and I adore you."

"No. I am too damaged. My eccentricities too insurmountable. I have been trying to behave as though I can attain a normal existence and have normal experiences and interactions. It is a charade. My past is indicative of who I am and who I will always be. You perhaps find my character temporarily amusing, interesting even, but you will tire of me, and this will fall apart." She looked at him now. "I do not want this with you. This relationship cannot survive. It cannot survive me."

Justin's face paled and he began shaking his head. "No. No, don't say that. No, no. You can't do this."

"Yes. I can. I have to. In my heart, I am weak. You have now heard about Flat Finn and about how I carried around a replica of my dead brother for years. That is bizarre. And because of my weakness and fragility, I am responsible for the destruction of Matt and Julie's relationship. The destruction of my brother, really. Matthew knew that I would disintegrate without him then and now, and he is likely correct. I will not let you sacrifice yourself for me the way that he did. And it will happen."

"What? What are you talking about?" He was panicking now, his voice shaking and his breathing irregular. "No, no. I am not sacrificing anything for you. And you are *not* weak. Do you not see that? You don't, do you." He stood up and paced in front of her. "You have more strength than anyone should. All those years that you were alone? That you isolated yourself? You didn't have friends, you didn't have anyone to be close with, to talk with, or... or play with. You were alone. That must have been painful, and yet you rallied anyway and kept going. It takes strength to stay apart from the crowd. You are brave, Celeste. So what if you found a way to deal with your brother's death that was a little unusual? Good for you. It was a smart thing. I don't care what you had to do to get through something so painful."

Celeste was shut down now, speaking in a monotone.

"You will never be able to look at me the same way now that you know. About Flat Finn, about how I have taken everything from Matthew. I am a drain on those around me. That will not change. I am weird. As I said yesterday, I am certainly diagnosable, and that makes for something too drastic for you to have to deal with." She inhaled the truth, choking on the conviction of what she was saying. "Do you see how quickly I come undone? With a snap of the fingers. I had a bout of temporary sanity. It was a joke. An illusion. Now I understand the nature of my character and the expansive impact that I have on others."

Justin put both hands in his hair and continued pacing, talking quickly, desperately. "You don't get to tell me what I want and don't want. God, we're all probably diagnosable. Look at the world around you. Look! We all have *something*. All of us. Every single person in this world has a quirk. The guy in my lit class who can't stop sniffing every time the professor mentions the words *thematic representations*? Or... or... or the way my friend Trent gets a new body piercing every time he gets an electric shock on the job? That's weird, right? But it's cool. It makes him who he is. I mean, I wouldn't do it because that's not me, but it's him. And... and... I never understood the whole piercing thing, myself. Seems a rather extreme and painful way to express yourself, but—"

"Justin, stop," she said quietly. He was coming apart. Another thing that was her fault.

"No, no, I will not stop. And how about me? What about how you are with me? What about the snowy owl? Remember that first night that we went out, and I spilled and tripped and babbled and made a huge disaster out of everything? You didn't care, right? Tell me you didn't care? I know you didn't. That's how you are. And I don't care about any of this stuff about you that you think is not okay. You have to stop hating yourself. And stop assuming that everyone else will hate you. Please, you have to. Look how much you've done this year? You have Dallas and other new friends. You were great at Barton yesterday. And you have me. Sometimes you need someone else to believe in you, to carry you, until you can do that yourself. Let me carry you. You're almost there. Damn it, Celeste, you're almost there. God, please, you have me, and I want you." He stopped walking back and forth and put both of his hands over his heart. "I want you so much."

She looked at him, utterly exhausted now. "You only think you do. It will pass. I will not allow you to be further dragged into my dysfunction. You know how to work with whatever you imagine are your challenges. I do not. I refuse to be a burden on you or anyone anymore. We are over."

"Stop it! Matt made choices and those are his responsibility. Don't blame him for loving you." Justin's eyes were red now. "And don't blame me either. What about this weekend? What about everything that has gone on between us?" He got on his knees in front of her and took her by the wrists, pressing her hands against his chest. "I love you. Do you feel that? I love you, Celeste."

"You are mistaken. You cannot possibly. And even if part of you thinks you do, I will not let you."

"Listen to me!" He pressed her hands more tightly to him. "Don't doubt my love. Don't doubt yourself. You don't get to do that. Remember we talked about the fight? You're in it again. So win. Fight for yourself, fight for me, for us. For…

for whatever you need to. But win this battle and win the war. This is not the time to give up; it's not. God, you've worked so hard this year; you get more and more comfortable every time I talk to you, so don't stop now. Everything is lined up in your favor, so I'm telling you, win the war. Finish it. You need this to be over." He tried so hard to smile. "You're a pacifist, anyway. You are. Let the past rest. Let there be a future. Find the peace."

Celeste stood up, her emotions dulled. She was unable to cry, unable to feel. It was time for her to go. She took the car keys from her pocket.

He put both hands on her legs, trying to stop her. "You are more capable of being loved than you understand. And— Celeste, this is important—you nurture and love and protect more than anyone I have known. Or could know. Don't take that away from me. From us."

She had to gasp for air. It took enormous effort to get these words out. "My future is to be alone. No one will get hurt that way. You believe that differences make the world go around? You are wrong. People die, people are cruel, people leave, people get hurt. They damage each other, reject each other, abandon each other, they break up, and they spiral downward. *Those* are the things that make my world go around. There is no allowance in my life for happiness despite my efforts. It is fleeting only and cannot hold. I have failed, and now I surrender. I cannot tolerate having anything to lose. So I choose to let you go before you are pulled into my darkness and lost. Because you, you of all people, Justin, deserve light."

Now she was drained. Now there was nothing left. She turned from him and walked away, leaving him on his knees in the wet sand. Looking back was not an option. Celeste could not bear to see what she had done to him. It was better to do this today than months from now, when their hearts were further entwined, when the pain would be even greater.

When Matt returned to the hotel, they would drive to the airport and take the first flight back to Boston. Life would resume as Celeste had known it—life before she'd had hope, before Justin, and before that enticing taste of joy had broken through her walls.

Only this time, she would not have Matt, because she would have to let him go, too. It was the only way that she could free her brother.

## CHAPTER 25
# ERASED

**N**OT THAT BOSTON was known for gorgeous weather during March, but this year it felt particularly brutal. In more ways than one.

At least Justin's endless voice mails, texts, and emails had subsided. Blocking his number had been nearly crippling, but she'd done it, and she never replied to any of his emails. She hadn't even read them. It was the only way to erase him from her life.

Matt was proving more difficult. He had respected her refusal to speak to him for the first few days after their disastrous trip, but he was showing up at the house for dinner more than she liked, pushing her to talk to him. She rebuffed all of his efforts. It was exhausting to behave in anything resembling a friendly manner in front of her parents, but she forced herself each time. She did not want to explain any of this mess to her parents. In fact, he was downstairs right now, having invaded the house under the guise of needing to borrow an iron because he had a job interview this week. No one in the world could have any confidence that he knew how to iron even a napkin, so Erin had taken pity on him and was currently ironing his brand-new dress shirt and pants. Celeste had made herself scarce and was in her room.

As she had done every day since her return from San Diego, she ran through her phone and computer looking for anything left of Justin. She was afraid that she had missed something, and she needed all physical evidence of him out of her life. The emotional evidence was taking work to erase, but she fought every minute to keep emotion at bay. She had a very practical search to do. Granted, it had neared obsessive levels, as she knew that her browser history had been cleared and photographs, emails, and texts deleted. Yet something nagged at her. There was something that she was forgetting.

Her bedroom door swung open. Matt.

She glanced at him for a split second before turning away. "Please leave."

But he strolled into the room and sat down on her bed. "Are you still giving me the silent treatment? That's got to be boring. I mean, passing over compelling discussions with someone of my intellect has to be killing you."

"I asked you to leave."

"Mom says you decided to go to Harvard."

She didn't respond.

"And you're going to live at home? Why would you do that? Don't you want to get out of here?"

"I would very much like for you to get out of here," she said flatly.

"Celeste, come on. Enough."

"Get out."

"I said I was sorry for what happened. Really. You can't just pretend that I'm not your brother."

"I can. I will."

"Look, I give you points for stubbornness. Really I do. You win, okay? Now tell me what to do to get you to knock off this game."

She swiveled slowly in her chair. "You can get the hell out of my room. Now."

He looked so sad. "Celeste…"

She raised her voice. "Get the hell out! Do not come back. Graduate with your degree, go on your interviews, and accept a job far away from me. I am toxic to you!"

"That is not true. I hurt you, and you're mad. I know that. Tell me how to make this up to you. Free burgers from Bartley's for life? Or… or… or I'll only type in Comic Sans for the next year." He held a hand up. "Swear on my life."

"I have no wish for your jokes. None. Stay away from me."

"You can't do this. You can't keep up this act. Pushing everyone away is a huge mistake. Are you even talking to Dallas anymore? Dad just told me that she's been calling the house saying that you're not returning the messages she left on your phone."

"That is not your concern. *I* am not your concern. Not anymore."

The truth was that she was still talking to Dallas, although mostly only in school. Ending that friendship would be more effort than she had now. They would graduate soon enough, and Celeste could slip out of the small social life she'd established. Arousing too much alarm now was impractical. So she smiled at school, she asked lots of questions, and she did everything that she could to keep the focus off of herself. She knew that Dallas wasn't buying it, but Celeste pawned it off as not wanting to talk about her break-up with Justin. It was enough to satisfy Dallas for now.

"You're my sister. You really think I can just stop caring about you?"

She slammed her hands down on the desk. "You will not be encumbered by me any longer! I cannot stand it!" She was panting, and it took a minute to regain control. "You will go and live your life as you were meant to. Without me and without restraint. I will ask you for a final time to vacate my room."

Matt looked at her for a long time, tolerating her steely glare, until he finally stood.

"I'm not giving up on you."

"You should."

"Never," he said as he walked by her, finally leaving her alone.

It was not easy to remain stoic and unaffected. But she did it.

Back to the work at hand.

Celeste walked the perimeter of her room, rooting through items, throwing everything that did not give her an answer into a heap. The floor of her bedroom was becoming progressively more and more covered as she cleared off shelves, the nightstand, her dresser drawers. Some piece of Justin remained, and she had to find it. She opened the door to her closet and sifted through each hanger. Then she searched the floor, hurling shoes behind her. Nothing. There was nothing. And yet, there was something, somewhere. She could feel it in her heart, and that feeling had to be eliminated. Celeste stood on her tiptoes and pulled down a stack of sweaters, hurling each one behind her.

And then she saw it. And remembered. The pink sweater that she'd had on for her date with Justin last December. The one that he had gently pulled over her head when she'd been so distraught, and the one that she'd had on when she walked through his winter wonderland. And when they had been lifted into the air to look down on the Christmas tree.

The Christmas tree. The star.

Celeste took a deep breathe in and out through her nose, shutting her eyes to keep her composure.

The box that had their notes in it. That was still out there in the world. And she needed to get that back so that it, too, could be destroyed.

Calmly she walked through the mess in her room, did a quick search for a phone number, and sat down in her big chair. She dialed the number.

"Good afternoon, Eastern Communications. In order to better assist you, may I have your account number, please?"

"Hello," she said brightly. "I am not calling about my account. I am endeavoring to contact an employee of yours. His name is Trent, and much to my dismay, I cannot provide you with his last name. Would you be able to be of assistance?"

"Sorry, ma'am, I am only in charge of account services. May I have your account number?"

"I do not have an account number. I have a need to locate one of your fellow employees."

"I can't help you with that, ma'am. Perhaps you'd like to upgrade your service to one of our new bundle packages? May I have your account number?"

Celeste hung up and redialed, reaching a different person.

"Good afternoon, Eastern Communications. In order to better assist you, may I have your account number, please?"

"Hello. I am not calling about my account. I am endeavoring to contact an employee of yours. His name is Trent..."

And so it continued. Until finally she had a phone number.

Two hours later, she was in the car and heading to Dedham.

The Christmas tree lot was, of course, empty. Deserted, covered in muddy slush, and dismal, it looked nothing like it had the last time that she'd been here.

That made the ache worse.

Celeste stopped herself. She would not go back to that night, to that hope. She slammed the car into a parking spot and began the walk. There were no lights this time, no halo cast over her, no boy there romancing her and easing his way into her heart. She was grateful for that, because she had no room for those memories. She couldn't. There were puddles, there was gray sky that broke through the evergreen arch, and there was emptiness. Those, those she had room for.

When she reached the clearing, she immediately steered herself to the driveway without looking up at the tree. The rumble of the truck was relaxing. It meant this would soon be over.

Trent pulled his phone company truck up next to her. "I was certainly surprised to hear from you," he said with a smile.

"Lordy, you must be freezing! No coat? No hat? It's goddamn sleeting like crazy out there."

He was right. Celeste hadn't noticed her lack of winter attire until Trent pointed it out. It was only now that she realized that her thin shoes and socks were drenched with ice water. No matter. She barely felt anything.

"I am fine," she said. "You also are not sporting appropriate clothing." She nodded in his direction. "You have on only a light shirt."

He winked. "So I guess we're both tough mother—" He winced. "Well, you know what I mean. But we are both tough, and I'll leave it at that."

He could not be more wrong. Only one of them was tough.

"So how is Justin? What's going on with that boy?" he asked. "I haven't heard from him in weeks, and he's not calling me back."

He might as well have ripped a knife through her chest. Of course he would mention Justin. It was incredibly stupid of her not to have considered this. And now she had no response for him. Celeste looked up at Trent. "Would you... would you..." She swallowed hard. "Would you be so kind as to help me retrieve something from the top of that tree? It would be most appreciated, as I surely cannot climb or otherwise rise to such heights, but it is of great necessity that I obtain an item left there." She could hear the crying start, the choking, but she could not stop it. "It is with great urgency... I simply had no one else to whom I could extend the request..." She wiped her eyes. "I am very sorry for putting you out, as I imagine that this weather is causing telephone wire damage, and your services must be needed elsewhere."

"Hey, hey, easy there, little love." Trent frowned, the confusion on his face clear. "I'll help you. You wait here, okay? I'll get you what you need." He put the car in gear. "Tell me what I'm looking for."

"Thank you. Thank you." Celeste caught her breath and turned to point at the upper branches of the tree. Justin's tree. The lights were gone, as was the star. With every ounce of her being, she needed the box to be there. "In the top branches, there should be a small plastic container."

He nodded. "Hold tight. I gotcha."

Trent drove forward and pulled the truck up next to the tree and lowered the cherry picker. Nimbly, he stepped into the bucket and steered the crane to raise him to the top. It was with great anxiety that she watched him lean over the side, his hand disappearing among the branches. It felt like an eternity, but eventually he held a hand in her direction and waved his arm. He had found their notes. The last piece.

She felt relief. She felt devastation.

She felt nothing, and she felt everything.

Trent lowered the bucket back to the bed of the truck and ducked back into the cab, then circled the truck back to her. He held out the box, but kept his hand on it when she tried to take it from him. "You gonna be okay?"

Celeste met his eyes. She didn't know what to say.

"I've known Justin for years," he said.

She nodded. "Yes."

"He's my best friend. Like a brother. I know what you mean to him."

She froze. "Do not tell him about this. I beg you. It will make it worse. I know that."

"And I know that it's not over until it's really, *unforgivably* over." He let go of the box and faced forward. "Make sure it's unforgivably over, or you're going to regret it."

## CHAPTER 26
# HINGES

THE BOX WITH their Christmas notes sat on her nightstand for a week. Celeste was unable to destroy it as planned. It would make sense to, and it would finalize everything. But it sat beside her bed. She lay on her side with her head on the pillow and stared at it. She would not open it; she would not read what he had written. She would not.

Her room was back to its overly organized state. She had spent the morning cleaning and doing laundry, and she could still smell the bleach on her comforter. Her parents had asked her to join them on a day trip to Cape Cod, but the last thing she felt like doing was going antiquing or eating fried fish. Or pretending to be happy. Or doing anything, really.

She could do nothing, feel nothing, and think nothing. She might as well be dead. This had to end sometime. If she waited it out, this would end. The peace that she reflected on the outside would seep into her soul, and she would feel it. That's what she'd thought anyway, but it had been a month now, a full month, and her despondence held strong. She needed help, but there was no one to help her. No respite, no comfort.

Before, in her darkest days after Finn's death, when she couldn't accept all that Matt tried to do for her, there had been Flat Finn. His arrival at the house immediately turned things around. Not that she had ever believed he was actually her brother. Her thinking had never been *that* twisted. But it had been as a young child is with a beloved blanket or stuffed animal. A transitional object one uses and imbues with the feeling of a relationship. One can feel loved and supported by unconventional means.

Celeste knew what she had to do.

She rose from bed and left her room, walking to the door to the attic. The light flickered when she turned it on, but did not go out. Confidently, she made her way up the creaky stairs and scanned the dusty room. Tucked in the messenger bag that Julie had given her, he was right where she'd left him so many years ago behind a hope chest. Rather amusing placement, she noted to herself. The bag was dusty, but she wiped it with her hand, hung the strap over her shoulder and marched back to her room. And then, with exceptional care, she slid Flat Finn from the bag and unfolded the cardboard cutout. She pulled out the flaps on the back and set him standing tall in the center of her room. Some of the photo paper had wrinkled a bit, but she was pleased to see that essentially he was in good shape. This was a positive sign.

Celeste backed up and sat cross-legged on the floor in front of him. The gold hinges that Julie helped her affix were all there, put on so that this life-size replica could be folded and tucked away when Celeste needed him to be less conspicuous and more portable. For the first time in weeks, she smiled. The familiarity of having Flat Finn stand guard in her room was overwhelming. "We are back together, my friend. Things are just as they are supposed to be."

She stared at Flat Finn and waited. This would work. *He* would work. Going back to what had helped in the past was quite logical. If only she'd thought of this sooner. No matter. At least she'd thought of it now.

So she sat, and stared, and breathed in the musty attic smell that rose off of Flat Finn and the bag. She sat for an hour. Then two. Then she decided that perhaps there was too much pressure this way and engaging in normal activity would help. It was a bit difficult to determine what was normal activity, though, since in recent days it had meant laying catatonic on the bed. What did she used to do? Celeste flinched. She was asking herself what she used to do before her life imploded.

Read. She could curl up in her chair and read. She pulled a book from her shelf and sat down by the window. Four chapters later, and barely comprehending a word of what she was reading, she glanced at Flat Finn. He was failing to console her. "Come on; you can do this," she encouraged him. "Work. Like you used to."

The sky outside began to darken, and Celeste's anxiety grew. "I am asking you to help me," she said forcefully. "Now!"

She felt as lifeless as he was.

A sense of fury rushed through her. She stood and hurled the heavy book at Flat Finn, knocking him to the floor. "This is unfair of you! This is a betrayal! You are failing me when I need you the most! This is a betrayal of the highest order!"

Enraged, Celeste rushed to her desk and searched through the three drawers until she located what she needed. Now, with a box cutter in hand, she moved so that she was on all fours on top of the cardboard brother.

And she started cutting, and cutting, and cutting.

With each shard she sliced, her heart pounded more, and the shaking in her hands intensified. Over and over, she slid the blade across Flat Finn, splicing his arms and legs into strands. A scream poured from her gut as she slashed his face, the face of the brother who had left and taken with him his vivacious, bold spirit. Whose death had traumatized the entire family. She wiped a hand across the only part of the photo not in fragments, smearing her tears across the red of Finn's shirt. "You are a piece of shit! You are a piece of shit! I hate you!" she yelled, unleashing every bit of her pain. "I hate you!"

"Celeste." Matt was there, kneeling on the floor behind her. "Oh my God."

Delicately, he took the box cutter from her hand and took her in his arms.

She sobbed, unable to stop. "He is broken, Matthew. Flat Finn is broken! He is a piece of shit! What am I going to do?"

Matt held her, rocking her back and forth as she cried.

Suddenly, she tensed. "What have I done? No, no, no. What have I done to him? Matthew, we have to fix him. We can fix him." She lunged from Matt's hold and crawled back to her desk drawer, grabbing a box of hinges leftover from Julie's endeavors so long ago. "We can fix him; we can fix him," she said over and over. "Help me, Matty. Please. Fix him for me; fix him for me! You can do this. You can do anything. Oh, please, help." With her hands shaking, she dumped the box onto the mess of cardboard shreds and bits of rug that she'd cut off in her fit.

"I can't, Celeste," Matt said quietly. "I can't fix him, honey."

She whipped her head to face him. "Yes! Yes, we can! You will help me! You will do this for me. I am begging you!" But when she looked down at the floor, she saw there were only five gold hinges. She shook her head, over and over. "No, no... Oh God, no." This couldn't be right. "There are not enough hinges. There are not enough hinges." Then Matt was holding her again, pulling her back into his body, surrounding her. "Why aren't there enough?" She took fistfuls of cardboard shreds in both hands and angrily threw them into the air.

Matt squeezed her. "Stop. Please, stop."

She panted and fought to get free from his hold. Celeste screamed in one final burst of despair. "I have destroyed him, and now there are not enough hinges!"

Her brother, the one who was here and who she knew loved her, dropped his head onto her shoulder. She felt her shirt get wet.

"Matthew," she said, calm now. "Matty, please do not cry."

"I think," he replied with his head still down, "I think we need to make our own hinges now."

She thought. "Yes. I believe you are right."

Together they stayed on the floor of her room, both recovering.

Celeste was drained. "I'm sorry I hurt you. I'm sorry that I wrecked everything for you and Julie."

"You didn't. I wish you hadn't heard what I said in San

Diego. It wasn't you, Celeste, it was me. I'm the one who screwed it all up. I used you as an excuse not to go with Julie to California because... I don't know... because..."

"Because you were afraid it would not last," she finished. "That she couldn't possibly love you as much as you loved her."

"Yeah."

"But you stayed with me to keep me safe."

"There's something wrong with me. It was a horrible thing to put on you. I didn't mean to."

She closed her eyes and listened to her own breathing. "You did a wonderful thing for me, Matty, because you were right. I did need you. Very much." She touched his arm. "I don't know what would have happened to me if you had left, and that's the truth."

"You are much stronger than you think, and you would have found a way to make things work. You always do. Sometimes it's a little... different..." He ran a hand though the Flat Finn remnants. "But you make it work."

She couldn't help but laugh a bit. "So now we need to find hinges for you."

"And for you."

"You first. You do still love Julie, do you not? I was right about that."

Matt sighed. "Yeah. Yeah, I still love Julie. She's moving to London. This summer. It's part of the foreign-study travel program at the college where she works. She's going to be in charge of settling students into campus life, acting as the head rep for the college. I didn't hear the details of it, but it sounds like a big deal. I don't think I got the chance to tell you that because of the whole shunning-your-brother thing."

"I feel terrible about that. About many things. Tell me, Matt, how did your conversation end with her?"

"Oh, I don't know. It didn't really go anywhere but in circles. We left soon after you did."

"I'm sorry."

"I made this mess, not you." Matt blew out a chest full of air. "And it hurts like a bitch."

"I am allowing your use of exceptionally bad language because you and I have faced extraordinary circumstances today, and therefore those sorts of words are appropriate. They capture the strength of our difficulties. And I, too, know that it hurts like that word."

"I know you do. You're not talking to Justin, I gather?"

"You gather correctly." There were tears again, silent this time, and she let them fall. It was nice to finally feel again. She needed that. "Why did you send in the Barton application on my behalf? Was it because you felt that you could pass me off safely into Justin's hands? Then you would be able to move on?"

"What? No, not at all. You have it all wrong. It didn't have anything to do with Justin, actually."

"I am confused."

"I just thought that… you might like it better at a school where the academic pressure was less strong."

"Because you do not have confidence that I could keep up?"

"Again, you have it all wrong. Celeste, we all know that

you could take those schools by storm, but even for you, it would still be a massive amount of work. And I know you well enough to know you just might take that opportunity to do only that. You'd drown in schoolwork, and there would be nothing else. I think that at a place like Barton you could still get a great education, and you'd know how to push the limits and get all you could out of it, but… I don't know how to explain it."

"I think I do. It is your belief that I would then have time for my emotional and social health and development."

"I think you could stand to give yourself a break. Who cares if you graduate from Yale, or Harvard, or Brown, or wherever if your life is missing important pieces? You could have so many more pieces. Do you get what I'm saying?"

"So your intention was not to pawn off your crazy sister on someone else?"

He hugged her and chuckled. "You're not crazy. I mean, you made Flat Finn confetti, but that's okay. Everyone likes confetti."

"That was quite the outburst I had. And rather embarrassing. I will confess, though, that I feel better after doing so. This needed to happen." She surveyed the scene before them." Although now we find ourselves in a rather extraordinary mess."

"Sometimes you have to make a mess."

"And then you clean it up," she said confidently. "You simply clean it up."

"I don't know where to begin."

"We have cleaned up our relationship. That is a significant start. I love you, Matt. You are an extraordinary big brother."

"I love you, too. Just don't ever turn me into confetti."

"I promise." Her body relaxed, and her mind eased a bit. And in that state, as the world came back into focus, an idea dawned on her. A question. She lifted from her slumped position in Matt's arms. Celeste began to brighten, just a touch. "Matthew Watkins," she said with surprise as an understanding began to seep into her soul.

"What? Why are you looking at me like that?"

"You had been saving your money..." she began.

"I am a big ol' cheapskate as you so kindly pointed out during what I remember of our cab ride to the airport."

"No," she said emphatically. "No, you are not. Not when it matters. I know you, and I know what you were squirreling away for." Matt looked decidedly uncomfortable, so she knew she was right. And now she had something to be happy about. "I know what you were saving money for."

"You do, do you?" He pursed his lips, but she could tell that the thought lifted his spirits.

"You have your hinges, don't you? You just have to use them. Or *it*, rather. You have one giant hinge! Matthew!" She was giddy now.

He stared at her. She could see a glint in his eye, but he said, "No. That's insane."

"It's not. It's perfect. It's the perfect hinge. This is stupendously exciting!"

He started and stopped a few times. "No... It's too... I couldn't possibly... Celeste, that's too risky." Then he rocked his head from side to side a few times, mulling it over and then finally letting himself smile. "You think?"

"I do."

Matt looked down, brushed away a bit of Confetti Finn, and then groaned. "I don't know…" Eventually he looked her in the eyes. "I'm scared to death."

"I know."

"And I should do it anyway?"

"Yes, Matt. It's your moment to fight. To win this war. And I will help you."

## CHAPTER 27
# LEVELING UP

THE ANDAZ HOTEL in West Hollywood was suiting Celeste surprisingly well. It was eclectic and historic—so that part easily matched up with who she was—but she even quite liked the rock-and-roll art that hung on the walls. And West Hollywood was undeniably full of characters. Yes, it was showy and she could hardly count the number of spray-tanned bodies that had paraded past her in shocking outfits today, but the truth was that the people were actually quite friendly.

Which was good, because it was giving her the confidence she needed to approach strangers to assist in the plan.

The hotel lounge was buzzing this Friday afternoon, so she had plenty of potential people to target. The ceilings were nice and high, and that helped ease the claustrophobic feeling that her nervousness was bringing on. Celeste took a sip of her ginger ale and then hopped from the bar stool and smoothed down her navy dress. She had to get moving. An hour better be enough time. She picked up the stack of poster board sheets that were leaning against the stool and tossed her hair back. She could do this.

The couple at the corner table looked friendly enough, although Celeste was hesitant to judge based on looks alone. A young man with long dreadlocks and a sleek, stylish suit sat with a woman whose hearty laugh had been echoing through the room for the past ten minutes. So at least one of them was in a jovial mood. Next to them were two Austalian women, and Celeste had been delighting in their accents since she'd first entered the lounge. She would start with this section of the room.

But her phone rang. "Dallas!"

"Hi! How's the plan moving along?"

"I am glad you called. I am zeroing in on my first set of candidates. Do you have words of support?"

"Kick. Ass."

"I do believe you have captured the spirit needed for this endeavor," Celeste said. "Dallas?"

"Yeah?"

"I apologize again for my sour attitude this past month. You have been patient with me, and you stuck by me when most wouldn't have. Thank you."

"We're friends. Friends go through rough stuff, and they come out better friends."

"I like that sentiment very much." Celeste smiled. "Send my greetings to Zeke, and I will report in with the results of today's event."

"Check ya' later, kid. Good luck!"

The poster board sheets were rather awkward to carry, but she did her best to look self-assured. Amusingly ironic, she thought, that she'd just rid herself of one cardboard item only to replace it with this stack. These cardboard pieces were for the future, though, not the past.

Her heels clicked across the wood floor, alerting the hotel guests to her approach. She cleared her throat. "Good afternoon. My apologies for disturbing your evening, but I am in need of cohorts who might wish to join me in a clandestine caper of the most fun sort."

"A caper!" The woman with the laugh clapped her hands together. "I'm intrigued!"

The man elbowed her. "By 'intrigued' she means 'tipsy.'"

"So then perhaps she'll be inclined to help?" Celeste asked with hope.

"What sort of caper?" The brunette Australian asked. "Is it illegal?"

"No, no. Nothing like that," Celeste promised. "It is more of the… fairy tale sort."

Her girlfriend scooted in closer. "Like Rapunzel?"

"There will be height involved, so you could say that."

"Well, grab yourself a seat, and do tell us all about this fairytale caper."

"Oh. Really? Thank you." She glanced out at bustling Sunset Boulevard. Sunset Boulevard! How could one not be inspired to go after one's dreams? It was then, as she looked at the wild chaos of honking cars, flamboyant locals, flashing billboard signs, and nightclubs, that she knew the plan was going to work out. Celeste sat on a bench between the two tables. "I will need to gather more volunteers for this to play out perfectly, but here is the story. It all started many years ago…" She detailed the best parts of what she felt to be a true epic saga, thanked her now-enthusiastic assistants, and with their help, found the necessary additional people.

At precisely two o'clock, she moved to the front lobby and took a seat on one of the leather loveseats—very much a fitting place to wait. She crossed her legs and watched her ankle bounce up and down. The minutes ticked by. Celeste frowned and clapped her hand down on her knee. It took a few deep breaths to calm her nerves.

But then the person she was waiting for appeared. The plan was now fully in motion.

She leapt from the cushion. "Julie! You made it!"

Julie was in red heels and a black sheath dress, looking glamorous with her hair and make-up done and a wide silver bracelet around her wrist. She rushed over and embraced Celeste. "You weren't kidding when you said to get dressed up, were you? Check you out, all glammed up for Los Angeles!"

"And you look stunning, as well. I am so glad you agreed to meet me while I'm here looking at UCLA. After that terrible visit in San Diego, I am pleased to the utmost degree that you are willing to show me around town and allow me to take you dinner."

Julie squeezed her hard. "I'm so sorry about that day, Celeste. I feel just awful. About so much." She sat down and patted the spot next to her. "Tell me how the college trip is going. Where are Roger and Erin?"

"Oh, my parents wanted to give us a night alone. You

know, just us girls!" Celeste sang out too loudly. "You and me, hitting the town,such as it may be!"

"Well, okay, then…" Julie said with a somewhat worried look on her face. "Should we get going? Where are we eating? I don't know why you didn't let me make reservations. I live here after all, silly."

"I just had a particular spot in mind, and it was fun for me to browse online through all that this city has to offer. Did you know about something called Yelp? Quite useful, that site."

She laughed. "I do know about Yelp."

"Do they have Yelp for London?" Celeste asked pointedly.

"Ah. You heard."

"I think it is wonderful for you."

Julie paused. "Matt told you."

"Matt told me a lot of things. Anyhow… I would very much like to show you my room here at the quirky and unique Andaz before we depart. Shall we?"

"Oh. I guess so." Julie followed Celeste out of the lobby, past the front doors, and to the area in front of the elevators.

Celeste hit the button and looked at the floor numbers as they lit up, as the elevator came to the lobby. She stared straight ahead. "Elevators are always so interesting, are they not?"

"I'm sorry, what?"

"One never knows who one might encounter, what wild adventures might happen."

Julie bit her lip and looked down, pretending to examine her shoes.

"Huh." Celeste touched a hand to her cheek. "I do believe

that you and Matt had a rather unusual elevator experience, did you not? When you were trapped in a broken one and having a bit of a panic attack. He was pretending to be Finn, for whom you had feelings, and I do believe there was a rather titillating message exchange."

"Oh God, Celeste. He told you about that?"

"Yes. I gather a thinly veiled skydiving metaphor was used to in an effort to conceal an intense romantic and sexual attraction?"

"Celeste!" But Julie could not help laughing as she pushed the elevator button again. "Come on, come on...."

"How does one begin a conversation like that? Just out of curiosity."

"Technically, it was two messaging sessions. One then, one a few months later." Her face sobered a bit now. "But I don't know how it started... I don't remember. It was ages ago. It doesn't matter."

"You must remember something," Celeste prompted softly. "A back-and-forth series of progressively heated prose, the outpouring and confessing of love? Those cannot be easily lost, no matter when they took place."

Julie allowed the hint of a smile to touch her lips. "I was scared. In the elevator, I was scared. Matt tried to reassure me. Distract me. Make me feel safe."

"And did he?"

"Yes. He asked... " Julie took a breath and then her eyes focused from the memory. "He asked if I'd forgotten that he was a superhero."

"How fascinating. Well, that situation is all dead and

buried now, isn't it? And lucky for you, you won't have to see Matthew *ever* again. I know how you are thoroughly finished with all of that nonsense. Delightful! Our elevator has arrived." Celeste gestured for Julie to go ahead and then followed. Celeste swiped her room key to activate the elevator and then punched a bunch of floor level buttons. "There. Look at all those pretty lights. Like a Christmas tree."

"What the hell, Celeste? Why are we stopping on so many floors?"

"Because this is a wonderful hotel, and we must appreciate what it is that various floors have to offer."

Julie was sullen as they rode to the third floor. "You know, I never said that I couldn't stand ever to see Matt again," she said without hiding her irritation.

"Whatever. Cool beans and all." When the doors opened, she pushed the button to hold them there.

Julie started to step off the elevator, but stopped sharply when she was blocked by the brunette Australian girl who stood in front of her on the landing. In her hands she held up one of the cardboard poster signs that Celeste had given her.

It took Julie a moment. Then she stepped back, wobbly on her feet, catching her balance on the rail. She was visibly shaking.

"Read it," Celeste encouraged. "Read aloud what the sign says."

The shock poured from Julie's entire being. She looked at Celeste with such confusion and wonder that Celeste had to nod and again tell her to read it.

"It says," Julie started. But she had to stop and close her

eyes for a moment before she continued. Even then, her voice broke. "It says, *Have you forgotten that I am a superhero?*"

Celeste nodded to her sign holder and then pushed the button to close the doors.

"What is happening?" Julie whispered more to herself, it seemed, than to Celeste.

They rode to the next floor. And when the doors parted, another helper was there with a sign. This time the man with the dreadlocks, and enthusiasm for his part in this had him struggling to stay still. Celeste widened her eyes at him, and he settled down.

Julie read the words printed on the poster board. "*Tell me that you trust me.*" They rode to another floor, and Julie reached a hand out to Celeste for support.

Celeste could barely take her eyes from her friend, but she had to focus on her role as director of this show.

The doors opened again, and Celeste held her finger on the open button.

Now Julie's eyes were wet as she read another quote from the messaging session that may have left her head, but never her heart. "*As much as you're terrified right now, you're also starting to feel the rush. The thrill from being on the brink.*"

Another floor, another sign. "*I want to feel like this forever, lost in this experience.*"

Julie was now leaning against the back wall of the elevator and holding Celeste's hand so tightly that, were it not for a good cause, Celeste might have shaken her off.

And the next floor. "*I want to drift together.*"

On the next floor, Julie laughed through her shock. "*I want to give you the slow version. The hot version.*"

They were lifted higher. The next floor couldn't come fast enough for either of them now. Julie read the sign held out for her. "*Right now, only one thing scares me. That you'll get up and walk away from me.*" Julie was shaking her head as she made Celeste look at her. "No, I won't. I couldn't. Oh God, where is he? Where is he?"

Celeste wiped Julie's wet cheeks. "Soon."

The hum of the elevator echoed around them as they rode to yet another floor. "*I think about you all the time, and I can't get you out of my head.*"

They were getting closer to the top. "*Julie, right now, today at this hotel, I am asking you to ignore everything you think you know and listen only to your heart, without doubting anything.*" Julie's hands were over her face as she shook, the full impact of what was happening hitting her now.

"You have to look up," Celeste instructed. "Do not cry so much that you cannot read. You are going to want to pay particular attention to this next one."

The doors parted and Julie let out a beautiful sob. "*Will you marry me?*"

Celeste was in awe. How could she not be? She was in the middle of life–changing bravery. Julie leaned into her, and Celeste put an arm around the friend who had once saved her. It felt remarkable to finally be able to repay—even if just a bit—what Julie had done.

And then—at long last and many years overdue—the final floor.

The elevator doors slide apart. And Julie nearly collapsed.

Matt, in a full suit and tie, was down on one knee. And in one hand he held a ring.

"Julie." He radiated relief. And love. "You... You stayed through every floor."

"Of course I did," she said through tears. She flew forward, and he stood, catching her in his arms. Matt held her, his body trembling because he was back with the person he belonged to and who belonged to him.

Now, through her tears, Julie reflected back more words that Matt had written to her. "And then you kiss me. Matt, then you kiss me, and make me feel everything that you feel."

So he did.

Celeste slipped out from the elevator and moved off to the side, watching from the edge of the waiting area. She didn't want to miss a moment. With her hands clasped with excitement, she welled with pure happiness for her brother and for Julie. They were going to get their happy ending.

But the kissing went on and on until Celeste was tapping her foot with impatience, and she couldn't hold it in any longer. "You must respond to his question, Julie! You must say yes, or it is not official!"

Julie dropped from her tiptoes, but kept her hands in Matt's hair as she moved her mouth from his just enough to respond. "I have to check something first."

"You do, do you?" Matt asked, so deliriously in love that Celeste almost didn't recognize him.

"This hotel is not you, but it's very me. And these clothes are not you, but they are very me. And I appreciate those things, I really do. But I just need to make sure..." Julie nodded mischievously and slowly slid her hands to the top of his shirt and began undoing the top buttons.

Matt raised his eyebrows. "Look, I seriously can't wait either, but to be completely honest, you shouldn't have high expectations because it's been a while, so the phrase 'eternal voyage' may not come to your mind when—"

"Matt!" Julie laughed, but continued undoing a few buttons and pulled open his shirt. She sighed with happiness. "Good. You're still my superhero under these dress clothes. You have on your *Nietzsche is My Homeboy* shirt. As handsome as you look in this suit, now I really know that everything is as it should be." She started to kiss him again.

Celeste tossed up her hands. "ANSWER THE QUESTION!"

This time Matt pulled away. "Yeah, let's hear it." He bunched his shirt closed. "No answer, no Nietzsche!"

Julie pulled open his shirt again. "I say yes to Nietzsche and yes to my favorite homeboy." She looked up at Matt. "That's you. Yes, yes, yes. I will marry you, Matthew Watkins."

Celeste jumped up and down and cheered as Matt slid the beautiful ring onto Julie's finger. It was not, as engagement rings often were, a diamond, but rather a purple stone much the color of one that Matt had given Julie years before. It was the perfect ring. Celeste could not stop clapping and celebrating. Not that Matt and Julie noticed at the moment due to the resumption of the kissing. And the groping. Granted, it was a little creepy watching her brother make out with someone so passionately, but she did know what it felt like to love someone so much that—

Oh no.

She couldn't do this now.

Or could she? Maybe it was the perfect time. Maybe there was a lesson here.

Celeste backed down into the hallway and walked the corridor to her room. Her suitcase sat on the bed, and very slowly she unzipped it. It was time. She rooted through her belongings until she located what she was after. Then she walked to the window that took up most of the far wall and sat down in the chair that faced Sunset Boulevard.

In her hands was the box from the Christmas tree. She'd felt compelled to toss it into her luggage, and now she knew why. She lifted off the top and took out the two pieces of paper, slightly water damaged and wrinkled, but still intact.

She reread hers first.

*Live the life you've dreamed.*

It was a quote from Thoreau. The sentiment had been her intention. That night she'd been at the top of the tree, so filled with the hope and the delight that came with Justin's romantic gesture, and she had meant with all her heart to do just that: to make the dreams she'd only just started to allow herself to have to become her reality. But instead, just when they were falling into place, she became filled with terror. That was when she should have known that she was on the brink of great change. That was when she should have bitten the bullet and continued on.

Justin's paper was folded into a small square, and she slowly pulled apart the paper, careful not to tear it. Celeste inhaled sharply and held her breath. He'd also written down a quote.

Of course he had. They were both quote people. His was an Emerson quote. One she knew well, but had never thought to apply to herself. But Justin had thought to.

*To be yourself in a world that is constantly trying to make you something else is the greatest accomplishment.*

Celeste stood, paper in hand, and walked to the window. Justin believed in her. She touched her forehead to the glass and looked down at the street. Out there, there were characters, and personalities, and interesting people. Some would be wonderful and magical; some would be awful and cruel.

And some, she understood, would not only love her, but would teach her to love herself.

# CHAPTER 28
# THE POWER OF CELESTE

CELESTE POUNDED ON Matt's hotel room door. Well, Matt and Julie's door. "I am terribly sorry to disturb you. Really, terribly, horribly, mightily sorry, but this is of an urgent nature!"

"Are you on fire?" Matt called after a minute.

"Well… no." Celeste admitted. "Not in a literal sense, but figuratively and emotionally, I am very much on fire!"

If this hotel had crickets, their chirping would be ricocheting off the walls.

"Matthew!" She hammered her hand on the door. "Julie! I am fully aware that I am interrupting you both, but in the name of love, I am begging you to open the door!"

She heard scuffling sounds, and Matt whipped open the door. "I do not see any figurative or emotional flames shooting from your head."

Celeste kicked her foot between the door and the doorjamb before he could shut it. "Julie!"

Julie laughed. "Matt, let her in."

He sighed and grandly gestured for her to enter. She covered her eyes and slithered past him. "I do not wish to witness anything I should not witness. I am simply here to retrieve the car keys."

"Where you going?" Julie asked.

Celeste paused. "I am going to San Diego."

Matt pulled her hand from her face. She loved the adoring look he gave her. "Are you really?"

She held up a hand, palm out, to partially block her view.

"What are you doing?" he asked.

"Shielding my eyes. You do not have on a shirt and we are not at the beach."

"Well, don't come knocking on the door an hour after a guy proposes marriage. And it's not my upper half you should be hiding from."

"Matthew, gross! I realize this is an inopportune time, but you'll have plenty of chance for that after I am gone. And for the rest of your lives. I need the car keys!"

"You're really going to San Diego?"

She held up the piece of paper with the quotes and waved it frantically at him. "I found my hinge, Matty."

He nodded. "Okay." Matt turned to Julie. "We gotta go."

"On it." She was thankfully still dressed, and immediately hopped off the bed and picked up her shoes from the floor.

"No." Celeste stopped them. "I want to do this alone. I need to. You two must remain here and allow me to handle this myself."

"I know you can handle it," Matt said. "We both do. We

just want to support you. Besides, you drive like a damn maniac, and you should arrive there in one piece, not eighty-seven."

She put her hands on her hips. "You will drive fast, though?"

"Yes," he agreed.

"Very, very fast?"

"For you, yes."

"We have that outrageous Tesla sports car that you insisted on, so you best not attempt to blame the car for any inability to break speed limits. I need to be there by sunset and that is at six minutes after seven."

"Understood."

"Drive as though your life depended on it," she ordered.

He shrunk back exaggeratedly. "Based on the look you're giving me, my life does depend on it."

"Suck it up." Julie appeared next to Matt and tossed his geeky T-shirt at him. "Let's go get her man."

Matt did as he promised, and he drove them to San Diego with the speedometer well over the legal limit. Granted, it would be difficult for anyone not to make good use of the car's capabilities.

Except for the music blaring from the speakers, the car was silent. Julie kept her hand on Matt's shoulder for the entire ride, occasionally running her fingers up into his hair and back down. They were both whole again.

Celeste needed to think.

Actually, what she needed to do was feel. The words that Julie read out loud today rang through her head. *Ignore everything you think you know and listen only to your heart, without doubting anything.*

Matt had it right, but she would not wait years to implement what she saw so clearly was the truth. She would act now. But she would need help.

Celeste started to text Michelle, Justin's roommate's girlfriend, whom she'd met that day at Barton. Then she stopped. A text was safe and impersonal. This called for a phone call. So she dialed her number. Michelle was surprised to hear from her, but friendlier than Celeste would have expected given what had happened.

"Michelle, I realize hearing from me may be odd, but I am throwing myself on your mercy."

Michelle's voice immediately soared. "Are you calling for the reason I think you're calling?"

"I am. I need your help, if there is any chance that you are willing."

"If you are going to restore order to my world, then I'm all yours."

"I am going to do my best." Celeste hesitated. "Thank you. Thank you so much. It means a tremendous amount that you are agreeing to facilitate this."

"We all screw up. We all run from stuff when we shouldn't. It's okay, Celeste. I get it. Maybe not exactly what you're going through, but I get it still. Everybody runs from something good sometime. Tell me what you need."

They talked for ten minutes, and then Celeste tucked her hands under her legs and looked out the back window of the car. She shut her eyes. There was no stopping now, and she didn't want to.

Matt got them to San Diego in under three hours. He made the stop at Starbucks that she requested and continued with the directions from the navigation system until they reached a spot on the coast. Matt and Julie got out of the car.

"It's going to be dark soon. You okay?" Julie asked.

"I will be, yes. Either way, I will be." Celeste scanned the area at the top of Sunset Cliffs. They were just past the spot where she had stood a month before. "You can go."

"What? We don't get to stay and watch?" Matt stomped his foot and pretended to have a fit. "You interrupted us just as things were about to—"

Julie clapped a hand over his mouth. "Call us if you need us. We're going to get dinner. And you know what? I'm proud of you. Really, really proud. You're doing what I couldn't do."

"Thank you, Julie. Matt?" She stepped toward her brother. "Matty?"

"You can do this." He was done joking now. "It's going to be fine."

"Okay."

"You can. You're the bravest sister anyone could have."

"Okay."

"I love you, Celeste."

She fell against him and let him hug her and rub her back. "I love you, too, Matty. You are going to have a wonderful life."

"You are going to also."

"But nothing has happened yet."

"A ton has happened," he said.

She squeezed her arms around him. "Yes. You're right. A

ton has happened." He took the Starbucks coffee cup from Julie and gave it to Celeste. Then he tousled her hair and smiled.

Celeste crossed the street and watched Matt and Julie drive away. But they were riding away together, and that was perfect. She waited only a few minutes. A car pulled up not far from her, stopped by the cliffs, and then drove slowly as it passed. Michelle waved and winked.

Celeste had to compose herself before she could look at the boy who was now less than fifty feet from her. Finally, she lifted her eyes.

Justin stood with his hands in the pockets of his jeans, a backpack slung over his shoulder, his hair blowing in the ocean breeze, and a look on his face that she couldn't read. It took all of her might, but she walked to him and he to her. They met in the place on the rocks where they had been once before. Her heart clenched when he was before her. Now she could see clearly that Justin's eyes were wet, his face pained.

Celeste struggled to hold back the immeasurable reaction to seeing him again, but it was impossible. After everything she had been through over these past months, with him and with herself, she couldn't. So she gave in, sobs erupting from her as she hung her head. She dropped her head as the tears fell.

Justin stepped in and put his hands on her waist. He didn't say anything, letting her get the worst of it out.

She finally spoke through her heartache. "Hey, Justin?"

He took forever to reply, but finally he said the two words that saved her from collapse. "Hey, Celeste?"

She looked up. This look from him? *This one* she knew. "I brought you a coffee." She held out the cup to him.

"Yeah?"

"Yes." She sniffed hard. "I had to special order it."

Justin knew what to do. He took off the lid and looked down. When a smile broke through, she knew that he understood. "This is the most beautiful peace sign I've ever seen." Then he read the marker writing on the side, scrawled in wobbly cursive.

*Make love, not war.*

Now he sniffed. "I told you that you were a pacifist."

"I won the battles, Justin. And I won the war. And now there is no more fighting. Now there is peace. You told me to let joy win out, and I am choosing to do that."

Justin took a deep breath. "This coffee looks, like, totally amazing and delicious, but I really want to kiss you. And for that I need two hands because I'm going to have to hold you up. That's how hard I'm going to kiss you."

Without hesitating, Celeste batted the cup from his hands.

He stepped in and immediately wrapped his arms around her waist. "I missed you. I didn't think you'd come back to me."

"But I did. And you waited, didn't you? You didn't give up."

"No, I did not."

"You could have. You likely should have. That would have been fair. I imagine that I hurt you significantly, that you were very angry with me, and for that, I am profoundly sorry. I pushed you away because I thought I needed to protect us, and instead I threw away what was protecting us, what was making us both stronger. Justin, I am so sorry. I will do whatever I can to make things better."

"Things are already better. You don't need to apologize, Celeste. I knew, even during that wretched talk on the beach, that what was happening wasn't really about us. It was about you. So I wasn't angry. Hurt and sad, yes. My heart shattered, yes. But you had stuff going on that was greater than us, and you had to go deal with that. I didn't know if that was really going to be the end or not. And when you never picked up the phone, or replied to my emails, or... Well, I really got worried when I texted you the coffee froth picture of the Mad Hatter that I, like, really labored over. Fine, I know that picture sucked, but you must have seen the effort that went into it, because I even used a toothpick and tried to swirl the chocolate into an expressive face, but—"

"I loved it. I absolutely loved it." Then her mouth was on his, and she drowned in the immeasurable scope of what it meant to be back with him. She touched his face, ran her hands through his hair, felt the skin on the back of his neck in the way that he loved so much.

When Justin stepped back, she almost whimpered, wanting more. Wanting everything. But he turned her to face the ocean. "We can't miss this sunset."

So together they followed the sun as it dropped, both imperceptibly and all too fast. Justin stood behind her and held her close, his chin resting on her shoulder.

Celeste took an empowering breath. "I'm submitting my acceptance to Barton." Before he could say anything, she continued. "It's where I want to be. Not because of you. Partially, of course. But truly, it's because I'm choosing a more important path for myself. Matt helped me see that. Just because I assumed that I would go to an Ivy does not mean that is the right choice for me. It's not what I want. Not anymore. In fact, I don't think I've wanted that for a while. I refuse to be left behind in this world, so I need to catch up. This is a smart step for me."

Justin's hold on her tightened. "I'm so happy for you."

"You have taught me, Justin…" She took some calming breaths. "You have taught me that I am allowed to like myself just as I am, at whatever stage I am in. I can change, I can stay the same, or I can be whoever it is that is right for me; but I can be satisfied. No, more than that. I can be *proud*. I can celebrate. That is what I am going to do."

"And you are going to do that brilliantly. I have no doubt."

"I have hope that you and I will continue this relationship, because I care so deeply for you, Justin. So much so that I withdrew. But I know that not every love is forever. That's the practical side of me talking. I do not want you to feel a responsibility because I am going to Barton. I am, very sincerely, going for me."

"And I want to you know that I get this, Celeste. I really do. Your choice comes from strength, not from dependence."

"Yes."

"And now I have a very important question for you," he said. "Why do I have a backpack? Michelle made me take it and wouldn't tell me anything. I thought maybe she was dropping me off for some sort of vile reality show survival game where I'd have to kill a pig in order to eat dinner."

Celeste laughed. Oh, how she'd missed him. "I was

hoping that you would lead me down the steep rocks and to the beach."

He kissed her cheek. "You want to sleep down there?"

"She brought me appropriate shoes, and a blanket and… I don't remember what else I asked for. I don't care what we have. I just want to sleep on the beach with you."

"Then that's what we'll do."

"And I am considering something else." She stepped from his arms and walked forward, closer to the edge of the rocky cliff. The view just before night hit was incomparable.

"What's that, my brave girl?"

Celeste watched as the sun threw the last of its light across the water. "One day, when the color of the sky is perfect, when I have spent the night in your arms, and when I am fully back where I belong, I may just jump from the cliffs to the water below. Maybe. Maybe I will; maybe I won't. But in either case, I will still be just fine."

She could feel Justin studying her. "You're going to do it, aren't you?" He clapped. "You are. That is the power of Celeste."

Celeste smiled without reservation and peeked back at him. "Maybe," she said coyly. She winked and raised both hands in the air, flashing the peace sign to the world before her. The world that used to terrify her and the world that now welcomed her.

"I am choosing a love that defies boundaries and a life that defies boundaries. That is the power of Celeste."

# ACKNOWLEDGEMENTS

SYDNEY DELORES HERRING and Maddie Round are two very special young women. They wrote me in December 2013 and absolutely gushed over the Flat books and me, and they did so at a time when I was discouraged and utterly confused and uninspired to write. After messaging back and forth with them one evening, I fell asleep hearing Celeste in my head. It was borderline creepy how clearly she spoke to me, but it was then that I knew I could—and had to—write *Flat-Out Celeste*. How could I not? Sydney and Maddie call me "*the* author," *Flat-Out Love* "*the* book," and Matt "*the* character." I'm humbled and curtsying like crazy over these girls.

This book would never have been possible without the endless help that Rebekah Crane gave Celeste and me. The hand holding, the yelling of, "Let it land!", and the unwavering championing were the reason I could write. Without Rebekah, there could be no *Flat-Out Celeste*. Smart, brilliantly funny, and loyal, she is everything one could ask for in book advisor, and even more important, in a friend.

Liis McKinstry, Mo Mabie, Whitney McGregor, Aestas, Whitney McGregor, Rob Zimmerman, Marlana Grela, Maryse Coutier Black, Jen Halligan, Jamie McGuire, Tracy Crawford Hutchinson, Rebecca Donovan, Tammara Webber, and Tracey Garvis-Graves have extended themselves in so many ways. All have proven to be generous, loving, and supportive over the past few years, and I thank them with all of my heart for their dedication to me and to my books. They continue to cheerlead enthusiastically when I am discouraged and whiny and have certainly earned wild applause.

There is not enough praise to throw Autumn Hull's way. What a stupendous job she's done for me with Celeste's promotion! As talented a publicist as she is, Autumn is equally kind and caring on a personal level, and I am very thankful to have her in my corner.

Antoinette Woodward pulled me from a ledge just before I jumped, and she has my eternal love.

Without Maria Milano, Justin would not have a last name. Also, she has a true knack for proofreading and can spot a missing word a mile away, and Celeste and I owe her dinner.

My friend Tom, while in the battle of a lifetime, still insisted on hearing about Celeste and giving me his time and creative input. I needed that hand-holding desperately, and he got me through a few huge struggles and desperate days. His patience for my babbling and thinking out loud cannot be underestimated.

Not a day goes by that Andrew Kaufman does not support me, challenge me, make me laugh, and offer me the most layered and remarkable friendship a girl could ask for. He knew what it meant to me to get this book written and published, and he never once gave up on me. Andrew manages to be the voice of reason and calm during my frequent hysterics, and he has the ability to talk me through even the most crazy of thinking. I would be, without question, lost without him.

Carmen Comeaux is so smart and fabulous that I was scared to send her my manuscript. Her sharp eye and immeasurable editing skills are much appreciated. College may be far behind, but friendship is not.

My longtime friend Alexa Lewis did a wonderful job line editing and included amusing comments, such as, "This line sounds like a Celine Dion song. Change? Unless you're going for that." So she caught typos *and* catastrophic word choices. I couldn't ask for more.

Thank you to Dawn Abby Gil and Dallas Fryer for letting me borrow their names. I hope I did them justice.

John Vosseler talked me through Sunset Cliffs, and on my next trip to San Diego, I'm there!

I've got a core group of twenty women with whom I fight the good fight each day. The publishing world is not easy, and it means everything that I have them to catch me when I fall and celebrate with me when I climb. I'm throwing handfuls of glitter at them right now, and each one of them looks positively stunning.

And as always, gratitude to my ever-patient family for allowing me to disappear for days and picking up the slack during crunch time. Apologies to my son who continues to suggest that I "should really think about writing something else." Perhaps one day I will write that epic science fiction book…

My readers and bloggers: Man, am I lucky. They give me more than I ever understood possible with their encouragement, and humor, and sending of unicorn paraphernalia and Wonder Woman pictures. They are the reason that I have a career, and I don't forget that for a second. Special love out to my Facebook and Twitter followers who are the most wild and wonderful crowd imaginable. Clearly I cannot list you all here (although I'd love to!), but I know so many of your names from our frequent interactions, and you all rock my world hard. See you soon, my friends.

And finally, thank you to The Coffee People for making Black Tiger k-cups, to Amazon for delivering my fuel at near light speed, and for the baristas at my local Starbucks for knowing to add an extra espresso shot to everything.

CPSIA information can be obtained at www.ICGtesting.com
Printed in the USA
LVOW05s1610301014

411271LV00020B/1184/P